Project Chiron

Project Chiron

by Ryan King and Dennis Griffin

Dennis - To my wonderful wife, Julie

Chapter 1

The day was as perfect as Jack Winters could have dreamed. The accumulated tension slowly seeped out of his body as he drove south along I-90 towards the Gulf of Mexico. He didn't normally like loud music, but he had found a station that played good blues and turned it up, singing along as the warm wind blew through the open windows.

His ringing cell phone broke the spell. Jack looked down and saw it was from the office. He groaned, turned down the radio, and answered it.

"Cindy," said Jack trying to hide his exasperation, "I've only been on vacation an hour. What could possibly be the emergency?"

"Sorry, Jack," she said. "Sonny Lyon's son got busted on a DUI and wants you to defend him. It will be his third strike if convicted and he'll see some time. I'm sure Sonny is more worried about his company stock possibly taking a hit over the negative publicity rather than little Dean Lyon."

Jack sighed. "Can't someone else do it? You know I've already got a full load."

"I know, but he asked for you specifically, and for what he's willing to pay, we're not going to tell him no."

Of course, thought Jack. *They always want the son of Supreme Court Judge Jeremiah Winter to represent them. As if his father's genius had been passed down to him like a prophet's mantel.*

"When is the hearing?"

"Next Friday," she answered.

Jack closed his eyes for a minute, but then snapped them open again remembering he was driving. "Next Friday, huh? What will I do with all that time?"

"I know," she said, "but it's fairly cut and dry. Dean Lyon is guilty; they got him dead to rights and the police reports are all in order. You'll argue to keep him out of jail. Suspend his license for five years and probation for six months, I would say."

Jack hated defending cases like this. It wasn't difficult, just not why he became a lawyer, but it was part of the job. Not every case could give you that sense of purpose while fighting or the feeling of exhilaration when it was won.

"All right," he groaned. "See if you can push as much as possible till the following week. Even though it's a simple case, it won't keep Sonny Lyon from sitting in my office agonizing and talking about it for hours at a time."

"Billable hours," she reminded him.

"Still not worth it."

"Maybe not to you," she laughed, "but we take it where we can get it. Business has been a little tight lately."

"Yeah, yeah, I know," he answered. "Was there anything else? You sure you don't need me to argue a case down here at some little town or something? Maybe give some legal advice to the Cajuns in return for discount shrimp or something? You know all you have to do is ask."

8

"Ummm, I like shrimp," she said. "You're such a dear to offer. ake sure they're the big ones. And deveined, too. I hate seeing all ick in there."

"Goodbye, Cindy."

"Bye, Jack. Enjoy your vacation. We'll try not to bother you ain."

"Thanks," said Jack putting his phone away and turning the music ck up. It was one of Stevie Ray Vaughn's early songs. It reminded ck of Rhino's, a blues bar he and his friends used to go to near the uisiana State University campus. On Thursday nights, they had arter-dollar Buffalo wings and three-dollar pitchers of beer. And ey always played good blues. That had been nearly ten years ago.

Ten years, Jack thought, *where did it all go?*

Jack and his friends had spent a lot of good times at Rhino's. oofing off and enjoying life and talking about how they were going change the world. This annual get-together was a way to recapture me of that magic. Jack looked forward to it all year long, and this as his year to pick the location.

Bog Island hadn't been a difficult choice. As a matter of fact, it d been on his mind lately with the recent death of his father. Jack d his dad used to vacation there in the summers to fish, but with remiah Winter's long fight with multiple sclerosis, they hadn't gone ce Jack had been in college.

Jack realized he missed his friends, too. The six of them had mehow come together at LSU, by chance and strange cumstances, from different backgrounds and locations, but they had

9

fit perfectly. Jack had friends and acquaintances at work, but none were as close as those from those sunny college years.

The miles rolled away as he reminisced and his smile slowly returned. Jack was surprised when he saw the sign for Avery Island ahead. He looked at the clock and realized it had been nearly ninety minutes since his call from Cindy.

He made his way through town to the marina where he spotted Charles Haywood instantly. It was nearly impossible *not* to spot Charles Haywood. The black man was nearly six foot six. Even a decade out of playing defensive end at LSU, he was still a rippling mass of muscle. As usual, he was surrounded by a group of young boys. Charles was an assistant principle in North Louisiana at Tallulah High School and had always had a way with kids.

Charles looked up and smiled as Jack got out of his car.

"...and that my friends is why you never, ever go coon hunting with someone crazier than yourself," he told the enraptured boys. "Now, I've got to go say hello to my good friend over there. You all stay out of trouble." The kids smiled and waved as he jogged over towards Jack's car.

Jack stuck out his hand, but Charles ignored it, engulfing him in a monstrous hug. The big man had always been a hugger, but Jack was also slightly claustrophobic and had to fight back the feeling of panic as Charles slapped him sharply on the back several times to emphasis his embrace. Jack waited it out, knowing from habit that three mighty slaps would signify the end of the hug and hopefully not knock his heart out of rhythm.

"Good to see you, my friend," Charles said after finally releasing Jack.

"And you," said Jack. He was grinning foolishly, but so was Charles.

"Sorry to hear about your dad," Charles said, his smile melting away slowly. "I wanted to come to the funeral, but my boss's wife went into early labor with twins. They needed me to play at being school principle for a week."

"I understand," said Jack. "The call meant a great deal."

They stood awkwardly for a few seconds.

"Soooo," said Charles finally, "this is your show, brother. What are we going to do? I got to tell you I'm a little nervous about what you're laying down right now. You ever see the movie *Deliverance*?"

"No, I don't think so," answered Jack.

"Well, it starts out a lot like this vacation," Charles said while shaking his head in slow motion for extra emphasis. "It did *not* end well, believe me. These Cajuns are just as crazy as those Kentucky hillbillies I bet."

"Don't worry," Jack laughed. "Besides, you're as big as a damn alligator; who would mess with you?"

"You know Cajuns eat alligators," answered Charles solemnly. "Maybe they want to see how ole Charles Haywood tastes cooked over an open fire smothered in barbecue sauce."

"Damn, that *does* sound good," answered Jack dreamily.

Charles punched Jack lightly in the shoulder, but it was still enough to knock him backwards.

"Let's go sign for our boat, then we can load up," said Jack rubbing his shoulder.

A half hour later their twenty-foot boat was loaded with coolers of food and beer. Jack also stowed away their fishing gear and bait.

"Hey! It's Heather," yelled Charles, jumping from the boat to the dock and in the process causing the twenty footer to rock noticeably from side to side.

Once Jack was sure the boat wasn't going to take on water, he looked up to see Charles hugging a beautiful redhead who smiled down at him. Charles let go of her and grabbed her backpack.

"Hey, Jack," she said, "permission to come aboard?"

"Permission granted," Jack answered, taking her hand to help her onto the deck where they also hugged. The sweet smell of Heather's hair caused pleasant memories to flood into his mind. Jack and Heather Daniels had dated for a while in college, and had been able to end their romantic entanglement without upsetting their little group dynamic.

"We picked a good time of the year to do this," Heather said once they had separated. "The New Orleans Port Authority shows clear weather all weekend."

"You still like working there?" asked Charles. "I've heard it can get pretty hectic managing all those ships coming in from all over the world. Not to mention having to deal with labor disputes, or new customs regulations, or an environmental scare."

"It does keep me busy," she answered, "but that's one reason I like it. Every day is different, and I know if we don't keep the ships moving that a farmer in Nebraska won't have gas or a mom in Tennessee can't put bananas on her kid's cereal."

"Yeah, you keep up the good work." Charles looked around as if something had just occurred to him. "Hey, where are we supposed to sleep?"

A new voice spoke from the dock, "I don't know about the rest of you, but I'm sleeping inside a tent with mosquito netting. Those buggers will flat out drain you dry this time of the year."

"Evan!" squealed Heather. "Come on down here!"

The tall, thin man handed an exceptional amount of gear to Charles and then climbed into the boat where he was hugged simultaneously by Charles and Heather. Jack held back, but then joined in with a smile.

"How's the accounting business going?" Heather asked after everyone had separated.

Evan looked a little embarrassed. "It's good. They've made me a named partner."

"A partner?" asked Jack. "That's a big deal. So instead of Simon and Kestler CPA, it's…?"

"Simon, Kestler, and Athers," answered Evan with a smile he could no longer hold back. "Biggest CPA firm in Port Allen."

"Well, I'll be," said Charles. "Good for you!"

"Thanks," said Evan. "Where's Brian and Amanda?"

Jack checked his watch. "Should be here any minute. Amanda was picking her brother up at the airport. He was able to get leave this year."

"How's he doing?" asked Heather. "I heard he got shot up over in Afghanistan."

"Amanda says he's doing okay," Jack answered. "He's more upset about losing a few of his men than his injuries."

Charles shook his head. "I can't imagine that kind of life, but Brian was determined to join the army. I bet he's good at it."

They all nodded. It had been a shock to all of them when Brian had enlisted the day after graduation. He could have done anything with his mechanical engineering degree, but he wanted to be an infantryman. Jack had suspected that Brian's choice had been emotionally driven based on the September 11th attacks and that he would leave the army or change jobs given time, but over a decade later, their friend was still serving faithfully.

"When was the last time Brian was able to come on our yearly get-togethers?" Evan asked.

"Been at least four years," answered Jack.

"Five," said Charles. "He was with us the year we went to Key West, but not the next year in Gulf Shores."

"I hope he's okay," said Heather. "They say a lot of vets are coming back...different."

"My gorgeous lady," said a booming voice. "Don't you worry about Brian Winston. I'm here and I'm as right as rain."

A short, stocky, muscular man with a shaven head walked down the dock towards them. He had a broad grin on his face and carried a gigantic camouflaged backpack as easily as if it were filled with nothing but pillows. A pretty blonde followed, and it took no more than a cursory glance to recognize the two were twins.

"Well, if it isn't the Winston kids," said Charles. "Up to no good, I bet!"

"You know it," answered Brian, tossing his pack into the boat and hopping down among them, surprising Charles with a hug before the big man could respond. Brian moved quickly from Charles onto the others, shaking their hands and hugging them.

Jack looked in his eyes when they came together. Brian's twin sister had been in pre-law with Jack, which is how he had met Brian.

The two hugged and Jack whispered to him. "It's good to see you. Are you okay?"

Brian pulled back; his face was serious. He looked around and spoke loud enough for everyone to hear. "I know you all heard what happened, but I'm fine. Seriously. This getaway is exactly what I need."

"You're not the only one," said Evan.

"Come on down here," Heather said, holding her arms out to Amanda who still stood on the dock.

After a second's hesitation, Amanda Winston hopped down agilely into the boat. Like her brother, she was short and muscular, but where he was stocky, she was wiry and lean, as befit her status as an avid tri-athlete when she wasn't working as a state prosecutor in Baton Rouge.

She received hugs and smiles from each of her friends. As usual, she wasn't nearly as outgoing and exuberant as her twin brother. Even so, Jack thought she seemed more reserved and pensive than normal.

"Okay, so it looks like we're ready to go," said Charles. "Jack, Mister Tour Guide and Master of Ceremonies, where is our destination?"

"Bog Island," answered Jack.

"What?" said Evan. "Sounds...swampy."

"It's fine," said Jack. "My father and I used to go there all the time. Don't worry, you'll see. Fishing is fantastic and hardly any people."

"Oh, hell," groaned Charles. "This *is* going to be like *Deliverance*."

"Like what?" asked Heather.

"Never mind," answered Charles. "Just whatever you do, don't ask me to squeal like a pig."

"I better write that down," said Heather. "Anyone got a pencil?"

"Don't worry," said Brian. "Any crazy locals had better watch themselves around this bunch. Bog Island doesn't know what it's in for."

"Yeah, we'll see," said Charles.

The small group cast off the boat lines and pulled out of the marina to a beautiful carefree sunny day.

For some of them, it would be the last day of their lives.

Chapter 2

Brian caught Charles looking at his bare legs again.

"You know you're starting to make me feel a little uncomfortable about wearing shorts, big man," said Brian. "We're friends and all, but that's all it is, just friends. I'm very flattered, you know, but I don't really swing that way."

"Are those scars from bullets?" Charles pointed, clearly fascinated.

"No, those are burns," answered Brian. He pointed to several smaller puckered wounds on his calf. "These are from shrapnel."

"Like from a bomb?" asked Heather.

Brian nodded. "The vehicle was armored, but a mine went off right under my feet; most was absorbed by the vehicle, but a few pieces got through."

"Sounds like you were lucky," said Heather.

"Luckier than my driver," said Brian. "He didn't make it."

An uncomfortable silence fell over the boat.

"Look, it's okay, guys," said Brian. "Really. I know there's a lot in the news about soldiers going off to war and coming back all messed up, but I'm fine. It was bad to lose friends, but we're soldiers. We talked about it and we all knew the dangers. We all accepted the risks. It's part of the job."

"And I think you've done your part," said Amanda. "You've been shot up and blown up. My brother has done enough. Let someone else take a turn. You don't need to go back anymore."

"Well, who *is* going to go?" asked Brian seriously. "We've talked about this. I get young kids every other month. Kids like I used to be. They don't know shit about shit, and if I don't prepare them, they don't have a shot at making it back home to their friends and family."

"We appreciate what you do," said Evan.

"I know that, and thank you," said Brian. "It's my job, guys. You don't have to feel bad for me or guilty. I chose this life and can quit any time I want."

"Then why don't you?" asked Amanda with barely suppressed anger. "You can get a good job, get married, have a real life."

Brian smiled sadly at his sister. "I *have* a real life. One that matters and makes a difference. I know you don't understand and that you worry about me, but trust me. This is my life. This is what I want for me."

More uncomfortable silence filled the boat. The hum of the engine and the slap of the waves on the bow seemed unusually loud.

"Hey, didn't we bring beer?" asked Charles, finally breaking the stillness.

"Now that's what I'm talking about," said Brian. "We're supposed to be having fun. Pass me one of those brewsters, big man."

Charles pulled out cold cans and handed them around to everyone except Amanda who waved the offer away, still angry.

"So tell us a little about this resort island we've never heard about," said Heather. "I bet it's just like Ibiza only without the clubs, hotels, people, or beaches."

"That's pretty much it," said Jack. "But keep an open mind. It's a nearly uninhabited island owned by the state. Much of the island is part of a national forest. Lots of wildlife and very peaceful. You'll love it."

"How come I've never heard of Bog Island?" asked Heather.

Jack shook his head. "It's not really popular since there's nothing to do but relax and fish. Could also be because the only way to get there is by boat."

"And you and your dad used to come here?" asked Evan.

Jack nodded. "My dad was always a big fisherman. We had an old black man from down in the bayou who worked for us around the house."

"Why's he got to be black?" asked Charles, pointing at his own dark face with mock offense.

"Anyway," continued Jack, "I grew up calling him Uncle Johnny, and he showed us Bog Island. He had a small house there. Said that back a hundred years ago it was owned by his family for generations. Part of a small settlement started by former slaves after the Civil War. Government eventually took it over, but left part of the island to those who didn't want to leave."

Brian pointed ahead of them. "That must be it. Doesn't look too bad. Bigger than I would have thought."

19

They all gazed towards an island that rose out of the early morning mists. Sunlight glinted off canopies of trees that stretched away as far as the eye could see.

Jack steered toward a shallow spot near shore he knew about. "It's nearly eight hundred square acres, most of it covered in woods, but there are some low-lying ground you have to watch out for."

"Like quicksand?" asked Amanda with a touch of unease.

"More like muck," Jack said, looking at Amanda's expensive leather loafers. "Might ruin your shoes. I recommend everyone put on sandals or be prepared to go barefoot in spots. We'll have to do a little bit of walking."

"Walking to where?" asked Heather.

"Why Uncle Johnny's house, of course," answered Jack.

"You mean he still lives here?" asked Evan.

Jack shrugged. "Sure, why not. He's retired, can live wherever he wants. Why not live on his family land? He has a little cabin and can go over to mainland for groceries whenever he wants. All he likes to do anyway is fish and drink whiskey."

"Then this is likely paradise for him," said Charles.

"He'll know where the fish are biting and the best places to camp," said Jack, easing the boat in slowly towards shore while watching the depth finder. When there was only three feet of water under them, he cut the engine and let them glide in slowly. When there was only a foot of clearance, Jack tossed an anchor out behind them. He felt the boat slow and tug at the line. Before it could start slipping back out towards the water, he tossed another anchor off the front of the boat and felt them stabilize.

"Looks like you've done this a few times," commented Brian.

"That I have," answered Jack. "Now just grab what you need for a little hike. We'll be back before dark for our gear."

"I got the beer," said Charles, filling a small cooler with ice and cold drinks.

"It's good to see a man with his priorities in the right place," said Brian.

"Hey, dude," said Charles seriously, "it's hot out there. Dehydration is serious." He studied the cooler before pulling sandwiches and snacks out and repacking in order to fit in an additional few beers.

Jack led the way by leaping into the shallow water with a light pack on his back. He helped Heather and Evan down while everyone else just jumped over the side. Charles nearly fell face first into the water while trying to wrestle with the awkward cooler.

"You need some help with that?" asked Brian.

"Don't even think about it," answered Charles. "This here cooler and I are going to be inseparable for the next few days."

"Ah, sounds like true love," said Heather, "so beautiful and so rare."

Jack looked at Heather, not sure if she was also making a quip at his expense, but she just winked at him and strode up onto the sandy bank.

"Okay, which way, our fearless guide?" asked Brian.

"This way," said Jack, walking into the woods. He had feared he might have forgotten the geography over the past ten years, but there was no hesitation. He knew this island better than he knew his own hometown.

The group of six walked in the light underbrush for half an hour. Birds joyfully called out to each other from the trees above them. The old trail was curiously grown up and the smell of clean damp earth filled the air. Jack always remembered the trail from the north bank to Uncle Johnny's cabin as being well worn.

A lot could change in ten years, Jack thought. *Uncle Johnny kept his fishing boat in a cove on the south side of the island, so maybe no one uses this trail very much anymore.*

Jack walked around a corner and into an open clearing and froze.

There was nothing there. He knew this was the spot, but the clearing was empty except for a few birds and insects playing in the light as it filtered in from the opening above.

"What's wrong?" asked Brian from behind him.

"This is where Uncle Johnny's cabin was," said Jack.

"Are you sure?" asked Evan. "You said it's been ten years. Hell, I can't remember where my car keys are right now, so maybe you misremembered or something."

"No," said Jack. A feeling of unease washed over him. "This is definitely the spot."

They all walked into the clearing and gathered around the old stone foundation of what had once been a small cabin.

"Maybe he moved on," said Heather.

"Or died," said Brian.

"Brian!" hissed Amanda reproachfully.

"I'm just saying," Brian answered with his hands out to his side. "It does happen on occasion, I hear. Uncle Johnny doesn't sound like a spring chicken to me."

"No, he was old even when I was a boy," said Jack, staring at the ground.

"Did he have any family?" asked Charles. "Could be he got where he couldn't take care of himself and they moved him in with them."

Jack shook his head. "Not that he ever mentioned, but I guess he could have had some distant relatives. If he had any, he never talked about them, though."

"So what now?" asked Heather. "Do we head back and go somewhere else?"

"Head back?" asked Brian. "We just got here, and I like the feel of this place. Jack was right, it is peaceful."

"You okay with that?" Charles asked Jack. "Maybe find someplace to sit and drink these delicious and so far unappreciated beers?"

"You have a one-track mind," said Heather.

Charles pulled the cooler up close to his face while caressing its hard surface. "Don't listen to them, little buddies, they just don't understand our love."

"Oh, good grief," said Amanda turning away. "Let's go find someplace with a stream or something. It's getting hot as hell, and I'd like to sit in some cool water."

Jack thought for a moment. "I think I know just the spot. Let's head that way." He pointed to a trail that led to the south.

They all began walking with Jack bringing up the rear. He was about to leave the clearing and looked back one final time at where Uncle Johnny's cabin used to sit. He saw the pattern in the grass all at once and walked over again. The ground was indented where the foundation of the cabin had sat. It was all gone except for hard indentions in the soil and a faint smell of ash.

Sun reflected for a moment off something in the tall grass and then it was gone. Jack froze and backed up a few steps and saw the shinny surface again.

He walked towards it and he sucked in his breath when he recognized the object.

Uncle Johnny had always been a sort of handyman. He proudly proclaimed that he hadn't made it past the sixth grade, but could build or fix damn near anything if given enough time, and Jack believed him. The old man had a small toolbox he frequently used, but often as not relied on a small pearl-handled pocket knife he said he had won in a poker game when he was younger. Jack had asked the old man what the initials JAT on the pearl handle stood for, and Uncle Johnny had just shrugged.

Jack reached down and pulled the knife out of the ground. It had been one of the blades sticking up that had caught the light. Jack rubbed his thumb on the surface to clear off the dirt, and JAT stood out clearly on the pearl handle. He rubbed his thumb across the dirty tip of the blade before pulling it away. He stopped and looked at the flakes of dried substance on his thumb.

Brownish red. Blood? he wondered, and the uneasy feeling returned.

"Hey, fearless guide," yelled Brian from the head of the trail. "You coming or what?"

He thought to tell them about the knife, but not now. Not until he figured out what it meant. He certainly didn't want to dampen the mood any further.

"On my way," yelled Jack. He folded the knife up and put it in his pocket before following his friends down the old trail that led into the heart of the island.

Chapter 3

The old adage said that some men were destined for greatness. That their rise to an exceptional life was somehow preordained, monitored and constantly tweaked by a steady and reliable captain. Governor Eric St Keel had always wanted to believe such a thing about himself.

But if someone or something was in charge, guiding me down this road, he wondered, *then why do I often feel so lost? Why can I see nothing but darkness ahead?*

"They'll be ready in five minutes, sir," said Lucas Ross, his chief-of-staff.

"Thank you," answered the Governor of the State of Louisiana. Eric St Keel opened his mouth to tell his chief-of-staff for perhaps the thousandth time that he could call him by his first name. After all, they had known each other since elementary school.

Lucas Ross looked at him, every facet of his formidable presence focused on the governor's needs and wishes. People called Lucas 'The General', but only behind his back. Colonel Lucas Ross had retired from the army after twenty-five years of service in a variety of specialized and covert units that Eric still did not fully understand or care to know about. He might have made general if not for the debacle in Oman.

It had been natural for the governor to offer his friend a job. Since assuming the post as chief-of-staff, Lucas had helped propel Eric St Keel from Congressman of Louisiana's 9th Congressional District to Governor.

"Did you need something else?" his old friend asked.

"Nothing," St Keel said, releasing him to do what he did best: take care of Eric and make sure that nothing nor anyone threatened him or the governor's office.

St Keel looked down at his notes. Today's televised interview was important. The network had wanted a live broadcast, but Lucas had argued adamantly against it knowing any misstep on live television could be a death blow to the governor's future political aspirations. If anything went wrong during a taped event, Lucas would make sure the offensive segment got taken out with or without the network's permission.

An aide brought Eric a cup of coffee at the same time a sound technician placed a miniature microphone on his jacket lapel and quickly conducted a sound check. Satisfied, he moved over to do the same with the arriving host of the *Our Nation* show, Miss Candice Stapleton.

She ignored the sound technician and strode up to St Keel, beaming a perfect smile to match her lean athletic figure, aristocratic confidence, and dark sultry eyes that made her just right for the television cameras.

"Good to see you, Governor," she said. "Thank you so very much for agreeing to come on my show."

"My pleasure." St Keel stood to greet her. "How is your dear mother, Beatrice, doing?" Lucas always prepared him for such events with information and names that endeared him to all he met.

Candice's calm slipped, and her eyelids trembled ever so slightly. "She is recovering; a stroke, they say. That's so very nice of you to ask."

St Keel patted her hand with a sympathetic nod, establishing what Lucas called an 'anchor', endearing the host to him even before the interview began. "Thank the Lord, such a wonderful woman. And an excellent dancer, if I might be so bold as to say. She nearly took my breath away at the Christmas party."

Candice laughed and then got sad again. "Yes, she always did love dancing. I fear she may never be the same again."

Eric St Keel moved close to her and lowered his voice, establishing an intimate and comforting moment that he hoped she would remember when discussing him to her considerable fan base. Lucas had told him that Candice had lost her father when she was very young and often sought out father figures. "Never fear, child. What we love can't be taken from us. The joy is always there, no matter what."

She turned a hopeful smile up to him. "Thank you, sir."

"We're ready whenever you are," the set engineer told them both from a raised and brightly lit platform.

"Excellent," answered Candice briskly, reassuming her businesslike role as the sound technician attached her microphone. "I trust you've had an opportunity to look over the questions. Any concerns or issues?"

"None," he answered. "I'm an open book."

"Very good then. Shall we begin?"

St Keel nodded, and the set engineer gave a few signals before pointing at Candice who fluffed her hair as the light on top of the cameras lit up bright red.

"Good evening. I'm Candice Stapleton, and tonight on *Our Nation,* we have the pleasure of talking to the Governor of the State of Louisiana, Eric St Keel. Welcome to the show, Governor."

"Thank you, Candice." St Keel beamed at the camera first and then at the woman beside him. "It is an honor to be here."

Candice looked at the teleprompter. "Let's start by talking about your Take Back the Streets program. The results have been extraordinary in some of Louisiana's largest cities, especially New Orleans. Violence in all categories is down, gang activity is practically a thing of the past, and homeless people are off the streets. Tourism is booming in a city that many gave up for dead. Bourbon Street is cleaner than anyone has ever seen it and safe to walk down at midnight. The entire state is experiencing a financial rejuvenation while the rest of the country is in the middle of a recession. How did all of this happen?"

St Keel looked at Candice with a concerned look. "Frankly, it starts with empathy and understanding, Candice. Many of the people in our state are not unemployed or homeless or driven to criminal acts because they want to be, but because they have no other choice. A big part of the Take Back the Streets Program is finding jobs and assistance for those in need. Although many said this program would be cost prohibitive, the increased tax revenues we have gained have more than paid for the program and have not cost a single citizen of this great state a dime."

"Empathy and understanding," Candice said. "Helping people find jobs and assistance, that's a fairly novel approach for a conservative, wouldn't you say?"

"Actually, no. Many politicians have suffered from an image problem for years, especially in this state. The members of my party care deeply for each and every American, and only want what is best for this country. It's about revenue of course, but it's also about service. The people of this great state hired me to perform a service for them, and I vowed the day I assumed office that I would do right by each and every one of them. I mean to keep that promise."

Candice smiled. "Speaking of assuming office, you're two years into your second term as governor. Although there has been talk of amending the Louisiana Constitution to allow you to run for a third term, it doesn't appear to have the opposition votes needed to carry it. What do you intend to do after this term?"

St Keel glanced over at Lucas who shook his head slightly. The governor looked at the camera. "Right now, I have no further aspirations other than leading this state. I wake up every morning asking myself what I can do to make the lives of my fellow Louisianans better. I frankly don't have the time or the inclination to worry about a political future. I still have lots of work to do for Louisiana."

Candice dug in. "There are some who have floated your name as a potential vice-president candidate for President Janice Wilkens. The latest polls have her popularity ratings dropping. Many believe it's because of the recent gaff by Vice-President Tipton with the Mexican government. Strategists are saying in two years President Wilkens' ballot needs to have you on it to stand a chance. Some have even gone so far as to suggest you as a presidential nomination."

Governor St Keel had to resist a smile. Candice had played this exactly as Lucas said she would. He frowned at her. "Candice, I frankly don't like that kind of talk. It is counter-productive. The president has my full support during this trying time."

"Governor, if I may..." Candice pulled out a sheet of paper. "Last year you spoke at the funeral of your dear lifelong friend, Louisiana Supreme Court Judge Jeremiah Winter."

"Yes," said St Keel, and he didn't have to fake the emotion that was in his voice. "He was a good man, a wise judge, and a friend I miss."

"You said in your speech, and I quote, 'Judge Jeremiah Winter exemplified a selfless life filled with honorable endeavors with the sole purpose of lifting up civilization and society from the animal baseness that is always roaming about our society. All men and women of such a society have an obligation to do whatever is called upon them, no matter how unwanted that obligation may be,' end quote."

Eric St Keel glanced at Lucas who had an intense twinkle in his eyes. Not only had his chief-of-staff written that speech, he had somehow planted the snippet in Candice's research team's notes without her being any the wiser.

Candice was leaning in close. Evidently, this was the moment she had been building towards. "With those words that you spoke at the funeral of your dead friend fresh in your mind, if you were called upon to serve as vice-president, or even president...would you accept?"

The governor sat back and looked uncomfortable. Lucas had made him rehearse for this potential event months ago. Inside, he was so excited he wanted to dance a jig, but instead he spoke slowly. "Candice...Candice...as I've said, I'm the governor. That's enough responsibility for any one man. I fully support President Wilkens. She is my president."

Candice leaned in even closer. "But would you accept, Governor St Keel? That is the question. Would you reject a nomination for the President of the United States of America?"

The governor was silent for a long moment as if the idea had never occurred to him. He looked at Candice and then directly into the camera. "Those words I said at Jeremiah Winter's funeral a year ago were from the heart. He inspired me by his example and he was one of the primary reasons I went into politics. I still believe that every citizen has a responsibility to sacrifice for the welfare of the whole and that sometimes means service. Sometimes grudgingly, sometimes unwillingly, but service does not wait for us to be ready."

"That sounds like a yes," said Candice, unable to contain a grin. She knew she would get tons of exposure over this clip. Networks like CNN and Fox would be sure to air bites from her interview.

"If I were nominated for such a position," Eric added, "I could not in good conscience decline the responsibility if the citizens of this country felt me worthy of it, but"—Eric held up a finger—"this country has a president. A woman of integrity and heart who needs and deserves our support. I for one will give her everything I've got, just like I have the State of Louisiana. It's the only way I know to live."

"I think we can all see that, sir." Candice saw the signal from the engineer. "Thank you very much, Governor. We have enjoyed having you on the show."

"The pleasure has been all mine," he answered.

Candice faced the camera. "Don't go away. When we return, we will hear from an expert who will discuss the threat to the coastal marshland ecosystem and what some are doing to try and save it."

The lights dimmed, and Candice and St Keel turned to each other as if talking until the lights came back on.

"We're clear," yelled the engineer. "Well done, everyone."

Candice smiled again. "Thank you, Governor. I hope I didn't make you too uncomfortable with that whole presidential run talk. It was on the topic list we sent."

St Keel gave her a disapproving look. "Actually, the *vice*-presidential bid was, not the presidential."

Candice smiled and shrugged. "I'm sorry if I put you on the spot." She didn't look sorry.

"No it's okay. It's good to talk about it here since others already are, I guess, but I meant what I said. I'm not looking for a job. I already have one."

"That's why you're so perfect for it," she answered.

St Keel waved his hand at her as if she were making a joke. This part of the interview was nearly as important as the televised part. Candice Stapleton would be invited on other talk shows and asked her impression of Governor St Keel as a possible presidential candidate. He had to appear the dutiful, yet un-ambitious, public servant.

He took her hand in both of his. "You tell that mother of yours to get well soon and not to let anything keep her down. Tell her I am looking forward to dancing with her again before the year is out."

"I will." Candice smiled, her face open and trusting.

He turned away knowing he had her. Candice Stapleton would be an advocate for Eric St Keel, a true believer. That was important in a politically divided state, especially where most of the media were skeptics.

Lucas fell in beside him as they walked off stage. They headed towards the underground parking lot that held his luxury sedan. St Keel wanted to laugh and cheer, enjoy the moment with his friend, but that would have to wait until later when they were alone. For now, they were stoic and all business.

Once in the car, St Keel poured them both a finger of dark highland scotch in expensive crystal tumblers from the specially designed mini wet bar. The governor couldn't help voicing a thought that had been nagging at him. "You know the president isn't going to like that broadcast. She'll have to react in order to secure her position within the party."

Lucas smiled darkly. "I'm counting on it."

St Keel shifted more towards Lucas and cleared his throat. "You know, I still don't feel completely comfortable not knowing what's going on. I'm impressed with the results you've achieved, but don't you think I need to know the details?"

Lucas stared hard at his friend. "Do you trust me?"

St Keel nodded.

"Then know I'm not telling you everything for you own good. If things happen to go badly, and they won't, I want you to be able to honestly say you did not know the details. This is for your own protection and good. Just leave it all in my hands."

They drove in silence though the clean safe streets of New Orleans that they had both changed so radically...and mysteriously. They knew that The General was paving a path for Governor St Keel all the way to the doors of the White House.

And I'll be in the driver's seat the whole way, thought Lucas, taking a sip of the expensive scotch. It almost made what they had done to him over Oman worth it.

Almost.

Chapter 4

Moses Mitchell was running and it felt good. He had always loved running. It was the only thing he'd truly been good at in his entire life. Five years before he'd been the state one hundred-meter champion and received an invite to the Olympic Village in Colorado, but that was all before the voices started.

He was the middle of three children. Their father had died shortly after his youngest son was born. Moses and his older sister Deborah spent much of their time looking after little Adam. Their mother often worked two shifts to make ends meet, and it was not uncommon for them to find her asleep at the kitchen table when they came down for breakfast.

His older sister was already at Tulane University when it happened. Deborah was the first person in their family to attend college and his mother had been immensely proud. Moses himself was at track practice when his mother picked little Adam up from school. The authorities later told him that she must have fallen asleep at the wheel, that the car had drifted off the road into the bridge embankment, killing them both.

Moses and Deborah had always been close, and she tried to help him. Moses had pushed her away while at the same time feeling so utterly alone without his family. Something inside told him he deserved to be unhappy after what happened to his mother and brother. How could he possibly be happy when they were dead? To feel any joy or pleasure seemed like disloyalty to them.

He ran away from home and even contemplated suicide for a time, but then the voices entered his head. And he was no longer alone.

A part of Moses knew the voices were not real, but another part insisted that they were. It didn't really matter except he wasn't by himself anymore. As the people around him became less real and inconsequential, the voices became dear friends.

Moses spent five weeks in a state psychiatric hospital, but it was overcrowded, and he was judged non-dangerous and released a few months after he was admitted. Moses had no trouble living on the streets of New Orleans, even liked it there. He learned how to find food, stay dry, and avoid the police. Even when he did get arrested, his big sister, now an FBI Agent out of the New Orleans Field Office, could usually smooth things over. Deborah would then try to get him to live with her for a while, but he always drifted away.

Now something entirely different had found him this time. Now it was just like running in high school, but the stakes were so much higher.

Moses slowed as his feet sank into soft mud. He made himself slow his breathing, taking deep open-mouthed breaths. He listened, but couldn't hear anyone coming after him.

They will be following, said Billy in his head. *Don't be fooled. They catch you again, they might kill you. Promised as much last time you got away.*

37

"I know, I know," said Moses, looking around furtively.

I don't know if you've noticed, said Delores, always the practical one, *but you kind of stand out.*

Moses looked down at his jumpsuit and saw that she was right. Although it was dirty, the bright orange still shone vividly. He started to take the uniform off.

Don't be stupid, said Nate. *You're going to need the clothing at night when it gets cold and the bugs come out.*

Moses didn't like Nate. Sure didn't like his attitude, but he was smart and usually right. Moses looked around and then zipped the jumpsuit all the way to his neck before throwing himself into the muddy pit in front of him. He rolled back and forth while rubbing muck into his short curly black hair and onto his already black face.

He froze. Men talking. Back the way he had come.

Time to go, said Billy.

"You got that right," whispered Moses, pulling himself out of the muck. He spotted dry ground on the other side of the shallow pit and carefully made his way there. Once on the other side, he started running again.

It felt good to be running. He wasn't afraid when he ran. It made him feel happy. Although he didn't notice, running made the voices go away for a while. It made him feel free.

"I'm running," whispered Moses. "This time I have to win. This time I need to win for sure." A broad crazy smile breached the face of the muddy thin wraith as he slipped soundlessly through the dark ancient woods.

Chapter 5

The small pool was exactly where Jack remembered it. Large smooth rocks formed a giant bowl where clear cool water collected before spilling out the southern lip. From there the clear water gathered into a stream that made its way to an inland lake below them brimming with fish. They had already laid out their gear on a clearing to the east side of the lake.

"Now this is nice," said Amanda, who had stripped down to a bikini. She drank a canned beer and lay on a rock in the water, her head tilted up towards the sun with her eyes closed.

"You ain't kidding," said Brian, opening his fourth beer.

"Pass me another one would you?" asked Jack as he turned up the music player.

Evan tipped his beer appreciatively at the electronic player. "Good thinking with the tunes, partner."

Charles reached into the cooler and emerged with a beer in each hand, a look of horror on his face.

"These are the last two, my friends."

The group let out wails of despair.

Jack grabbed one of the beers out of Charles' hand. "Don't worry, folks, I brought plenty more."

"But...it's back at the boat," said Evan.

Charles opened the other beer and drank deep. "Yeah, and we can't possibly be expected to find our way back there on our own, especially now that we just got comfortable."

"I propose that our fearless guide go get us more beer," said Brian.

"Second," said Heather quickly.

"All in favor?" asked Charles, and five hands went up in unison.

Jack killed the rest of the open beer in several long swallows. He then climbed out of the water and grabbed the empty cooler. "Okay, okay, be back in a little bit."

"Bring some food too," said Charles. "We missed lunch, and all this beer is making me feel a little lightheaded."

"We might just take advantage of you," said Heather with a mischievous grin.

"Yes," said Brian, running his hand along Charles' thigh, "we just might."

Charles slapped Brian's hand away. "Jack, *please* come back quickly."

Jack chuckled as he walked away. "I will. Ya'll play nice until I return." He stumbled a little climbing up the hill. His head spinning slightly, Jack realized that he was a little buzzed. He hadn't drank this much in several years.

"You okay, Jack?" asked Evan. "Want someone to go with you?"

Jack waved his hand. "No, I'm good, be back soon," he said, making his way over the hill and out of sight.

Feeling relaxed and happy, Jack enjoyed the stroll to the boat. When he got there, he found a dignified pelican sitting on the bow looking at him.

"I'm sorry, buddy," said Jack, not wanting to disturb the bird, "but I got to get the beer." He moved slowly toward the boat.

The bird looked at him reproachfully and with a squawk lifted off to glide smoothly over the flat water.

This is why Dad loved this place, thought Jack. It had nothing to do with fishing. It was the peacefulness. Getting away from the courtroom and people's troubles. Jack and his father had started coming after Jack's mother died. Bog Island had made things better somehow.

I should come more often, he thought. *It's nice here with my friends, but I can come down alone on the weekends. Recharge. Relax.*

Thinking about getting away more often caused Jack to look at his cell phone to see if he had missed any calls. He realized he couldn't remember the last time he had gone this long without his phone ringing.

"Of course," said Jack, seeing no signal on his phone and putting it back in his pocket. He filled the cooler with ice and beer before picking up a small duffle bag and packing it full of food and a few more six packs of beer. Jack debated grabbing the tents and sleeping bags, but dismissed the idea. He was already carrying a lot and they would have time to come get the rest of their gear before nightfall. He slung the duffle bag across his shoulder and decided to grab his fishing tackle box and a couple of poles. Maybe they could catch some fish for dinner.

His hands full, Jack made his way back up the trail. He paused at Uncle Johnny's clearing as an odd thought struck him. He walked over to look at the cabin foundations more closely. Something didn't seem right, and after a few more minutes, Jack finally figured it out.

The area was clean. There were no old stones where the house had fallen down. No burned supports or evidence of a fire. Nothing except the bare foundation, almost as if the cabin had been lifted right off the ground and taken away.

He thought of the pearl-handled pocketknife in his pocket. *Something isn't right here.*

Jack's thoughts were interrupted by laughter to the south. Instead of following the trail, Jack decided to take a shortcut since it wasn't that far. His friends sounded like they were having fun without him, and Jack wanted to be a part of it.

If Jack had only had to deal with the vines or the affects of the beer, he probably would have been okay, but the combination of both was debilitating. He struggled and pushed through the undergrowth dragging the cooler, duffle bag, and fishing gear with him. Soon, he was exhausted and sweating heavily. Jack inched up the hill and saw his friends below him singing along to the music from the player, which was certainly near maximum volume.

Jack opened his mouth to yell at them to come help him when his feet slipped out from under him in the soft soil. He fell in a heap of gear onto his face. Jack looked up and could still see his friends.

"Hey!" he yelled. "Give me a hand here!"

His friends kept singing and talking loudly over the blaring music.

Jack started laughing at the absurdity of it all and struggled to stand.

Something made Jack look down the hill again. It took him a moment to realize what was wrong. A dark horror of a figure, dirty and gaunt, stood on the edge of the clearing, nearly blending in with the background. He appeared to be wearing what was once an orange prison jumpsuit, but it was difficult to tell with all the mud and dirt covering him. Jack yelled out a warning, but it was lost in the sound of the music.

Brian either heard Jack or sensed something was wrong. He stopped singing, stood slowly, and turned to face the figure. A few seconds later, the others did the same. Charles stepped protectively in front of the two women while Brian moved to face the dirty wraith.

Words were spoken by Brian and the dirty vagabond, but Jack couldn't hear anything. He struggled again to free himself, but only became more thoroughly entangled.

The muddy figure was suddenly startled and turned his head behind him as if listening to the air. Without warning, he darted between Brian and Charles with amazing quickness, leaped over the pool of water, and vanished into the far edge of the woods. Jack's friends were talking to each other and looking around. Jack started to yell again, as there was a break between songs, but stopped.

Something was coming out of the trees from where the ragged man had emerged. Jack's friends saw it also and stood together to face whatever was about to emerge.

Intuition made Jack yell out without thinking. "Run!"

It was too late. Another song blared over the scene below. It was Golden Earring's *Twilight Zone*.

Chapter 6

Something was coming through the woods towards them.

"I don't like this," said Heather.

"Just take it easy," said Brian. "And, for the love of God, turn that damn music off. We're probably drawing attention from all over the island."

Evan reached over to turn off the player as more than a dozen men with assault rifles and camouflage uniforms emerged from the brush. Both groups stopped and stared at each other.

"Good afternoon, folks," said a man in the middle after some hesitation. "I'm Captain Brent Urchart of the local park service. Sorry to disturb you, but have you seen a man run through here recently?"

"Why?" asked Charles. "He do something wrong?"

Urchart shook his head. "Not at all. He's part of our security exercise here; he got bitten by a water moccasin. He was getting treatment, then while in delirium ran away. We need to get him back before he hurts himself or before that snake poison does any further damage to his system."

"Security exercise?" asked Brian, looking at their military gear and unmarked uniforms.

"Yeah," said a pale man with blue eyes, "but we ain't got time to screw with you civilians. You seen the man or not?"

"He went that way," said Amanda, pointing to their rear.

"Thank you kindly," said Urchart, signaling for his men to move forward.

"Want me to call for a medical helicopter?" asked Evan, holding up his cell phone.

Urchart shook his head sadly. "I wish we could, but there's no signal out here."

"No problem," said Evan, holding the phone up to his ear. "This is a satellite telephone. 911 is ringing. We'll get help here in just a minute."

"Put that phone down!" screamed a blond man with blue eyes, pointing his rifle at Evan.

"Hey, take it easy," said Brian and Urchart at the same time.

"Now!" screamed the blond man at Evan.

Evan froze with his eyes wide, the phone to his ear.

"You boys aren't on a security exercise, are you?" asked Brian, his face hard. "You're some kind of mercenaries. I've seen your type before, my friend."

Evan's look of fear was replaced by one of concentration. "Yes, this is Evan Athers. We have an emergency situation here at—"

His words were cut short as the blond man sprayed bullets into Evan's chest. The cell phone flew out of his hand and landed in the pool of water.

"What the hell!" screamed Amanda, rushing out from behind Charles to fall on her knees beside Evan. Her friend's eyes were wide; blood bubbled from his mouth.

"Get away from him!" yelled the blond man, pointing his rifle at Amanda's head.

"Jimmer!" yelled Urchart in an authoritative voice. "Put that rifle down now."

"Not till she gets away from him," he answered, his finger tightening on the trigger.

Amanda didn't even look at him. Instead, she was applying pressure to the chest wounds. She had taken an EMT certification course at LSU when she had contemplated pre-med. That had been twelve years ago, but everything came back quickly.

"I'm not going to tell you again, bitch!" screamed Jimmer.

"Go to hell, asshole," responded Amanda, working to stop the flow of blood.

Everyone's attention was focused on the standoff between Amanda and the maniac with the rifle. No one noticed as Brian stood up and pulled a long knife from the small of his back. He darted past the other soldiers and pushed the rifle away from his sister's head just as Jimmer pulled the trigger. With his knife hand, Brian jammed it deep into the blond man's neck before yanking it free and turning to the nearest soldier rushing his way. With a vicious upward swipe, Brian stabbed him in the groin.

Urchart felt movement to his left and turned to see a gigantic black man trying to escape up the hill with a redheaded woman. "Stop them!" he yelled pointing towards the two. "Don't let them escape!"

Urchart spun back to find a third soldier down with a knife sticking out of his right eye and Brian now had one of the assault rifles in his hands. He expertly cleared the rifle before dropping to one knee and sweeping the clearing.

Oh shit, Urchart thought, *we've got a problem here.*

Brian was about to turn the rifle in Urchart's direction, but there was a noise to his rear and he swept back around. The soldier behind him got off two shots, but they were rushed and went wide. Brian took a deep breath and put a shot into the soldier's chest

Now or never, thought Urchart. He drew his pistol and moved out from behind a tree toward the killer on his knee with the rifle.

Brian heard him at the last minute and spun with the rifle, but it was too late. He turned to look into the barrel of a large caliber pistol just before it blew his head off.

"NONONONONO!" screamed Amanda, moving away from Evan to cradle what was left of Brian's head.

Urchart motioned to one of his remaining men to take Amanda. He spun to find another holding the redhead down while five of his men were trying to subdue the huge man who was fighting with a fury and had already injured several of them badly.

Determined not to let the situation get any further out of control, Urchart strode up to the struggling mass of men and slammed the barrel of his pistol down on the black man's head.

The giant slumped and then tried to get up. Urchart hit him again, and the man became motionless.

Urchart focused on calming himself. "Situation report!" he barked.

Lyles spoke from beside him, "Three of ours dead and one badly wounded. We also have two dead civilians and three prisoners."

Brennan ran up from the lake area. "Sir, they had gear down by the lake. Doesn't look local, probably came in by boat. I'd bet at that cove a half mile north of here."

Urchart holstered his pistol and ran his other hand through his hair. "What a mess," he finally said.

"Yes, sir," answered Lyles. "And we still don't have Moses Mitchell."

Urchart had forgotten about Mitchell. "He's the least of our worries right now. We'll let him be until morning. I'll take Brennan with me to check out the north landing, see if there's a boat," he told Lyles. "You get the rest of the men, these bodies, and the prisoners back to camp ASAP."

"Should we initiate Chrome Protocol?" Lyles asked.

Urchart thought for a moment. Activation of that contingency would be an admission of failure by the security company he represented. Failure at his hands that could cost him dearly. "No, not yet," he answered. "We don't know if there was any compromise. We may be able to contain this all here."

"Roger, sir," answered Lyles, moving to get the remaining soldiers organized and ready to move.

This is bad, thought Urchart. *A homeless crazy person was not credible even if he were to escape and tell everything, but five missing civilians might be noticed. What if someone knew they had come to Bog Island?*

"Lyles," yelled Urchart, "one more thing."

The man turned back to the captain. "Yes, sir?"

"Just to be safe, let's go ahead and activate Iron Protocol."

Lyles looked a little uncertain. "Are you sure, sir?"

Urchart nodded. "I'm sure. Quarantine the island until further notice. No one gets on or off."

Chapter 7

Tiffany had been excited when the temp service called her to help cover a 911 line. Most of the jobs were boring and demanding. People treated part-time help with disdain and did all they could to work them to death until they left for some other thankless job. Tiffany couldn't wait until she graduated and could get a real job. Hell, a real career. Unfortunately, the temp job was the only real way to make ends meet while she finished up at the University of Arizona.

But this job had promised to be different. Manning the city's 911 operators during the summer vacation season certainly couldn't be boring. And how demanding could it be sitting in a chair and answering a phone for a few hours? After three weeks, she was sick of it.

Most calls were from drunks, or college kids looking for a ride home, or kids trying to be funny. Only once had she taken a call from someone who needed help, but by then, it was unnecessary. The whole switchboard had been lit up by people calling to report the warehouse fire.

Tiffany looked at her watch. Only an hour left, then she had to go take her biochem final. She felt ready for the test. One good thing about the 911 job, there was plenty of time to study.

She heard the ringing in her headset, meaning a call was coming in. Tiffany pulled out the official script. It was all choreographed. Say the same things. Get certain information. Remain calm. Call for help if needed. Boring and monotonous.

Tiffany's hand froze as she was about to initiate the call. The incoming number wasn't local. That wasn't too rare since cell phones were so prevalent and not tied to particular area codes, but she had never seen a number like the one on her display. 881-320-6513.

"An 881 number? What the hell is that?" she said aloud to Glenda, the lady beside her, but the older woman had a call of her own.

Taking a deep breath, Tiffany pushed the button to answer the call while looking at the script. "911, what is the nature of your emergency?"

The seriousness of the voice made Tiffany sit up straighter. "Yes, this is Evan Athers. We have an emergency situation here at—"

Then machine gun fire and then the call ended.

"Hello? Hello?" Tiffany paused at the dead line. She stared at the computer in front of her before she punched in the number attempting to return the call

A robotic female voice connected, "The Iridium subscriber you are attempting to contact is temporarily out of service. We apologize for the inconvenience."

Punching keys on her keyboard, Tiffany pulled up the digital recording of the call and listened to it again. Eight seconds in all. Tiffany's three second greeting. Evan Athers' four-second response. Then one second of gunfire.

Tiffany flipped the control switch, taking her offline for incoming calls and emailed the digital recording to her shift supervisor Randy. She then took off her headset and ran back to Randy's office. She knocked once on the frame of the open door to get his attention before walking in.

"Tiffany, how you doing? Are you okay?" Randy asked, seeing the tenseness in her face.

"I just got a strange call," she said. "I emailed it to you. I think you should listen to it."

"Sure." He pulled up the email and opened the file. "An 881 number."

"Yeah, what is that?"

"It's an Iridium satellite phone number," Randy answered. "We get them occasionally because one of their three ground stations is here in Tempe. That call could have come from anywhere in the western hemisphere. The low orbit satellites simply download calls to the nearest ground station. For a normal call, it doesn't matter, but 911 is a local call so it comes to us by default."

Tiffany was stunned. "Anywhere in the western hemisphere?"

"Sure," answered Randy, shaking his head. "I once took a call from a guy on a cruise ship off Chile. He was pissed because their cruise had cut off his line of credit at the blackjack tables and wanted the Coast Guard to come helicopter him to land."

She pointed at Randy's computer. "This one sounds serious. I think you should listen to it."

Randy clicked on the file while turning up his speakers. Concentrating, he listened to the file. Then he did the same a second time and then a third, taking notes the last time.

"Well, what do you make of it?" he finally asked her.

"Me? That's why I brought it in to you."

"Yes, but you actually spoke to him," he said. "Did it seem real to you?"

Tiffany didn't hesitate. "Hell, yes. I think we just heard someone get shot, maybe killed."

Randy nodded. "I think you're right. Hopefully, it wasn't this Evan Athers."

"So what do we do now?" she asked.

Randy shrugged. "Not much we can do. We don't even know where the call is coming from."

"Can't we at least call the police?"

He shrugged. "Which police? Tempe? Arizona State Troopers? Mexican Federalies? Canadian Mounties?"

Tiffany put her hands out to her sides. "There must be something we can do? Maybe we can Google Evan Athers and at least find out who he is."

Randy nodded and began typing on his computer before shaking his head. "Yep, just what I thought. There are at least two thousand hits for that name."

She dropped her hands beside her and sighed in exasperation.

"I'll email the file to my friend at the state police," he answered. "He can probably get the satellite phone company to give up information on the number, especially given the nature of the call. With any luck, the registered user is this Evan Athers, which will be tied to an address. The police can then send the info to that local police station to check into."

"How long is that going to take?"

Randy's lips tightened. "I'm not going to lie to you. Probably at least a week given the other things everyone has going on. And that's if there's a positive hit."

Tiffany's stomach sank. "I don't think that caller has a week. Hell, I'm not sure he has an hour. He could be badly hurt or dead by now."

"I know," answered Randy, "but there's nothing more we can do."

"This sucks," she said. "The one real call I get, the one chance to help someone, and there's nothing I can do but listen to possibly his last words."

"It's not your fault," he said kindly. "We can only do so much. It comes with the job."

"Yeah," she said standing up, "that's what I'm afraid of."

Tiffany walked out of the office and went to her desk to grab her book bag. She still had a test soon and needed to focus, but after that, she intended to call the temp service and tell them to find someone else to do this crappy job.

Chapter 8

Jack lay as still and silent as he could, fists clenched. His tears and grief went unheard. Waves of coldness flooded through him. He hated himself for staying hidden, although he knew there was nothing he could have done to stop the murder of his friends. Now his job was to escape and get help, and he knew he could only do that if he avoided those soldiers...or whatever they were.

He waited as the men called Urchart and Brennen went in search of the boat. Part of him wanted to rush ahead of them, but that would be folly. He was still hidden in the underbrush less than fifteen yards from the soldiers.

Jack watched the one called Lyles direct his men to bind a dazed Charles to the handles on the front of a metal fold-out stretcher. They piled the three dead soldiers on the stretcher, and two soldiers each took a handle at the rear while forcing Charles to carry the front end alone. Jack could tell it was immensely heavy by their straining, but even with what was likely a concussion, Charles appeared to be having an easier time handling the load than the two soldiers to his rear.

They stacked Brian and Evan on another stretcher carried by two more soldiers. They put the one wounded soldier, gray from blood loss and unconscious, onto another. Jack doubted the man would survive much longer. Brian's knife to the man's groin had likely severed several arteries and, although they had staunched the outward flow of blood, he was certainly bleeding internally.

Heather and Amanda were bound at their wrists by plastic flex cuffs and then to each other. The soldiers loaded all of Jack's friends' gear into their own backpacks. Lyles grabbed the bound wrists of the two stunned women and signaled for the rest of his men to follow him. With groans of effort, they picked up their stretchers and struggled up out of the bowl of rocks to flatter ground.

Then they were gone. Jack looked down and except for several pools of blood already fading brown into the undergrowth, there was no sign that he had just seen two dear friends murdered and three others kidnapped. Jack suddenly had an overwhelming desire to take a nap. Part of him recognized that this was ridiculous, but another part hoped that when he awoke everything would be better. Nothing but a bad dream. In reality, he actually was tired. He had consumed a lot of beer and his body was now reacting to a post-adrenaline flood. Just a little nap would do the trick.

Get going, son, said his father's voice in his head.

Jack's eyes snapped open. He hadn't even realized he'd gone to sleep. How long had he been out? Jack pushed himself backward out of the underbrush, finding it was much easier to extract himself than it had been to push forward. After a few moments, Jack managed to untangle himself completely from the thick undergrowth. Leaving the cooler, duffle bag, and fishing gear, Jack turned north and began running through the woods.

The two soldiers would likely use the trail, but it wasn't the shortest route. Jack hoped by cutting through the forest he could beat them to the boat and escape. He turned on an extra burst of speed, ignoring the thorns, vines, and mud attempting to slow him down.

He started to see an opening in the trees ahead of him and then water further beyond. Jack nearly burst through the trees onto the shore, but stopped as he heard voices. He crept forward silently and saw Urchart standing on the sand while Brennen climbed around on the boat.

"Sir," Brennen said, "it looks like we have sleeping bags and gear for six, not just five."

Urchart stared at Brennen. "Damn it to hell! Just when I thought this day couldn't get any worse. Now we're possibly looking for another civilian out there."

"Could just be an extra," Brennen said.

Urchart shook his head. "I doubt it. Regardless we can't take that chance."

"What do you want me to do with the boat?"

"How well do you swim Brennen?"

Brennen smiled. "Like a fish, sir."

"Good, strap all the gear down, take the boat out into deep water and sink it. Then swim back here. Should have just enough light left to do it before dark."

Jack groaned in despair, much too loud.

Urchart slowly turned in the direction where Jack was hiding and held up his hand to Brennen. "You hear that?"

"Hear what?" asked Brennen.

"Someone. Close." Urchart started walking towards Jack's hiding spot, his pistol out before him.

Jack held his breath, willing the man to go away, but Urchart kept creeping closer and closer. Fighting the urge to flee, Jack crouched down lower. A branch snapped loudly beneath him.

Urchart froze. He turned slightly towards the sound and moved with purpose towards Jack.

Indecision flooded Jack's already exhausted brain. He felt like a rabbit, pursued by dogs. Like the rabbit, Jack willed himself not to be.

Urchart moved nearer still. He felt he was close. Someone was here. With any luck, it was the missing civilian or maybe even Moses Mitchell.

Jack was trembling now. He couldn't help it. Adrenaline was flooding into him again. Death was hovering over him. He could smell it.

Urchart's face came into view. They were only separated by a few branches now.

Urchart stopped again and stood searching. His eyes were locked on the ground and trees. His head kept turning from one side to the other as if something was off. His eyes froze and began to move up towards Jack's head. Urchart locked eyes with a face looking fearfully out at him.

"Hello, friend," said Urchart. "Why don't you come on out of there now. You're safe with us."

Jack bolted. He ran as fast as his legs would carry him, not even looking where he was going. He felt a sharp blow and then searing pain in his right shoulder that almost knocked him off his feet. A loud gunshot echoed behind him.

I've been shot, Jack thought. *Holy shit.*

You're going to get shot again if you don't pick up the pace, his father's voice said.

Jack followed the advice, somehow finding the energy to speed up. Two more shots followed, but both went wide. He could hear Urchart crashing behind him.

Legs and lungs burning, Jack wasn't sure how long he ran, but when he fell jumping over a log, he found he didn't have the strength to get back up. He lay there in the grass heaving great gasps of air, waiting for the bullet that would end his life.

His breathing slowed, and Jack noticed it was getting dark. He listened for his pursuers, but heard nothing but nocturnal insects and frogs. Pushing himself up, Jack cried out from the shooting pain in his shoulder. He reached around to the back of his shoulder and probed at the seeping hole until he could no longer stand the pain. When he pulled his hand back, his fingertips were covered with blood.

"I need to get to a hospital," he said out loud and was a little frightened at how weak his voice sounded.

He was also starting to shiver. The temperature was dropping with the sun going down, but that couldn't be all of it. Jack recognized that he likely had a fever and could even be going into shock as a result of blood loss and physical trauma.

Pulling himself carefully onto wobbly feet, Jack saw a nearby pool of standing water and realized how desperately thirsty he was.

"No," he croaked. "Get sick. Need to find running water. Clean water."

But Jack ignored the advice. Falling forward into the stagnant pool, Jack slurped up muddy water. It was the most delicious thing that had ever passed through his lips.

When he was unable to drink any further, Jack carefully got on his feet again, mindful of not using his wounded shoulder.

"Need to find someplace to wait out the night," he heard himself say. "Someplace safe. And dry."

Jack looked around. He knew much of Bog Island from years roaming its wooded slopes and marshy lowlands as a youth, but nothing looked familiar. He turned until he could find the setting sun. They had chased him from the north; maybe he should keep heading south.

Staring longingly at the setting sun, Jack turned left and proceeded south down a small valley path. He looked for any shelter that would protect him all the time conscious of the lengthening shadows and waning light.

He was beginning to despair when he spotted a darker than usual shadow in the nearby hill. Climbing with difficulty up the wooded slope, he found a depression in the earth. It wasn't as deep as some animal dens he'd seen as a child, but it would have to do. Jack lay down in the hole and pushed himself as far back as he could while pulling leaves and branches in after him. Hopefully they would provide him some insulation from the night cold and the ground.

And prevent any pursuers from seeing him.

Jack thought about his friends, and he had to hold back tears.

I'm sorry I brought to here, he thought. *All my fault, so sor—*

A troubled sleep pulled Jack into a deep embrace.

Chapter 9

Moses Mitchell had learned during his short life that it was important to be grateful for the little things. Big things were often unattainable or a mirage. Little things were what made life bearable.

So he was grateful for the setting sun and another night of freedom.

They'll stop searching for you in the dark, said Billy. *They're afraid of the night.*

Moses wasn't afraid of the night. He'd become comfortable with it living on the streets and appreciated the safety darkness could provide.

Still have to be careful, said Delores. *You break a leg or something in the dark and you're as good as dead.*

Slowing slightly, Moses made his way back towards where he'd seen the group of young people in the water. He'd heard the gunshots and knew they were likely captured by the bad men or worse, but maybe they had left something useful for Moses. The sky was hazy, but enough moonlight filtered through trees to allow him to find his way.

Better watch for booby traps, you booby, said Nate. *They've done it before.*

Nate was right. That's how they had caught him the second time. Moses squatted down to look ahead through the grass. If they left a surprise for him, it would probably be around the waterhole where they had likely killed those others.

Moses stopped and studied the terrain more and more often as he got closer, but didn't see anything. He moved up slowly until he could look down into the rocky bowl filled with water.

"Oh, those dirty bastards," whispered Moses. They hadn't left him anything. Not even the music player.

He started to back up into the security of the forest shadows when he noticed something to his right. Square and burnt orange in color.

Moses had to make his way slowly to avoid getting tangled in the thick vines on the north side of the bowl. Whoever had put the orange thing in the vines must have really wanted to hide it.

Moses chuckled when he saw the tackle box. He popped it open and saw lures, fishing line, hooks, weights, and even a long, sharp dressing knife. He could do a lot with this bounty.

Look around, dummy, said Nate.

Moses did and his eyes got wide. Not only were their two collapsible fishing poles, but a black duffle bag and small cooler. He felt the outside of the cooler and found it was cold.

Don't open it, said Delores. *This isn't a safe place. Let it stay cold as long as possible, whatever it is.*

"Good idea," he whispered reaching for the black duffle. He unfastened it slowly to minimize the sound. He couldn't believe what he found.

There were two packages of hot dogs along with buns. Bags of potato chips and boxes of snack cakes. He even found a couple of cans of mixed nuts. Moses' mouth flooded with saliva, and his stomach rumbled loudly. He reached for the nuts.

Don't do it, said Billy. *Take it all away to a safe place.*

Moses whined indecisively and then picked up the can of nuts anyway.

You want to get caught and end up back in the camp? Dolores asked. *They'll take not only all of this, but your freedom too. This time they are going to kill you, Moses.*

"I'm so hungry," Moses whispered. "Just a little bit, that's all."

Paaaleease, said Nate. *You've never been able to do anything halfway in your life. You start eating here, you won't stop until you make yourself sick as a dog. At least get someplace else first, you dumb shit.*

Moses hated it when they teamed up on him, but knew they would keep at him unless he did as they wanted. He collected up all his treasures and then slowly melted back into the forest's protective darkness.

Chapter 10

Jack's friends were in trouble. Something was coming through the woods, menacing and evil. Jack screamed at his friends to run, but they ignored him. Loud music blared from the very heavens, the sun thumping to the beat of the drums.

He was running through the forest toward them, but they were impossibly far away. His feet were sucked into the muddy ground and thick vines reached out to wrap around him. Jack was a child again and his father was in trouble somewhere.

"You got to help 'em," said Uncle Johnny.

Jack looked over and saw the old black man whittling away at a branch with the pearl handle pocketknife. The letters JAT glowed eerily on the handle.

"How?" Jack asked.

The old man smiled. "You'll figure it out, I wager." He turned back to his whittling. "Or you won't, but you gotta try. Otherwise this island will chew you up and spit you out. It ain't a place for the weak or the unworthy. You want to make it here, you better be prepared to spit in the devil's eye."

"I don't understand," said Jack. "Where's Dad?"

"Your father's dead, boy," answered Uncle Johnny, not unkindly. "Time to grow up and be a man on your own. That time comes for everyone. Be strong, son."

"If they catch me," Jack said, "they might kill me."

The old man stopped whittling. "Ain't you been listening to me, boy? There's far worse things than dying. Everybody dies, you only get to chose whether it's lying down or standing." Uncle Johnny then threw the pocketknife at Jack's feet where it stuck in the ground with the pearl handle pointing up in the air.

Jack reached down and pulled the knife out of the ground. When he looked up the old man was gone. Folding up the pocketknife, he saw that it now said "Bog Island" on the handle. Jack put the knife in his pocket and started walking towards where he knew his friends waited.

Soldiers with guns fell in beside him. Jack tried to get away from them, but his feet were not his own. He was dressed as they were and carried a rifle with a bayonet attached. They all giggled and smiled in anticipation of what was coming.

His friends were waiting for them in the rocky bowl, but each was stripped naked and bound to a stake in the earth. Their eyes were wild and pleaded with him for help. Jack felt the pressure of the soldiers behind him. He knew what was expected. What he had to do. He shook his head, tears pouring down his face.

"No," he said. "I won't do it."

A ghoulish half-dead version of Urchart laughed. "Jack, you've already done it."

Jack looked back at his friends and saw they all had blood pouring out of their chest and stomach. Their accusing eyes pierced him. His hands dropped the rifle with the bloody bayonet.

The ghoulish soldiers laughed, and Jack ran. He heard them chasing him, not just the soldiers, but his dying friends. They shambled through the brush, falling and climbing back up, determined and eager for his blood.

Running for what seemed like eons, he burst out of the forest onto the cove where they had left their boat. The water was peaceful and still, but there was no boat in sight.

"You know this isn't real, right?" said a voice to his right.

Jack turned to see his father sitting on a log, fishing. His father, not as he had been when he died, but young and vibrant. The night had suddenly been replaced by early morning.

"Dad?" Jack asked.

"You're having a nightmare," his father said, casting his line far out into the water. "Brought on by fever from that gunshot."

"Gunshot?" Jack looked at his shoulder and saw the blood and felt the pain anew. When he looked up, his father was gone. Jack turned to find Urchart standing there.

"I bet it hurts," he said. He pulled back his fist and slammed it into Jack's injured shoulder.

Jack fell backwards in agony. He looked at his shoulder and saw Uncle Johnny's ivory-handled pocketknife sticking out. On the handle, it read, "Jack's gonna die!"

Water was seeping up over his face, pulling him out into the water. It was hard to breathe. Jack flailed and struggled, but it was no use.

"Wake up," said half-dead Urchart gleefully. "Wakeup wakeup wakeup." His voice slowly changed from the rough rattle to a young girl's. The water closed over his face and pulled him down deep.

Jack struggled up out of his delirium and opened his eyes to morning light and waves of dizziness. The next thing he saw was a pretty waif of a girl with jet-black hair shaking him.

"Wake up, wake up," she said. "You're sick, got to get you some help."

He stopped struggling and felt like he was going to be sick. Jack pushed himself up on one elbow with a herculean effort. After a moment, he was able to keep himself from vomiting. He lay backwards again, breathing heavily, and looked at the girl.

"Who are you?" he rasped.

She smiled. "Don't worry, I'm a friend."

Jack shook his head. "I don't have any friends. All my friends are gone."

Before she could answer, he lost consciousness again.

Chapter 11

Lucas Ross was an avid chess player. He relished out-thinking his opponent and always staying a few steps ahead. So often, he was able to do the same in real life. Being surprised was enough of a novelty that Lucas could appreciate it, but President Wilkens had not surprised him.

In fact, she had made the worst of three available moves. She could have done nothing in reaction to Governor St Keel's interview and talk of a presidential campaign, allowing the speculation to run rampant. She could have been receptive and supportive of St Keel as a future VP candidate and thereby abandoning Vice President Tipton. Instead, she had publically supported Tipton and renounced St Keel.

Her political advisor should be fired, he thought.

Lucas studied the numbers again. Janice Wilkens' approval ratings had dropped five points since her latest emotional press conference. Better yet, the leading candidate challengers weren't terribly popular either. The American people wanted something different. They wanted someone who was about results, not just empty promises. Someone like Eric St Keel.

Bridgett, one of his aides, knocked on his open office door. "Sir, you wanted to see me?"

Lucas waved her in. "Did you leak that story about the governor avoiding a bribe when he was a young intern?"

His aide smiled. "Yes, sir, there should be an exposé on the virtues of the governor next week."

"Good work," he said. "Don't let that reporter stray too far. We need him for a while longer. Also, don't give it up too easy. Make him work for it so he doesn't get suspicious."

"Allen doesn't suspect anything," she said with a smug smile, "and he's not going anywhere."

Lucas nodded satisfied, and Bridgett left. He had orchestrated the meeting between the two a year ago, and now they were lovers. In addition to planting storylines in their favor, Bridgett was able to obtain valuable information about what would be published days before the public ever knew.

Devin Coldwell strode into Lucas' office, closed the door, and sat down without permission. Lucas' former deputy in Oman was one of the few men who would dare take such liberties. The General tolerated these things from Devin because the man didn't read too much into them and was very good at what he did.

"Sir, we have a development you should be aware of."

Lucas sighed. "You know it's never good news when you use the word *development*. Why not expand your vocabulary, try *catastrophe* or *disaster* or *upheaval*?"

Devin shrugged, impervious to sarcasm. "I like the word development. No point in making too much of something until we know what we have."

"Okay," said Lucas, "so what do we have? What is the *development*?"

"They've initiated Iron Protocol at Site Iaso," Devin said. "Our hired gun there, Urchart, is claiming it is simply a routine drill."

Lucas sighed. "What is Iron Protocol again?"

"Quarantine. The locals are used to it," Devin explained. "Being a national park, they'll explain this is to protect the spawning or migration or breeding of some obscure endangered turtle or bird or fish."

"And those people buy it?"

"For short durations, sure. Plus, there are only a handful of them on the island anyway."

"So, why are you telling me about this *development*?" Lucas asked.

"Because my sources tell me this is not routine. There's at least one escapee, and somehow they've lost four men."

"Lost? You mean dead?" asked Lucas, sitting up straighter.

Devin nodded. "I talked to the company customer rep this morning and replacements are en route with the next group of prisoners. Urchart will certainly come up with a story about a tragic accident or the like."

"But that's not what happened?"

"Still not certain," answered Devin, "but it looks like the men were killed in a fight somehow. Not sure if it had to do with the escapee or each other. You know isolated soldiers with too much time can get violent."

"I know that only too well," growled Lucas ominously.

"Yes, of course," said Devin. "Anyway, Urchart is motivated to keep a tight lid on things, but he will be forced to let us know if anything goes too badly."

Lucas sat back and thought. Chess moves within chess moves. He smiled and sat back up.

"Let him keep thinking we are none the wiser," Lucas said. "Take steps to ensure everything ties back to Urchart if the situation should deteriorate."

Devin nodded and stood. He turned to walk out the door.

"And Devin," Lucas said before the man could open the door, "make damn sure things do not deteriorate. At least not until after the next election. After that, we can do whatever we want, but for now, the Chiron Project and everything that ties to it needs to stay totally covert. You understand?"

"That's what I'm best at, sir." Devin grinned before turning and walking away.

Lucas stared after his former deputy. Was he putting too much power in the man's hands? Could Devin take them down?

Chess moves within chess moves.

The General made a mental note to dig into Devin's background a little deeper. He had significant leverage over the man, but it never hurt to have more. As a matter of fact, it wouldn't hurt to do the same with this Urchart character.

Is there a connection between the two? Lucas wondered. *Now why haven't I asked that question before?*

Lucas reached over and buzzed the intercom at Bridgett's desk.

"Yes, sir," she answered instantly.

"Hold all my calls for the rest of the day, and no visitors," he said. "I need some time to think."

Chapter 12

Jack woke at times to find himself stumbling, carried along by the beautiful dark girl. Other times he was somewhere else, and yet sometimes these two worlds merged. He even talked to his friends and father while the girl supported him through the shadowy woods.

"You're hallucinating," said her oddly musical voice. "It's from the fever."

Jack roused himself enough to look at her. His initial hazy impression had been grossly inaccurate. This girl wasn't beautiful; she was stunning. Her face had the high cheekbones of the French, but the coloring of the escaped slaves who settled the island. She had a look that made it impossible to determine her age, and she could have equally passed from anywhere between eighteen and twenty-eight. Her black hair was pulled back and gathered together into a long braid and secured by a bit of cord that accented her dark olive-shaped eyes and full lips. Even in rough and slightly dirty clothing, Jack thought she was the most gorgeous woman he had ever seen.

"Who are you?" he rasped.

"Rena," she answered. "My father and I live on the east end of the island."

"How did you find me?"

She laughed. "How could I not? I was out collecting roots and mushrooms, and I could hear you from a hundred yards away yelling in your sleep."

Jack stumbled over a limb and felt the wound on the rear of his shoulder open up again. He moaned as fresh blood ran down his back.

"I'd say that's a bullet wound," she said while helping him up. "And you look like you've been running from something. What happened?"

Careful, son, whispered his father's ghostly presence beside him.

Jack remembered one of his first trials as a young lawyer. Levi Timmons had shot and killed his fishing partner over a drunk dispute about whose turn it was to buy fuel for their boat. He'd been able to get the man off with only a year. His partner had shot first after all, at least according to Levi's testimony.

"My friend and I had a fight while fishing," said Jack.

"That looks like more than a fight," she said.

Jack grunted. "We'd been drinking. A lot. Said some things we shouldn't have. We fought, and then he chased me through the woods."

"And shot you?"

"Levi Timmons tends to take things personal," answered Jack. "He'll cool off and everything will be okay. He wasn't trying to kill me; he was just mad."

"Sounds like you need some new friends," she said.

Jack nearly choked on her words. "I'd settle for getting my old ones back."

Rena stopped and shrugged him off her shoulder while easing him down onto a dry patch of dirt. She laid him back against an ancient tree and looked around worriedly. She put her hand on his forehead while giving him a drink from her canteen.

"You're burning up," she said. "I've got medicine back at our cabin, but it's gonna take a while to get there carrying you like this." She gazed around carefully and with a nod of approval moved to a tall dark tree. She pulled a hunting knife from her belt and began scraping at the bark.

"What are you doing?" he rasped. The wispy forms of Brian and Evan walked over to stare at her actions as if curious.

She drew her knife down in careful strokes. "This is a black willow tree. It's not as good as real aspirin, but might get your fever down. Don't want you going into shock or having a seizure before we can get home."

"Are you a doctor or something?" he asked.

Rena smiled. "Not exactly. I'm the closest thing to a doctor on this island. My mother was a nurse and taught me everything she knew before she ran off and left Poppa and me. The island taught me the rest."

"You stayed here with you father?"

"Sure." She smiled, walking back to him. "We like it here. She just wasn't made the same way we were."

Jack looked at his friend Brian who stood behind her. Brian gave Jack a wink and thumbs up gesture, whereas Evan just shrugged.

Rena carefully peeled the exposed inside of the bark away and put the thin strips into her mouth. She kept doing this until her cheek was sticking out so far she looked like it contained an exceptionally large wad of chewing tobacco. Rena then pulled the wad out of her mouth and held it before his face.

"Open up," she said.

Jack hesitated. He hadn't ever considered himself a germophobe, but he was still a little grossed out.

Rena smiled. "Come on now, city boy. I ain't got too many cooties, and it's either this or I can give it to you rectally. Won't make any difference to your body."

Jack's mouth snapped open.

"There we go," she said in a soothing voice as she plopped the wad into his mouth. "Now chew that and don't swallow it, or choke on it. Tastes bad I know, but it will get your fever down."

The bitterness nearly made Jack gag, but he chewed nevertheless. Having her saliva in his mouth seemed so strikingly intimate that Jack suddenly felt awkward around this mysterious woman.

As if reading his thoughts, she looked at him curiously. "I just realized I don't even know your name."

"I'm Jack," he answered in a muffled reply. "Jack Winter." The words were out of his mouth before he had to time to consider if it were wise to tell her his real name.

Rena smiled. "Nice to meet you, Jack Winter. And in case you die on me and I don't get a chance to tell you, it has been a pleasure."

Jack would have laughed if he could. Rena was the most interesting woman he had met since...well, since Heather. The thought of his captured friend sobered him, and his smile vanished. Jack looked up to see Rena studying him closely.

"Come on," she finally said, helping him up to lean on her shoulder and moving carefully east

He realized after a time that he no longer had chills and his dead friends and father were noticeably absent. The willow bark must be helping his fever. He also noticed that the pain in his shoulder wasn't as great.

"How much farther?" he asked.

"Best if you don't know," she answered. "Not as far as it was and further than it will be in a minute. Just keep putting one foot in front of the other, and I'll handle the rest"

Jack struggled along on leaden legs, keeping his eyes on the ground and moving forward. After what seemed like weeks, he felt Rena stop. Jack lifted his head with effort and spotted a small stone and timber cabin covered in moss and vines through the trees. A thin line of smoke rose from a chimney.

"Your home?" Jack asked in little more than a whisper.

"It is. Poppa's out fishing, but will be back before dark." She laughed. "He'll want to show me his catch, but I think mine will be bigger than anything he got."

Jack grimaced. "Is that supposed to be funny?"

"I think so," she answered with a smile. "Our humor probably isn't as sophisticated as you are used to on the mainland, but you'll eventually come to appreciate it. If you survive that is."

"More humor?"

Rena shook her head. "No, that's serious. This will be the first bullet wound I've ever treated. Not too worried about that. The problem is you've been out in the woods all night and most of the morning, and I don't have antibiotics. If you die, it will be the infection that gets you."

"Your bedside manner is awful," he croaked.

"Just wait until you *see* my bedside manner," she answered.

Jack groaned and limped towards the entrance to the cabin on Rena's shoulder. He realized that she was panting and that this trip had to have been exhausting on her. She had supported most of his weight for what was likely two or three miles at least, and he estimated he outweighed her by fifty pounds.

"By the way, I wanted to say thank you," he said.

"Don't thank me yet," she said, helping him through the door. The interior was surprisingly large compared to the outside impression. The inside was rustic, but clean and neat. A main room huddled around a large fireplace, which was adjacent to a kitchen that was dominated by an old wood-burning stove. The furniture was homemade, but sturdy and comfortable looking. The walls were hung with tools, traps, supplies, and fishing gear. Two open doorways led off the main room, and Rena guided him towards the one on the right.

"Over this way," Rena said, steering him towards a small wood-framed bed. Jack started to lie down, but she pulled him back. "Nope, need you to lie on your stomach so I can work on that shoulder."

Jack complied. "Maybe you should call a doctor or take me to the mainland."

Rena shook her head. "Phones don't work here, and I'm not sure you'd survive a boat ride in your condition. As a matter of fact, I'm surprised you're still alive at all."

"Humor?" asked Jack.

"A little bit." She smiled. "See, you're starting to get it." She left the room to boil water over the fire and returned with a small table and a canvas bag. She set the table beside his wounded shoulder and pulled up a three-legged stool from the corner to squat on. Rena unzipped her bag and pulled out a small glass bottle of clear liquid. Inserting a syringe into the end, she carefully pulled out an inch of the contents before putting the bottle away.

"What's that?" asked Jack.

"This," she said, sticking it into his arm and injecting the contents, "is to knock you out while I patch you up. You should have a nice little nap, and when you wake up, everything will be just wonderful."

Jack grunted. "If only that were..." His voice drifted off as he slipped into unconsciousness.

Rena carefully stripped Jack of his clothes and slipped a plastic sheet under him before starting an IV. Carefully laying her instruments on the table in front of her, she then began dropping them

81

in the pot of water over the fire. She looked at Jack's pants on the floor bulging with the distinct outline of a wallet.

Don't worry, Rena thought. *He's who he says he is, no threat to us.*

She reached over and pulled the wallet out anyway and began writing down information on a notepad and then methodically went through the rest of his pockets. The ivory pocketknife caused her to catch her breath, and she looked at the man before her more carefully.

Her father would not be happy she had brought this stranger to their home. He was cautious and protective by nature. If he thought the stranger was even a possible threat, he might take him out in the boat, weight him down, and sink him in deep water. Rena didn't like it, but she understood that on the island, you were on your own and handled your own business.

Rena chewed her lip and looked down at Jack's profile. She reached out and carefully stroked his hair before letting her hand drop. His breathing sounded strange, and she noticed that he still had the wad of willow bark in his cheek. She pulled it out and dropped it into the boiling water with the instruments, figuring it couldn't hurt anything and might help.

That was good enough reason to do something on the island—it didn't hurt and might help. Hopefully, that was the case with her helping this stranger.

Pushing a loose strand of dark hair out of her face, Rena retrieved the pot of boiling water she had hung over the fireplace that contained her operating equipment. She pulled out a hot scalpel and forceps with tongs and began probing for the bullet.

Chapter 13

Jack woke to the smell of food and a rumbling stomach. He opened his eyes and saw the lengthening shadows of approaching evening through the window. Sitting up slowly, he carefully pulled out the IV line and swung his feet to the ground.

It felt as if he had been asleep for days. He gingerly rotated his right shoulder and felt pain and soreness, but not as much as he would have expected. Jack pulled back the blankets and realized he was naked underneath. Yanking the blankets back quickly, his face reddened thinking of Rena.

"Hello?" he called out. "Rena?"

A large black man with a short beard stepped into the doorway staring down at Jack. Appraising him.

Jack was at a loss for words and just looked at the imposing figure.

"You're better, I see," the man finally said.

Jack rubbed his shoulder. "Yes, thank you."

The man shook his head. "Don't thank me; it was all Rena."

"She said she lives here with her father. Is that you?"

He didn't answer immediately. "It is. I'm Deloy Dequese, and this is my cabin."

"Yes," answered Jack looking around, "do you know where my clothes went?"

"Where did you put them when you took them off?" Deloy asked seriously.

Jack's face must have shown the horror he felt. "I…uh...I..."

The big man's face finally split into a wide grin. "Just playing with you. Rena laid out some fresh clothes for you there." He pointed to a pile of worn but clean clothes, his personal affects stacked neatly on top.

Jack moved to get dressed, expecting the big man to give him some privacy, but he just remained there watching. Doing his best to ignore Rena's father, he stood on unsteady legs and began dressing, the clothes only slightly too large for him.

"Where'd you get that pocketknife?" Deloy asked.

It took a moment for him to realize what the man was talking about. "I found it in the ruins of an old house north of here." Jack answered, pulling on pants.

Deloy eyed him closely. "I once knew a man who carried a knife just like that."

Jack froze. "Uncle Johnny?"

"He was Johnny Crittenton to us," said Rena's voice from behind her father.

Stunned by both the fact that they knew Uncle Johnny and that Rena had likely been standing there the whole time he had been dressing, Jack just stared at them.

"How did you know Johnny?" asked Deloy.

Jack continued getting dressed. "He worked for my father when I was young and used to bring us to this island to fish in the summers. I was coming to visit him, but I see his house is gone."

"You and your friend?" asked Rena pointedly.

"Excuse me?" Jack asked.

"You and your friend Levi were coming to see him right? That good friend of yours who shot you and then left you for dead?"

Jack smiled. "It sounds bad when you put it that way."

"I'm not judging," she answered. "Mainland ways are mainland ways. Just because we don't shoot our friends here doesn't mean that's the best way. To each his own."

"Do you know what happened to Uncle Johnny?" Jack asked. "I was here ten years ago after he retired from working for my father. He was in that cabin and doing fine. He hasn't died, has he?"

Rena and Delay looked at each other before the big man spoke. "I'm afraid to be the one to tell you, son, but John Crittenton died six years ago. Stroke, I believe."

Jack's heart sank. He hadn't realized how much he hoped to see and talk to Uncle Johnny. The man had been a tie to his father and could have answered so many questions. "What happened to his house?" he asked.

"He had some distant relative who got the house and sold it to the park," Rena answered. "Park service tore down the house after adding the land to their holdings. Johnny would have been okay with that, I'd say."

"Yes," murmured Jack. "He loved it here."

"You have to, otherwise you go elsewhere." Deloy looked at his daughter after saying this and then turned away awkwardly. "Anyway, let me go check on dinner. Are you hungry?"

"Very," said Jack as the man moved away to the stove. Jack cocked his head at Rena. "Wait a minute. Dinner? Have I been out cold all day?"

She laughed. "Noooo, you've been out two days. You got here yesterday morning."

Jack's mouth dropped open. *What's happened to my friends?* he wondered. *Are they even still alive?*

"Do you happen to have a telephone I could use?" he asked.

Rena shook her head. "Afraid not. Like I told you, they don't work here. We go to the park station if we need to make a call, but never do. You can use the CB radio, but not sure who you could reach on that; the range is pretty short."

"Could I call the police on it?"

Rena didn't answer for a moment. "About your friend shooting you?"

Jack paused, still cautious. "No, I don't want to get him into trouble, just wanted to make sure he's okay since I can't call him. He was acting strangely, not at all like himself."

"Food's ready," Deloy called.

Jack moved toward the kitchen and felt his legs wobble beneath him.

"Easy there," Rena said, reaching out to steady him. "You're going to be weak for a few days. I couldn't give you any blood, not

87

even plasma, so you need to take it slow while you recover." She sat him down at a chair beside her father and in front of a plate piled with fried fish and what appeared to be beans, cooked squash, and rice.

Deloy led them in grace and then dug into the food. Jack tried the fish first and found it delicious. "This is good," said Jack appreciatively.

"Caught it this morning," said Deloy. "Fish is always better the same day it's caught. That's why I never eat fish when I'm on the mainland."

"How often do you go there?" asked Jack.

Deloy chewed slowly and eyed him. "Three or four times a week. That's where I go to sell my fish and get supplies."

"Can you take me there the next time you go?" Jack asked.

Deloy started to answer, but Rena jumped in. "The open boat is no place for you in your condition. You need at least a few more days to heal up."

The big man looked at his daughter curiously and then back at Jack. "She's right. A lot can happen in a boat and not all of its good. Best to wait a few more days; we'll take you then. You need me to take a message to anyone or make a call for you?"

"Maybe Poppa can check on your friend Levi," Rena offered.

Jack shook his head. "No, that's fine. I'm sure he's okay. I'll look him up once I get back."

Rena and her father exchanged a sidelong glance, and Jack sensed they suspected something. He tried to think of anything to say that would make everything all right.

"Fish is really good," Jack muttered.

"You already said that," said Rena. "If you want more, just ask."

Jack realized he did want more. Rena piled fried fish on his plate, and as he ate, his mind kept drifting off, worrying about his friends.

I've got to find them and get them back to the mainland, he thought. *I started this nightmare and it's up to me to end it.*

Chapter 14

"I need you there," said Eric St Keel. "Nothing goes according to plan unless you're there to make sure of it."

Lucas closed his eyes and tightened his hand on the telephone. One of the downsides of being essential was that you were *always* needed. Even when you weren't really needed.

"Sir, this is just a routine fundraiser," Lucas explained. "I've sent you your speech, and I've been assured everything is ready to go."

"They always say that," said St Keel a little peevishly, "but you know it's never true. We're in the homestretch, Lucas. You said so yourself, we can't afford to let anything go wrong now."

Taking a deep breath, Lucas pulled up the calendar on his computer. "You're right, I'll shuffle some things and see you tomorrow night."

"Very good," answered St Keel. "Gotta go, see you then."

As soon as the call ended, Bridgett buzzed him.

Lucas suppressed his slight annoyance. "Yes, Bridgett?"

"Sir, Devin is asking to speak to you on the secure line. He's holding now."

"Yes, thank you," he answered. "Please make sure I am not disturbed during this call."

"Certainly, sir."

After the door was closed, Lucas picked up his secure phone. They had to pay a fortune for the service, but the extra security had certainly paid off before. "Devin, this is Lucas."

"Yes, I have a few updates on our earlier situation at Site Iaso. We might have a problem."

"No. We do not," said Lucas. "Whatever it is, we cannot allow it to be a problem."

Devin sighed. "My source at the Avery Island Marina said someone rented a boat a few days ago and hasn't brought it back."

Lucas' mind worked at the information. "You think the person who rented the boat went to Bog Island? Maybe that's why Urchart initiated the quarantine?"

"Possibly, although we've worked hard to make that place seem like a malaria infested quagmire to the public" answered Devin. "The boat was supposed to be back last night. The owner told my guy he's charging double for the extra day, and if it's not back by tomorrow morning, he is going to report it stolen to the police."

"Did he say how many people were on the boat?" asked Lucas.

"Two women and four men," answered Devin.

"Shit," hissed Lucas. "Wait until dark, and have every car that is still in the parking lot towed. Make sure the tow truck driver keeps his mouth shut about where the vehicles came from."

"Will do," answered Devin.

"Also," continued Lucas, "get a copy of that boat contract and see who he rented it to."

"Already done," said Devin.

Lucas continued. "If we can pay the guy to forget the whole affair that might even be best. How much can a boat like that cost anyway?"

"More than you'd think," answered Devin.

"But cheaper than dealing with a police cleanup," said Lucas. "The last incident nearly wiped out our discretionary fund."

"Understand, do you want me to do anything about Urchart?"

Lucas thought. "Does he still have the situation contained?"

"He does, but by procedure, he's supposed to report these sorts of incidents," Devin explained. "So far nothing."

"We can use that to our advantage," Lucas answered. "He'll do anything to keep us from finding out, which means keeping everything bottled up. With that said, you might want to be thinking about who to replace him with should things go south."

"Got it," answered Devin. "Uh, there's something else."

"Like all of this isn't enough?"

"The name on the boat contract is Jackson Winter," explained Devin.

Lucas shook his head. "Is that name supposed to mean something? Oh shit...no, it can't be."

"Yes," answered Devin. "Jackson Winter is the son of Jeremiah Winter. Jack's a lawyer in a firm up in Lafayette. Pretty good one from what I can gather."

Putting his hand over his eyes, Lucas murmured. "The only son of Supreme Court Justice Jeremiah Winter is missing after renting a boat near Bog Island?"

"That's about right."

"Okay," Lucas said, "you do everything to control things at the marina. Are you there?"

"On my way."

"Good, I think you need to stay there until this is under control. I might even need you to go over to Site Iaso if this gets any worse."

"Understood."

"Call me tonight on this line to give me an update," Lucas directed.

"Got it," Devin answered and hung up.

Lucas Ross sat thinking. Eventually, they wouldn't be able to keep the lid on the disappearance of Jeremiah Winter's son. Jeremiah was one of Governor St Keel's longest and dearest friends, and some reaction might be expected. The question was did this in any way endanger operations at Site Iaso or the Chiron Project itself?

Lucas pushed the page button.

"Yes, sir," answered Bridgett.

"I need you to come in here," he said. "We need to work on a potential situation."

Bridgett walked in and closed the door behind her.

"Can you be subtle with your journalist lover?"

The beautiful and leggy brunette smiled and looked offended at the same time. "Sir! Really?"

"Okay, I figured as much," he said. "Now listen, you tell your boy that you have it on good authority from a very reliable but unnamed source that the only son of Jeremiah Winter is missing."

"Missing?" she asked. "How? Where did he go?"

"Your source doesn't know," he answered, "but there have been some whispers that he's never really gotten over his father's death. Had trouble at work supposedly. Dealing with grief, dabbling in drugs, that sort of thing. Wouldn't surprise anyone if he just ran off. Poor man might have even had a nervous breakdown. Totally understandable, lots of people worried, hope he's okay. Might even be suicidal, that type of hype. Got it?"

"Easy," she answered, giving him a sexy smile that promised more if he wanted. "Anything else?"

"No, that's all," he answered briskly. He wouldn't fall into that trap so easily. Bridgett was good, one reason he'd recruited her, but not that good.

Bridgett nodded before turning and walking out of the office.

Lucas pulled up his non-attributable Internet connection and logged into their private security connection. It gave them access to a wide variety of databases only available to law enforcement and government officials.

He needed to know everything he could about Jackson Winter.

Chapter 15

FBI Special Agent Deborah Mitchell stared at the man hard. "Are you sure? It gets crowded here I know; maybe you missed him."

"I wouldn't miss Moses," said Cliff, who ran the Kingston Shelter in the Vieux Carre section of New Orleans. "He always makes a point of saying hello when he stops by. It's got to be at least six months since I've seen him."

Deborah hung her head. She had heard the same thing from a half dozen other shelters Moses frequented on occasion. He often disappeared for stretches at a time, but never for this long.

She handed him her card. "Give me a call if he comes in?"

"Sure will," Cliff answered. "Hope your brother is okay."

Deborah walked back to the car where her partner Justin waited. "Well?"

"Well, what?" she asked.

"Oh, come on," he said. "You're asking about your brother, aren't you? You'll get in trouble with the chief again if he finds out."

"I didn't use my badge," she said with a snort. "I won't claim the hours if that makes you feel better."

Justin looked back over his shoulder as his partner pulled their sedan away from the curb. "What would make me feel better is getting out of this part of the city. Unlike you, I don't exactly blend in."

She looked at him in shock. "That is a damn racist thing to say, you know that, right?"

"I'm just saying that I'm the only white person I've seen in an hour. These folks look at me like they're wondering how I'd taste slow cooked and slathered in hot sauce."

"Well," she answered, "it wouldn't hurt you to get a little sun every now and then you know. A tan would do you good."

He pulled at his sleeves. "I told you before my skin is very sensitive."

"That ain't the only thing," she muttered.

"What was that?" he asked.

"I said let's drive on over to 7th Ward. We don't have anything else going on. We go back to the office and we'll just get more paperwork."

Justin knew why she wanted to go to 7th Ward but decided not to say anything. If it had been his crazy brother missing, he would likely have done the same.

"At least it's not as bad as it used to be," he said.

"What's not?"

He waved his hand at the rundown neighborhood they were driving through. "Everything. That whole Take Back the Streets campaign has really done a number on cleaning the place up."

"A little too good to be true if you ask me," she said.

Justin shook his head at his partner. "You have to be one of the most pessimistic people I've ever met."

"It's not pessimism," she said. "Its suspicion. Which is a good trait in our line of work."

"Whatever it is," he answered, "why can't you just accept that it's a good thing?"

"Who runs it?"

"What? The program?" Justin asked.

"Yeah."

Her partner shrugged. "I don't know. Who cares?"

"I can tell you that no one and everyone is running it at the same time," she answered. "Department of Labor has a piece but will send you to Department of Social Services, who will send you to Department of Interior, who will send you to the Department of Corrections if you're not careful."

"What's your point?"

"My point," she stressed, "is that no one is really in charge. When everyone is responsible, no one is responsible."

"I'd say it's working just fine," Justin answered. "These lots used to be filled with people living out of shopping carts and cardboard boxes."

"Where did they all go?" she asked.

"Some work program somewhere," Justin answered, waving his hand vaguely in the distance. "Most are probably working an oil rig in the gulf or repairing levees up north. Regardless, they're better off, as is everyone else."

"You ever see anyone recruiting?" she asked.

"Recruiting? They're not joining the military."

"Right, but they're also not getting drafted or taken against their will. That means someone is convincing them. How?"

Justin shrugged again. "Don't know. Don't care." He snapped his fingers as he thought of something. "And to answer your question, I have seen some of these recruits. Over in the north part of the French Quarter, there is a place where they get classes, medical care, food, and shelter."

"I've seen it, too," answered Deborah, "but there was something missing. Did you notice?"

"Live music and free beer?"

Deborah dropped her head and sighed. "How in the hell did you get hired by the FBI? You don't notice shit."

"But I got a great personality," Justin answered, cutting his eyes at her. "Unlike some other people I could mention."

"Those people at the French Quarter are all old or young or sick."

Justin thought for a long moment. "Yeah, I guess you're right. Just means they're taking good care of them. It's not like you could push them out into the fields to pick cotton against their will or anything."

Deborah hit him in the shoulder. "How did I end up with a partner who was a racist bigot? A bunch of black homeless people picking cotton in the fields against their will?"

"Wait a minute," he protested. "I'm sure some of them are Hispanic. That's not racist."

Deborah let out a long breath. "Anyway, my point is, where is everyone else? Where are the healthy men and women over eighteen and under sixty?"

"Like I said, somewhere better off I'm sure."

I wish I could be sure, Deborah thought.

Moses Mitchell would be twenty-two the next day.

Chapter 16

Jack spent the next two days recovering, sleeping as often as he could. Although Rena said his wound was healing nicely, his ordeal had taken a lot out of him. Guilt and worry for his friends was never far from his mind.

"Rena, I'm ready to travel," he urged the second night.

"Are you so ready to leave us?" she asked, teasing while checking his bandage by the light of an oil lamp.

Jack felt an odd tension around Rena. He often noticed her looking at him when she didn't think he was paying attention. He found himself doing the same, and it was hard to get her out of his thoughts.

He found himself staring at her and she returned the look. "I'm grateful for everything you've done, but I've got to get back."

Her lips tightened. "So, I guess you'll go off. Maybe have your other fishing trips with Levi? Shoot each other with abandon and not even think about us?"

Filled with uncertainty, Jack dropped his head.

She suddenly reached out, grabbing his face in both hands, and kissed him forcefully.

Jack's surprise turned to eagerness, and he deepened the kiss, his hands tightening around her slim waist

Pushing him back, she placed her hands on both sides of his face again, her eyes only inches from his. "There is no Levi, is there?"

He opened his mouth to deny the lie, but saw in her eyes that she knew it wasn't true. Jack shook his head and dropped his eyes.

"Who really shot you?" she asked, her hands trembling slightly.

Jack hesitated then shook his head. "Some mercenary-looking guy; they killed two of my friends and took the others somewhere as prisoners. Shot me while I was trying to get away." He felt a surge of relief at being able to tell Rena the truth. "I'm sorry I lied to you, but I didn't know you. I didn't know if I could trust you. It's so crazy, I'm not even sure I believe it all myself."

Rena nodded. "It's okay, I understand."

A thought clicked in Jack's head. He looked closely at Rena. "You understand why I didn't tell you and you're not surprised by my story. You know about these guys?"

Standing up, she turned away from him. "They came a few years ago. Said if we keep to our business they'd leave us b, and, so far, that's the way it's been. We even get an annual stipend."

"The way what's been? And what the hell does it have to do with me and my friends?"

"I don't know for sure," she said. "I've heard they have a camp where they keep people. Poppa says not to ask questions we don't want to know the answers to."

Jack's jaw tightened. "They killed my friends! Who knows what they're doing to Charles and Amanda and Heather? I've got to get them help. Can you help me get to the mainland?"

"What will you do when you get there?"

"I'll go to the police," he said. "They'll come here, shut this all down. You can't do something like this in America. It's insane!"

Deloy filled the doorway. "Rena, time for bed."

Rena said, "Be there in a minute."

Her father stood there staring at them before walking away.

She turned back to Jack and gazed at him for a long time. Finally, she seemed to make up her mind and whispered, "We'll leave tomorrow morning in the boat. Don't mention anything to Poppa, okay?"

"You sure?" he asked. "I don't want to get you in trouble with your father."

She nodded and stood. "I'll deal with him. You just be ready."

Jack reached out and took her hand in his.

Rena nearly pulled away from him, but then she came back and kissed him almost frantically before turning away and leaving.

He thought for a moment he had seen tears in her eyes.

It took Jack a long time to get to sleep. He wondered if he should ask Rena to come with him, to stay with him. They had only known each other for a few days, but he had feelings for her that he hadn't had for anyone in a very long time.

He drifted off to sleep thinking of her.

Waking with a start, Jack saw the morning light filtering through the window. He quietly dressed and crept out of his room to find Rena at the stove fixing breakfast

"I thought we were sneaking out," he whispered.

"No need," she answered flipping eggs. "Daddy went out early. He's going to work on the traps, said I could borrow the boat for the day."

Jack sat and poured himself some coffee from the pot on the table. "Um...Rena...you know..."

"Just eat, Jack," she said, putting a plate before him and turning away and then walking outside.

"Uh, okay," he said, making a note to talk to her more later.

Rena returned as he was finishing his breakfast "You ready?" she asked, not smiling.

Jack nodded. "I guess so. Look, Rena..." He tried to pull her into his arms, but she moved away.

"Don't, Jack," she said. "We're different people from different worlds. It was fun to pretend for a while, but it's over."

He stared at her, his heart sinking. "Rena, I wasn't pretending. I really think I care about you...I think you're the most amazing woman I've met in a long time. I don't want this to be the end."

She was crying now. "Damn you, don't say that! Don't! You don't mean it!"

Something wasn't right. "Why are you acting this way?" he asked.

Looking out the window, she answered quietly, "Poppa was sick. Would have died if not for the medicine he got from the camp they built. I owe them everything for saving him."

"I'm sorry...I guess, about your father," mumbled Jack, "but he seems fine now, right?"

"Let's just go," she said, wiping her eyes as she strode outside.

Jack followed her and saw her father standing on the porch waiting. In the clearing in front of the cabin was a flatbed truck painted green. It had a large metal cage in the back. Standing in front of the truck was Urchart and three men.

"Hello, Mr. Winter," he said. "We parted so poorly."

Jack felt as if he were going to faint, "Rena, wha—"

Deloy grabbed him by the arm and led him roughly down the steps. "Don't talk to her. She saved your life and took care of you. No need to make her feel bad. She didn't ask to be brought into this, and neither did I."

"But why?" he asked. "I don't understand."

"Because," Urchart said, "what we are doing here is more important than you or I or any of us."

Mercenaries came forward and took Jack by the arms and bound his hands in front of him with plastic restraints. He cried out in pain as his shoulder wound pulled against the stitches.

"You killed my friends, you bastard," Jack grated through gritted teeth.

Urchart smiled. "Not all of them. They miss you, I'm sure." He walked up, turned Jack around, and poked painfully at his healing wound.

Jack couldn't help but cry out.

"I *knew* I hit you! Told them as much. Damn good shot if I don't say so myself."

"Yeah, well done there," said Rena sarcastically.

Urchart looked at her hesitantly, as if uncertain if she were serious or not.

"That's island humor," Jack said, staring hard at Rena. "It's an acquired taste."

They loaded him into the cage in back of the truck and locked it shut. Urchart and the soldiers climbed into the front four-door cab and pulled away leaving Rena and her father standing in the grass.

Jack locked eyes with Rena as they pulled away.

I'm sorry, Jack, she mouthed at him, tears in her eyes.

His last image of the cabin was Deloy trying to put his arm around her. She threw it off angrily and ran inside.

Chapter 17

Moses couldn't believe he had evaded them for this long. Two days was the longest he had previously been out and he was now going on four.

Don't get cocky, said Billy.

"No," whispered Moses, looking out on the sad scene before him. "Must be as still and quiet as a mouse."

This is why you haven't been caught yet, said Delores. *Chasing others, probably figure they'll get around to you in due time.*

The bad men were loading the young man who looked like he was injured into the back of one of the camp transport trucks. Moses knew the vehicle intimately. Each time he'd been captured he'd been taken back to his cell in it.

Or one like it, said Billy.

And they'll likely do it again soon, said Nate. *Unless you figure things out.*

Moses' eyes narrowed at the dark-haired girl on the porch. She had also tricked him, offered him friendship and shelter and food, but the next morning had betrayed him. Moses rubbed the back of his head, remembering where the girl's father had hit him with a club.

Do you like being free, or would it just be easier if you go and turn yourself in? asked Nate. *We both know they'll likely kill you this time, but maybe that's for the best, right? Surprised you're not dead already with all the things they've done to us."*

"No," whined Moses, shivering at the horrible images of sterile white rooms filled with pain. "Not going back."

Then we need a plan, said Delores. *A way to get off this island.*

And not get caught, said Billy.

The voices were silent for a time as Moses thought. He watched the truck pull away with their new prisoner and then watched the girl run inside. Strangely, she seemed upset.

How far are you willing to go? asked Nate.

"I don't want to hurt anyone," whispered Moses.

You may have to get dirty in order to stay free, said Nate, not unkindly. *Better start preparing yourself now. They won't have any mercy with you if they catch you.*

Moses suddenly remembered Old Slimy. The drunkard had smelled to high heaven but had been kind to Moses and helped protect him when Moses had been new to the streets. Most of the time the man was out of his mind, but he talked about his three tours in Vietnam as part of something called long-range reconnaissance, and he never tired of telling Moses stories. Many of those stories were disturbing, but Moses had listened all the same. Slimy had been a master at setting booby traps in Vietnam and used those skills to keep others away from his underpass. In time, Slimy taught Moses how to set and tend the booby traps and even showed him more deadly snares.

Yes, said Nate, *you have everything you need.*

The image of the fishing gear and tackle box came to mind.

But be careful, warned Billy again.

And find a way to get us off this damn island, said Delores.

First things first, my dear, said Nate.

Moses turned and melted into the woods.

Chapter 18

The truck followed a narrow trail through the woods that was really no more than a wide path. Easing around tree trunks and soft spots in the mud and dirt track made for slow going and gave Jack time to think.

They haven't killed me yet, he thought, *so maybe I'm going to wherever Heather, Charles, and Amanda are...if they're still alive.*

Realizing he only had a certain amount of time before he got to his destination, Jack tried to come up with a plan. As a lawyer, he had some experience with the prison system, and something told him he was about to be acquainted with a similar pleasure. They would search him, strip him, take everything from him, and then lock him away safe and sound.

Jack ran his hands through his pockets. A cell phone that was low on battery and couldn't get a signal, keys for his car, a wallet and...Uncle Johnny's pocketknife.

Part of Jack shied away from the idea. He tried to tell himself that this was some sort of elaborate hoax or that someone would come to save them. But then he remembered the bodies of Brian and Evan. He remembered Rena's last look, as if she knew he was going off to die.

Before he could hesitate, Jack cupped the knife in his hand. He looked to make sure none of the soldiers were looking his way, but they were all focused on the road and each other. With difficulty due to his bound hands, Jack carefully slid the knife down the back of his pants and pressed it in between the cheeks of his ass. It was uncomfortable, and not as secure as putting it in his anus as convicts did, but he couldn't go that far. It would hopefully escape any casual search, but nothing extensive. With any hope they wouldn't be expecting a lawyer from Lafayette to have any tricks up his...well, up his sleeve, per se.

Sitting back and trying to relax on the bumpy trail, Jack began to detect an odd stench. Like rot mixed with vegetation. He gazed ahead and saw a fenced compound with barracks-like structures and several tall radio towers. A cheerful sign at the front gate declared, "U.S. Government Department of Agriculture Canine Training Facility. Trespassers Will Be Detained and Prosecuted."

The vehicle stopped at the gate, and a guard approached from a nearby shack. Jack now heard the sounds of barking dogs, dozens of them, and spotted rows of single run kennels. Each contained an inside portion and a gate to let a dog outside into a twenty-by-five foot section completely enclosed by chain-link fencing. Rows of these dog runs ran adjacent to each other with large working-type dogs barking and jumping at the sound of Jack's vehicle.

"Badge, please," said the guard.

"Good god, Fred," said the driver. "You know it's us."

The guard's face scrunched up tight. "Lyles, you're supposed to show your badge. Those are the rules."

"He's just doing his job," said Urchart, flashing him a laminated card from inside a wallet, "and a mighty good job, I should say."

The guard smiled and proceeded to unlock and pull open the gate for them to pass. After the vehicle had pulled through, Jack watched the guard lock the gate back up using a ring of keys in his pocket before retreating to his guard shack.

The compound appeared to be composed of nothing more than barracks-type buildings and dog kennels. Stopping in front of one of the barracks, the four soldiers exited the truck.

"You three get him processed and settled," Urchart said, walking away. "I'll go check on things."

"Yessssir," said Lyles slowly. He then motioned for another soldier who unlocked Jack's cage.

"Come on out of there, little doggy," said the man with a cruel smile.

Jack stood and moved forward slowly, trying not to let the knife slip out. He attempted to look wobbly on his feet, which wasn't too hard considering he was still recovering from his bullet wound. Two of the soldiers reached up and grabbed him by the upper arms and helped him out of the vehicle to the ground. They led him up a set of wooden stairs and into a Spartan room where a man sat behind a desk. He looked up tiredly from a magazine he was reading.

"Got one for ya, Keith," Lyles told the man behind the desk.

"I can see that," he answered and then looked at Jack. "Place the contents of your pocket on the desk here."

Jack laid his wallet, phone, and keys on the table.

Keith picked up a clipboard and pen. "Name and address?"

"I'm Jackson Winters," Jack stammered. "From Pens Street, Lafayette."

He paused in his writing. "You don't say? I went to high school in Lafayette."

"Stop fraternizing, Keith," said Lyles, pushing Jack in the back. "Just get him processed so we can have lunch."

Keith looked the other man up and down. "Like you've ever in your life missed a meal. I know you're skinny, but you eat more than any two normal men."

"All the more reason to hurry the hell up before they run out of food," Lyles responded.

"Okay," said Keith, handing Jack a trash bag. "Take off all your clothes and put them in this bag."

Jack hesitated, but saw they were serious. He slowly stripped, turning his backside to the wall whenever he had to bend over, but they were in a hurry. When he was finished, Jack handed the bag to Keith who attached a note card to it before he tossed it into a pile of similar bags behind him.

"Go over there and shower," Keith pointed to a large communal stall without curtains. "You'll want to clean off real good, might be the last shower you have in a while, but be quick about it."

Jack turned on the water, and it was ice cold. He waited a few seconds for it to warm up but felt the point of a baton in his back.

"This ain't the Ritz, sweetheart," said one of the soldiers. "Hurry up unless you want us to crack your skull."

Jack moved into the frigid water and gasped. He picked up the dirty bar of soap and quickly washed himself before turning the water off and stepping out.

Keith had moved out from behind his desk and tossed Jack a threadbare towel. "You're about six foot, aren't you?" he asked.

"That's right," said Jack.

The man moved over to a shelf lined with stacks of orange jumpsuits and pulled one off the ledge along with a pair of socks, underwear, a white t-shirt, and Velcro shoes. "Try these on."

Jack quickly got dressed. He could feel the knife slipping out. The underwear just cleared his rear before the pocketknife slipped free. Jack quickly put on the jumpsuit to hide the odd bulge, but none of the men were watching him closely.

Fully dressed, Keith handed him a rough wool blanket and a stained pillow. "This way," he said, walking to the rear of the building.

Jack followed and felt two soldiers fall in close behind him. They went through a door and were back outside. There were a series of locked gates in front of them set side by side. Jack realized these were dog kennels like the ones he'd seen in the front of the camp, but there was no sound of dogs.

"That one there, where the old crazy spic used to be," Lyles said, motioning towards the third cell from the left end and unlocking the door with a set of keys.

Jack walked in and saw a small cot against the wall with a thin mattress, a bucket in the corner, and another door at the opposite end.

There was a faucet on the wall that fed into a small depression in the concrete.

"Use the bucket as a toilet," Keith said. "You trade out every morning when you get breakfast." He pointed at the other door, which opened to the enclosed dog run. "That will be opened for one hour each day; use it wisely. Now enjoy." He shut the door and locked it behind him.

Jack stood feverish and dizzy. His chills had returned with a vengeance. He looked around uncertain what to do. Eventually, he lay down on the cot and pulled the blanket up over him.

He tried to think of what to do next but quickly fell asleep.

Chapter 19

Jack awoke from a troubled sleep long enough to pull the pocketknife out of his underwear and hide it in a hole in his mattress. Thirst racked him. He crawled over to the faucet and stuck his mouth under the opening while turning the handle. The water tasted like iron, but his body craved it, and he drank until he thought he would be sick. He then climbed back under the wool blanket trembling with fever.

The next morning he awoke to banging on the door and angry words about his bucket, but Jack couldn't move and wasn't even sure if anything around him were real. He kept trying to find his cell phone so he could call Cindy at work and tell her maybe she should put someone else on Dean Lyon's hearing, but nothing was where it was supposed to be.

Hazy figures entered his cell and then carried him out into sunlight. Soon, they were lying him down on a real bed with medical equipment.

"Am I at the hospital?" he asked, a dark-skinned man inserting an IV into his arm.

"No," the man answered with a curious Caribbean accent. "You are in the infirmary. I believe you have a fever due to an infection from your injury." He unzipped Jack's jumpsuit and examined the shoulder wound.

Jack laughed as memory flooded back to him. "It's not an *injury*. I was shot."

The man shrugged. "You still have an infection."

"Thirsty," Jack rasped.

He shook his head, pointing at the IV. "The saline will hydrate you better than water. Besides, you need to rest." Reaching into a medical cabinet, he pulled out a small vial of clear liquid and a syringe. He then turned and pressed the liquid into his IV."

"No!" said Jack. "Must stay awake."

The man patted Jack's arm kindly. "You need to rest my friend. Plenty of time for you after you rest."

Jack started to argue, but he slipped into oblivion.

He later awoke gradually to the sound of classical music. Opening his eyes slowly, he saw the same dark-skinned man reading a book.

"What are you reading?" asked Jack with a raspy voice.

The man looked up with a smile and showed Jack the cover. "Dostoevsky's *Crime and Punishment.* Have you read it?"

Jack nodded. "In high school, one of the things that made me want to become a lawyer."

The man looked surprised. "You're a lawyer? I knew you didn't look like the normal inmates here."

"Inmates," Jack asked. "What is this place?"

Shrugging, the man started to examine his IV. "They tell me it is a rehabilitation camp for political prisoners."

"What?" Jack exclaimed. "That's ridiculous. There's no such thing. Not in America."

He shrugged again. "What do I know? I'm not from here."

"Not from here? Who are you?"

The man smiled. "Forgive me, I am Dr. Xavier Simone. I am from Haiti."

"What are you doing here?"

Xavier sat and looked around to make sure they were still alone. "I was on a large boat from Haiti. We were trying to make it to Florida, but your Coast Guard picked us up and questioned us. Everyone else was sent back, but once they found I was a doctor, they offered me this opportunity."

"Opportunity? What kind of opportunity?"

Xavier smiled. "I serve as the camp doctor and they make me an American citizen. I'll even be able to send for my wife and kids."

"And if you don't mind me asking, what kind of doctor are you?" Jack asked.

"Pediatrician," he said proudly. "When I leave here, I will help children instead of political prisoners."

Jack sighed. "I am not a political prisoner."

Xavier shook his head. "All political prisoners say that."

Clenching his fists, Jack closed his eyes and let out a slow breath. "Can you tell me about my friends? Are they here? Are they okay?"

The doctor looked at the closed door. "I'm not supposed to—"

"I don't want to get you in trouble," Jack said. "I just want to know if they are alive and okay. Two pretty women and a big black man."

Xavier's eyes lit up. "Ah, yes, Charles. Very big man. I see him often. He fights with the guards, and they bring him to me to patch him up afterwards. I try to tell him he should not do that, but he is a very angry man."

"Actually he's not," said Jack.

"He should not fight the guards," Xavier insisted. "They are only here to protect you until you have been rehabilitated...or..."

"And then they are released?" Jack asked. "Is that how it works?"

The doctor looked confused. "It is a long process, I am sure, all for a greater good—"

"You've never seen anyone get released from here, have you?"

"I am just the doctor," Xavier hissed. "They do not consult me about when to take someone. How would I know when you prisoners come and go? Prisoners are here, and then they are not. That is all."

Jack thought he heard voices in the hall. He whispered frantically to Xavier, "If you see Charles again, tell him I am here. Tell him his friend Jack is okay."

Xavier looked torn, but the door opened and he looked away.

Jack recognized Brennen as the soldier who searched their boat before Jack was shot by Urchart.

"How is he, Doc?" Brennen asked.

Xavier consulted a chart. "His fever is under control, but you should bring him to me every other day at least to change his bandage. Also, light duty for now."

Brennen looked at Jack. "Hear that, light duty, you lucked out, partner."

"Yes," answered Jack. "I've got to be the most fortunate person in the world."

Chapter 20

Captain Rory Flannigan sat on the edge of a chair and fidgeted outside the office of his commander. Lieutenant Colonel Abraham was reputed to be the best battalion commander in the entire brigade, but he wasn't one to overlook mistakes. Flannigan was afraid he had made one.

1st Battalion of the 187th Infantry Regiment, the Rakkasans, was expected to ship out of Fort Campbell, Kentucky for Kandahar, Afghanistan in less than six weeks. They had a ton of training and pre-deployment checks and not much time to get them done. And now his most experienced platoon sergeant hadn't returned from leave and the platoon leader was a cherry lieutenant.

"Rory," called out Abraham from his office. "Come on in here. What's going on? Your men ready?"

"Sir, I'm afraid one of my men hasn't returned from leave and we can't get in touch with him," Flannigan said nervously, standing before his commander's desk.

"How long overdue is he?" Flannigan asked.

The captain sighed. "Seventy-two hours, sir."

Abraham looked at him sternly. "Seventy-two hours is AWOL. Hell, twenty-four hours is AWOL. I should have known about this immediately."

"Yes, sir," Rory stammered. "I'm sorry. I just thought Sergeant Winston got hung up or something."

"Sergeant First Class Brian Winston?" Abraham asked.

"Yes, sir."

Abraham nodded. "A good man. Not someone to run off before a deployment. I'm presuming you tried all the contact numbers we have for him."

"Yes, sir," Rory answered. "No answer on his phone. The leave address has a sister in Baton Rouge, but no answer there. We pulled family data from his military life insurance, and I talked to his mother."

"She any help?"

"A little," Rory answered. "Said Sergeant Winston and his sister Amanda were meeting some college friends down at Avery Island for the weekend. She said her daughter pulled a lot of camping gear out of their garage."

Abraham thought for a moment. "He could be in some sort of trouble. Maybe in a hospital or something. Have you reported this yet?"

Rory shook his head. "Sir, I didn't want to get Sergeant Winston into any trouble. He's my best soldier."

"I understand that," answered Abraham, giving the young officer a stern look, "but this is about more than protecting the soldier's career. What if he's lying in some ditch or floating on a broken boat in the Gulf? Go ahead and report him as AWOL to the Provost Marshal. Make sure they have all the info you have given me; they'll reach out to the proper authorities in Louisiana. If Sergeant Winston has a good reason...a damn good reason...for being AWOL and not calling in, we'll be able to take care of him."

"Yes, sir," answered Rory. "Sir, about first platoon...without Sergeant Winston, they're real light on experience."

Abraham shook his head. "I don't have anybody to give you. Tell that lieutenant to get his head out of his ass; it's about to get real serious in a couple of months. And pray hard that Brian Winston shows up."

"Yes, sir," said Rory.

"Keep me informed."

Rory saluted and fled, grateful he had gotten off so easy.

Lieutenant Colonel Abraham sat and pondered uneasy thoughts. This was no time to be without one of his most experienced combat leaders. Something clicked in Abraham's mind and he snapped his fingers.

He'd run into an old West Point classmate of his while at Fort Polk, Louisiana the previous year on training exercises and gotten his card. Abraham dug around in his top desk drawer, shuffling papers and offices supplies back and forth.

"There you are!" he cried out, holding up the business card. He reached for the phone and called the number on the card. Maybe his old friend could pull some strings and figure something out.

The card read, "Lucas Ross, Chief of Staff, Louisiana Governor."

Chapter 21

Charles Haywood had grown up so closely acquainted with anger and resentment that it had become a close friend. That anger protected him when others tried to hurt him. It provided justification whenever he felt uncertainty or shame at some of the things he did. Daily life was an arena where he was the animal dragged out of its cage to die again and again for the enjoyment of the world.

That was until Coach Mac, the revered old football coach at Tallulah High, had sat down next to him one day at lunch. The cafeteria was crowded with smiling and laughing teenagers, but none sat near Charles' brooding hulk. At only fourteen, he was already bigger and stronger than even the senior class boys who used to beat him up years before.

Coach Mac eyed him with a small smile. "You're a big one. Heard you like to fight. What if I gave you an opportunity to do it without getting into trouble?"

Charles normally would have laughed or responded sarcastically, but Coach Mac was a legend. He had played guard for Coach Bear Bryant at the University of Kentucky and helped them win their only national championship in 1950 before going on to play a few years professional football for the Cleveland Browns. The old man's hands were gnarled from countless smalls breaks, but that only made them stronger. This was someone Charles would not cross lightly, someone worthy of respect.

"You want me to play football?" Charles asked. "Forget it. Those prima donnas don't want nothing to do with me."

Coach Mac looked over at a crowded table of loud jocks in school letter jackets. Pretty girls crowded around vying for their attention. "They *are* a bunch of prima donnas. You're right about that"—he turned back to look at Charles—"but I can see you're not."

"No, sir," answered Charles, taking a bite of food that would only quiet his ever-present physical hunger for a while. He was almost always hungry, and his mother rarely thought to buy anything to put in their refrigerator or cabinet.

"When I was your age"—the man smiled at Charles wistfully— "I'd knock the dog shit out of little punks like that. Do everything I could to put them in the freaking hospital. That's what I loved about football."

Charles had stopped eating and was watching the table of jocks.

"But I'm old now and happen to be their coach. I try to talk some sense into them, but what they really need is someone to put a serious butt whipping on them. Unfortunately, I don't have anyone on my team big enough, or strong enough, or just plain mean enough to do that."

Charles' mind started to turn, and his legs quivered with the idea of crushing those pretty boys into the dirt. "So you want to use me to teach your boys a lesson?'

"Partly," answered the coach. "My team has talent, but no toughness. This season is going to be rough because we're not ready for it. I'd like you to help prepare them, and then I want you to destroy the teams that we play against."

Charles shook his head. "They'll never let me in their circle. Sure, I could come to a few practices and stomp them for you, but they'll find me later and gang up on me."

Coach Mac looked at him for a long moment. "You come in and be who you are, and stick with us, they'll do more than accept you. They'll follow you."

Charles Haywood had scoffed at the old coach, but nevertheless, he came out for the two-a-day practices in the blazing Louisiana summer for the opportunity to inflict punishment on others. What he had found was just what the coach promised, a place he could be violent and angry and hurt others without getting into trouble. Hell, they had praised him and, like the coach said, accepted him...eventually.

By his junior year, he was All-State and Second Team All-American. His senior year, they won a state championship, and Charles was recognized as the best defensive end in the country. Two months after that state championship, Coach Mac died of cancer. None of the players even knew he had the disease but learned he had been fighting a losing battle for nearly a decade. By then, Charles was a different person and he recognized the gift that the old man had given him.

He'd gone to play football at LSU and, when on the field, was a fierce force of nature, filled with fury and determination. He had terrorized opposing offensive players. Off the field, he'd been calm, gentle, and funny. The dark angry side of him rarely showed itself anymore.

Until now.

Charles flexed his hands convulsively looking at the guards. He breathed in deep gasps, and he could imagine himself snapping their necks with his bare hands. A few saw his menacing look and pointed their rifles at him.

"Get back to work," said Dick, one of the younger guards with false bravado.

Charles' return smile was chilling, but he picked up a large rock nevertheless. He mentally calculated the distance and decided the soldier was outside of his throwing range. Instead, he heaved it into the back of the truck onto a pile of other large rocks. They had put him to work over the last few days collecting rocks from the high ground to fill in a washed-out area under the north fence line. He had majored in civil engineering and could have told them, had they asked, that the fence would only wash out again somewhere else. The problem was they had built the camp in the path of a major water run-off from the high ground. Most of the time it was a dry ditch, but when it rained heavily it became a raging torrent. Blocking the water's path would only make it go elsewhere, maybe take out the fence's foundation.

He slowed in his movements. This wasn't the first time he'd thought of escape, but he sensed there was something there. Some idea just beyond his consciousness and it had to do with the run-off and the rocks he was putting into the hole.

"That's enough, you goon," said Dick, showing off for his partner. He pointed at the truck. "Climb up in the back; we're done here."

Charles did as he was told. When the guard came close to shackle him to the ringbolt at the rear of the truck, the big man's smile caused the guard to slow in his tracks.

"Now don't you try anything," he warned. Turning to his partner, he said, "Hey, get ready to tase this asshole should he try anything."

"My pleasure," answered Cam, pulling out a baton-sized cattle prod.

Dick cautiously handcuffed Charles to the bed of the truck and then motioned for him to sit down on one of the wheel wells. Charles had little room for his legs with all the large rocks and had to rest them awkwardly on top of the pile.

The ride back to camp was painfully bumpy, but Charles enjoyed the time out of his cage. Just the thought of going back inside made his heart beat a little faster. He hated being cooped up. They parked near the washed-out area of the fence they had been working on, and the two guards exited the cab.

"Want to unload before dinner?" Dick asked his partner.

"There's no hurry," answered Cam. "We can have the goon do it tomorrow. Let's just lock him back up."

They unlocked Charles from the ring on the truck bed, but kept his hands cuffed in front of him, leading him back to his cage.

"Be just in time for your dinner too, big boy," said Cam.

Charles' breathing started to get faster as they walked down the line of cells. *Heather and Amanda are in two of those*, he thought.

"Hey, Heather, Amanda," he yelled loudly. "It's me, Charles."

"Shut your mouth!" said Cam poking him with the butt of the cattle prod.

Charles ignored him. "You in there, girls? Hang in there! You're not alone!"

Dick jumped in front of Charles, anger on his face. "Damnit, you're not supposed to—"

He never finished because Charles reached up and grabbed the man's throat in his shackled hands and began squeezing tightly at the same time he lifted the guard off the ground. Dick punched and kicked at the big man, but it did about as much good as a mouse struggling in the hands of a giant.

Charles heard Cam power up the cattle prod behind him, and he turned away, putting a weakly struggling Dean between them.

"You drop him now," said Cam, holding the cattle prod out between them.

"In just a minute," answered Charles with a smile as he gripped tighter.

Cam lunged at Charles with the prod, but the big man swung Dick out like a rag doll and the prod hit the guard's leg. Charles felt a mild jolt, but nothing more.

Cam was starting to panic. He pulled a radio from his belt. "Code Red! Code Red! By the north cells, we need help now!"

"Code Red is right, motherfucker," said Charles with an evil grin.

"I need help!" Cam screamed into the radio.

"They won't make it in time to help little Dick here," said Charles, looking at the man's purple face. "They might not even make it to help you."

Cam lunged with the prod again, and Charles danced out of the way. The guard ran at him, and Charles, using Dick as a shield, batted the prod away and then kicked Cam savagely in the groin. The guard dropped to the ground, his mouth a soundless O and wide eyes staring at Charles unbelievingly. Charles stepped closer and stomped down on the fallen guard's face and felt a satisfying crunch under his heel.

Hearing running feet behind him, Charles spun around, a limp guard still in both hands. The fury and anger had taken hold of him now, and it was a glorious feeling. Preparing to either kill as many as he could or make them kill him, Charles only got far enough around to see Lyles out of the corner of his eye. The man had a riot gun leveled at him from about fifteen feet away. Charles tried to put the flaccid Dick between them, but Lyles fired first

Charles felt a powerful blow to his side, just under his armpit. Without knowing how he ended up on the ground, he looked up to see men standing over him menacingly.

A smirking Lyles was standing over him with a smoking shotgun. Charles tried to say something. All went mercifully black.

Chapter 22

Heather Daniels heard Charles and yelled back to him, grateful to know she wasn't alone. She had seen him on occasion from a distance, but it sounded like he was right outside her door.

"Charles!" she yelled, beating on the heavy door. "I'm in here. I'm okay."

Is that true? she wondered absently before hearing angry turned fearful.

"What's going on?" she asked, but expected no answer and got none.

Running feet and then more angry talk. A gunshot. Then silence.

"Charles!" she screamed. "What happened? What's going on out there?"

A heavy slap on the other side of her metal door made her jump backwards.

"Shut up in there."

"What did you do to Charles?" she yelled out even louder. Other fainter voices could be heard but not understood. *Could they be Amanda or other prisoners?*

She screamed out at the top of her lungs. "What is going on out there?"

There was a low conversation outside her door and then a key rattled in the lock. The door swung open on squeaky hinges, and rough hands dragged her outside and slapped plastic flex cuffs on her wrists.

Heather swung her head around in the glaring sunlight, trying to find Charles. She saw two limp uniforms on the ground, one with a sheet partially covering him and the other in a pool of blood with two men trying to help him. Heather finally saw Charles through a mass of men in uniform struggling to pick him up. Lunging towards the men, she caught her captors by surprise, and two men gave chase and tackled her to the ground.

"You killed him, you bastards!"

A shadow loomed over her. Looking up, she recognized the one called Urchart.

"We didn't kill him," he said slowly. "Just knocked him out." He turned back to look at the two men Charles had attacked. "Although, he would certainly have it coming if we did."

"Screw you!" she screamed, trying to struggle up off the ground while the guards held her down easily with their body weight. "Whatever this place is we're not supposed to be here, you asshole!"

Urchart nodded. "I don't disagree with you, but you're here now nevertheless."

"Let us go," she pleaded. "Just let us go."

"Not going to happen," he said, not unkindly.

"Can we move this along?" asked an elderly woman in a lab coat holding a clipboard. "The doctor has a schedule to keep and doesn't like to fall behind."

Urchart motioned to the two men holding Heather, and they lifted her up onto her feet. Heather was propelled after the woman in the lab coat as the two guards carried her forward by hands under her shoulders. Her feet barely touched the ground.

They proceeded to the far edge of the camp. Buildings and structures slowly disappeared in direct proportion to the increase in trees and vegetation. Heather saw a shed ahead of them with a steel door and security code touchpad on the front.

"Where are we going?" she asked nearly in a whisper.

"Time to earn your keep," said one of the guards.

The other one snickered. "Yeah, you didn't think these fine accommodations and dining experiences were free, did you?"

The woman turned and glared at the men, and their smiles vanished. She focused on the touchpad and entered a series of numbers resulting in a cheerful *beep* and *click*. The woman pushed the door aside and walked down steps.

The two men dragged a struggling Heather forward and down a long flight of dim stairs.

Heather's heart sank as he heard the heavy door slam shut above her.

Chapter 23

Port Allen Chief of Police Andrew Bolton decided he had been through enough for one day. The morning had started with having to read a suspension to one of his best officers for drinking and driving, then an arson call at an apartment building where there had been three burned bodies, one of them a child, and finally that afternoon having to chase down reports of some pervert flashing old ladies and young girls downtown.

Right now, Bolton just wanted to get home, crack a beer, pop a Healthy Choice TV dinner in the microwave, and watch the Atlanta Braves game. He looked at the clock and saw it was within the acceptable window to depart. Normally a late worker, he knew when he was reaching burnout and his brain felt like mush. Grabbing his lunch cooler, he stopped at the desk of Gina his secretary.

"I'm going to call it a night," he told her. "Dispatch can give me a call at home if anything should come up."

"No problem, Chief," she answered with a flirtatious flip of her blonde hair. "We got it from here. You need anything else?"

He was tempted. Gina was beautiful, and they had been dancing around each other for several years, but he had instituted a strict policy against dating relationships within the police department, and Chief Bolton prided himself on not being hypocritical.

"Appreciate it," he told her, "but I'm fine. Have a good night and get out of here soon."

"I will and thanks," she responded.

He almost made it to the front doors when Sergeant Tooms intercepted him with a serious look. "Chief, you better come listen to this."

"Can it wait until tomorrow?" Bolton asked. "This has been one hell of a day."

Tooms shook his head. "Sorry, boss, but I don't think so."

Chief Bolton sighed and followed Tooms to the man's desk.

"You remember that missing person's report we got a few days ago?" Tooms asked him.

The police chief had to think for a minute. "The accountant?"

"Yeah," said Tooms. "He's from Simon and Kestler, which is now Simon, Kestler, and Athers. They called it in."

"Right," said Andrew remembering. "The new partner there, Evan Athers. Did he turn up after a long weekend at Biloxi like I predicted?"

"Not exactly," answered Tooms, pressing a button on his computer.

"911, what is the nature of your emergency?" said a young lady's voice.

A seriousness voice answered, "Yes, this is Evan Athers. We have an emergency situation here at—"

The voice stopped talking when the telltale sounds of machine gun fire erupted, and then the line when dead.

Chief Bolton looked at Tooms with wide eyes, his fatigue forgotten. "Is this for real?"

Toom's nodded. "Yes, had our techs check it out, and they confirmed it's a real call. That sounds like real machine gun fire."

"Wait a minute," said Andrew, "that's a 911 call. Why are you getting it in an email?"

"Yeah, that's also interesting," said Tooms. "This is from the Louisiana State Police, who got it from the Arizona State Police. The call itself was made last Friday."

"So, our missing person is in Arizona?" Andrew asked. "Presuming, of course, that he's still alive, which I'm inclined to think he isn't, given that call."

"Me neither," said Tooms, "but this might not have been in Arizona. The 911 call was made from a satellite phone. Actually, I checked with the provider, and it was one of those new phones that works as both a regular phone and satellite phone. All iridium satellite calls get routed to the ground station in Tempe."

"But it only works in the satellite mode if there isn't regular cell coverage," Bolton said.

"Right," answered Tooms. "But it also has to be someplace outside where you can get clear lines of sight to the sky."

Chief Bolton thought for a moment and shook his head. "That doesn't really help us much. He could literally be anywhere. We should probably upgrade his case from a missing persons to possible homicide."

"Already done, Chief, but that's not all," Tooms said with a smile. "We got lucky with a hit on Mr. Athers' car at a tow truck lot down at Avery Island."

Bolton looked at Tooms and then over at the wall map. "What's down there that's outside of cell coverage?"

"Lots and lots of open water," answered Tooms. "Might have gone on a fishing trip or something, maybe ran into some crazy Cajuns or pirates or something."

"Any reported missing boats in that area?"

"I've called the local PD and they're checking. Nothing yet."

Chief Bolton looked at the map closer and saw a small smear south of Avery Island. "What's this?"

"I saw that too," Tooms answered. "I asked the Avery PD about it. They say it's a nature reserve. A few people live on it, but it's mostly just a bunch of protected birds and turtles."

"Bog Island," Bolton read out loud. "Ask the Avery PD to check out the island for us."

Tooms nodded and made a call.

Chapter 24

Eric St Keel was sometimes shocked by the fact that he was an actual state governor. He'd grown up in a small middle-class home and his parents hadn't aspired to anything greater than annual vacations to the beach. Eric felt as if he were an imposter, playing a role that could end at any time. But he didn't want it to end. Eric enjoyed the position and the power. He was good at it.

His mother told him before she died that his father would have been proud. Eric had wanted to believe her, but was too much of a realist to fool himself. Tyler St Keel was a morose man, who probably would have been diagnosed with severe depression or bipolar disorder had he been born a generation or two later.

"All men seek the approval of their fathers," Jeremiah Winters had told him during one of their talks. "It's hardwired into us, and a man has a tough time seeing himself as a man until his father validates that fact."

Jeremiah had been more of a father to him than Tyler St Keel and had treated him not just as a friend. In the end, Eric had detested his father but still craved his approval even knowing it was worthless and would never come.

How pathetic, he told himself as the introduction speaker droned on.

What would Jeremiah Winter think of him? That was a much more important question. The man had been proud of Eric's accomplishments and told him as much, but Judge Winters hadn't known everything. Hadn't known the compromises and moral sacrifices that were necessary to achieve so much.

Thoughts like this made him uncomfortable. He smiled purposefully while focusing on the man at the podium.

"Eric St Keel is a new breed of leader, but also a throwback," said the Chairman of the National Health Society. "While working together with all parties towards a vision, he is also tough and can see any task through. He is a man who believes in America and what we can all do together. Most of all, he is a man of integrity and selflessness." The speaker paused and smiled at Eric. "There hasn't been a public official like Governor St Keel in a very long time, and that is a shame."

The speaker looked back out over the large crowd. "It gives me great pleasure to introduce my friend, Governor Eric St Keel."

Eric pushed that annoying feeling of shame away, put on his winning smile, and walked forward at the applause. He shook the speaker's hand and then turned to the audience.

"Ladies and gentlemen, thank you," he said to the applause. "Thank you, thank you very much. It is wonderful to be here."

He made a point of picking out a few familiar influential faces in the crowd and making eye contact and waving at a few. They would remember this gesture and likely donate more money to his future campaigns because of it. Eric gripped the side of the podium and let the applause die down completely before speaking. He had learned that patience in public speaking was often as powerful as the spoken word.

"As you all know, the National Health Society holds a special place in my heart. My wife Brenda has long worked in the medical field and understands the important work of the NHS." Eric purposefully put on a look of slight embarrassment. "In fact, Brenda couldn't be here tonight because she had to work. As she so often tells me, she works so that I can engage in my hobbies."

Eric hung his head and nodded with a wry smile as the laughter rolled through the banquet hall.

"But seriously, the NHS has been at the forefront of medical research for a decade. Much of that is due to the innovative work of Dr. Christian Zimmerman who, as you know, died just last year. He was a brilliant mind and a true healer."

The governor paused respectfully in memory of the Nobel Prize Laureate, who had been the genesis of the Chiron Project. The man's death had been sudden and carried an air of oddness that made Eric uncomfortable if he thought about the details too much.

He inwardly shook himself and continued, "The NHS has been crucial to sharing ideas, innovations, and life-saving techniques and medicines in a cut-throat business world. In many ways, the NHS has put the focus of medicine back where it should be: off of money and onto the sick and dying."

He stopped talking and waited until the room was still and expectant. Tilting his head and looking up, he made a show as if something had just occurred to him. He reached back and pulled out his wallet and retrieved a worn and faded photograph of a grim man.

"Many of you can't see this, but the picture I hold is of my father," Eric said, allowing emotion to seep into his voice. "He died far too young from cancer. A highly treatable form of cancer today, but back then, all cancer was deadly."

He looked at the photo pointedly before laying it down and gathering himself and continuing on.

"The most precious resource in the world is people," he said. "How sad is a barrel of oil compared to a symphony? How droll a bar of gold compared to a miraculous innovation? When someone dies because medicine just isn't there yet, it is a tragedy. The world will never know what that person might have done. How many Einstein's, or Newton's, or Beethoven's, or even Christian Zimmerman's have we lost without knowing it? How many parents, spouses, brothers, sisters, friends…and even children have we lost?"

Eric could sense he had them in the palm of his hand. He felt a wave of power wash through him.

"Medical research is one of the most critical endeavors and responsibilities we have. Will our next generation be no further along than we are? We owe it to them. *I* owe it to them."

He looked in the back of the room and identified the five men who had gotten him elected. They sat at separate tables, but anyone with an eye for power could pick them out. They owned the five largest pharmaceutical and medical research companies in America.

These men had squabbled and fought for years until Eric was able to bring them together. Until the Chiron Project.

One of the five men smiled and nodded slightly at Eric. It was enough. He knew he had done his part. That he continued to do his part. His support was safe. Powerful allies were what made Eric powerful in his own right.

"A life. That is what we are talking about," he said. "A cure for a disease or new treatment is too big. We must remember and think about the one life we are trying to save. Just look around you and find someone who is important to you, possibly even precious to you. What would you do without them?"

He let them look around and waited until the movement subsided.

"Most of you know me, some too well." He smiled, cueing those in the crowd to laugh. "I've made medical research a priority. Today I reassert myself to doing more. To strive for extraordinary results and breakthrough. Not for myself or the recognition, but for that one life."

Eric held up that hated photo of his father to the crowd and saw tears in many eyes. Lucas had made sure there were a few reporters in the audience who would carry his speech. It would have an incredible impact since they knew from sources in the White House that President Wilkens was about to cut funding to medical research.

"Thank you all for having me here tonight and thank you for what you do," Eric said, carefully putting the photograph in his shirt pocket. "We are all in a battle, one we must win. I am honored to fight it with you. Thank you all, and have a great night."

Applause and a standing ovation. Eric walked off-stage and shook several hands. Things were falling into place nicely.

The only cause for concern was Bog Island. It was the key to everything. Eric pushed these thoughts from his head. Lucas said he had it under control.

And when had Lucas ever lied to him?

Chapter 25

The heat was the worst part. There was a small air vent, but unless it caught a breeze, the tight concrete cell was as stale and oppressive as a crypt.

Jack lay on his back, his eyes closed. The concrete floor at least was cool. He was concentrating on the sounds of the frogs and the night birds. If he concentrated enough, he could forget where he was. He could even forget what had happened.

He shivered despite the heat and waited for the stomach cramps, but there weren't any this time. Xavier gave him some antibiotics that morning to help his severe diarrhea during a checkup for his bullet wound.

Xavier had also given him something else. He'd palmed a small piece of paper into Jack's hand while taking his pulse.

Jack wanted to go pull it from the hiding place in his mattress, to look at it again and know he wasn't alone. He resisted the temptation. Besides, he knew the contents of the letter by heart.

Jack,

I'm glad you are alive, but sorry you are here. I've seen Heather and Amanda for only brief moments. They look okay, although I'm sure Amanda is still traumatized.

I want you to know that none of this is your fault. I know how you are, and you're probably beating yourself up. We stumbled into a spider's web, that's all. Now it's our job to find a way out before we get eaten.

Xavier can be trusted, I believe. If he wanted to betray us, he would have already done so. Besides, he knows I'll kill him if he does...isn't that right, my little Haitian friend? Choke the life right out of you, I will.

Stay strong, Jack. I don't know yet what these bastards are up to, but something big is going on. You don't go to all this trouble to keep people locked up unless it's for a good reason.

I'll make sure I do something to end up in the infirmary every three to five days for us to pass messages through the good doctor. Take care,

Your friend, Charles Haywood

Jack sighed. Charles' words almost made him cry. Despite the reassurance, he did feel responsible. He would need to harness that feeling to find a way out and to save his friends. And he was worried about Charles.

Xavier told Jack that they hadn't been able to save the guard Charles had attacked. The man's windpipe had been crushed, and by the time, they'd gotten a chest tube into him, he'd slipped into a coma and died. The guards had taken turns beating Charles, but he had only laughed and jeered at them, mocked their sadness at the loss of their dead comrade. The other guard would eventually recover, but had a broken nose and mangled face.

"They'll make your friend disappear," Xavier had told him in a hushed whisper.

"What do you mean disappear?" asked Jack.

The Haitian had simply shrugged. "I don't know. They are here in the evening and then in the morning their cells are empty. No one is concerned. Sometimes the person comes back, but never the same. Most of the time, they are broken."

"Broken? You mean like hurt?"

Xavier struggled for words. "No. More like something important has been taken from them. Sometimes they are just sick, but not everyone comes back."

"Where do they take them?"

He shook his head. "Not sure. I don't hear trucks, so it must be close."

Jack had started to ask another question, but Lyles had walked in, and both men knew the guard sometimes looked for any opportunity to inflict pain.

As an attorney, Jack had a habit of tapping as he thought. Normally, it was the end of a pencil. He'd even discovered it was hard to think as clearly without this physical act. Jack had picked up a small stone from the yard and was using this to tap rhythmically on the metal floor drain.

Tap. Tap. Tap. Tap. Tap. Continuously, for long minutes at a time.

Thumpthumpthump, came a faint response.

Jack froze. His first thought was that maybe another prisoner in an adjacent cell was making the noise, but he'd long since given up hope of being able to communicate. Although the cells were next to each other, the guards never put prisoners in neighboring cells. They always left empty kennels between them.

Jack tapped slowly again and waited for the response, but nothing came. He put his ear against each wall and the floor, but heard nothing.

He lay back tired and frustrated. Jack closed his eyes and concentrated on the frogs and the birds. He could almost imagine he was camping out with his father.

Opening his eyes, he found himself looking at the drain.

The drain.

Jack crawled over and carefully laid out flat on the floor. He pressed his ear against the cool metal floor drain.

Nothing...except maybe...humming.

Why would there be humming down in a drain? Jack sensed it was machinery, more due to the feel of the noise than the noise itself.

He put his finger over his other ear and concentrated. Definitely a humming...and something else. Something out of place. Something lovely.

Jack sat up and shook his head. He must be imagining things. Been in a concrete box for a long time. Jack had been shot, betrayed, sick, and feverish. He'd witnessed some of his best friends being murdered. Was it too much to think that maybe he was a little delusional?

Laying his ear back against the drain, Jack took a deep breath and then cleared his mind.

There it was. Very faint. Music.

Not just any music. It was his father's favorite classical composer.

The hauntingly beautiful sounds of Vivaldi floated up from the earth.

Chapter 26

Dr. Edward Massengill prided himself on his professional detachment and rarely even noticed the test subjects, but he had to admit the woman on the table before him was especially beautiful. He'd always been more of a brunette guy himself, but the woman's deep red hair and high cheekbones were striking. Especially now, when she looked so peaceful.

He glanced up at his assistant, Helga. She had been with him from the beginning of the project and never shown a trace of moral consciousness, something that Dr. Massengill associated in his mind as synonymous with weakness. The middle-aged woman looked back at him calmly and with no hint of nervousness. *Very good*, he told himself.

"I saw the previous subject still on the table," said Massengill, nodding towards the storage room. "Why haven't we disposed of her yet?"

"There was a passing oil tanker to the west," Helga answered. "I was told it wasn't safe to dispose of the subject until later tonight."

"Did we get all the samples we needed from her?" he asked.

She consulted a chart. "Yes, doctor. We have blood, tissue, and spinal fluid. Initial tests show her white blood count off the charts."

Massengill nodded. "The subject's immune system sees the medicine as a virus. Something to be attacked. This current batch will hopefully rectify that issue."

"Doctor," said Helga tentatively. "If you don't mind me asking, how does the medicine work exactly?"

He looked at her and then nodded. "This is the first time you have ever asked me such a question. Why the sudden interest?"

"I apologize," she said, turning away to prepare the instruments. "I have overstepped my place."

Massengill frowned and sought for words. "That's not what I meant. I'm just been surprised you've never asked before. I presumed you simply had no interest. Do you understand what we are doing here?"

"Curing cancer," she said almost in a whisper.

"In a sense, yes," he answered, "but it is more than that. Eventually, we will prevent it from existing at all. It will be an evolutionary blip that is here for a short time and then gone forever."

"But how?" she asked.

"We have finally reached a point where our technology is advanced enough to treat the disease from the inside. It is as simple as that, yet far more complex."

"I've heard the lab techs use the term nanotechnology," Helga said.

Massengill felt a quiver of excitement run through him. As a biochemist, nanos were the Holy Grail. They could fight and cure any disease, or even perform internal surgery. The technology was still experimental, but showed great promise.

"How does it work?" she repeated.

"We have developed nanoparticles that are fifty nanometers in diameter," he said, growing animated and using his hands to describe the creation. "The particles are composed of a careful combination of polyactic, copolylactic, and glycolic acids, which hold cancer-fighting drugs within their molecular meshes. A peptide coats the nanoparticle causing it to bind to cancer cells and ignore healthy cells. These nanoparticles roam the bloodstream until they attach to cancer cells, which they treat with cancer medicine."

Her face showed she understood the implications. "No more chemo or radiation," she said.

"That's correct." Massengill smiled, pleased. He had always suspected Helga had a sharp mind. "In a few years time, those practices will be considered barbaric. Cancer will be an obsolete disease since even healthy people will be vaccinated with the nanoparticles against cancer."

"And the nanos will destroy the cancer cells as they first form, before they can grow or spread," she said.

He nodded. "Now you are beginning to see the potential implications of what we can accomplish."

She smiled. A sight so rare that it made Massengill hesitate.

"What is it?" he asked.

"The Chiron Project," she said. "I finally get it. Chiron was a centaur skilled in medicine. We are in a sense making a creature that is not completely human by combining other parts. To heal them like Chiron did in the stories."

"I see you know your Greek mythology," said Massengill. "Never cared for it myself, but my mentor Dr. Christian Zimmerman was crazy about it. Site Iaso is even named after a Greek goddess of healing and cures."

"You actually worked with Dr. Zimmerman?" she asked in awe.

Massengill nodded curtly. Growing bored, he looked at the clock, Massengill wanted to proceed so they could complete the full cycle of treatment that night. "Has the subject been prepared?"

"Yes, doctor," Helga responded businesslike. "The subject was injected with fully developed ovarian cancer cells a little over twelve hours ago. Blood transfusions have aggressively fed the cancer cells and the lymph nodes are already beginning to enlarge."

"Very good," Massengill answered. He reached for the latest specimen of NCF-102, but his hand froze. Tilting his head upward, he asked. "Do you hear that?"

Her face was blank. "What, doctor?"

"That blasted tapping," he answered. "Like metal on metal or something."

"I don't hear anything," she said. "Could be the guards up above."

He picked up an empty IV pole and raised it up in both arms, hitting the ceiling with the end several times. Standing still, he listened carefully.

"Nothing now," he said.

"Must have worked."

"Put on the music please," he said.

"Vivaldi?" she asked.

Massengill nodded. "Yes, Four Seasons. Let me see the subject's chart."

She started the music before handing the clipboard over. Twenty-eight-year-old female in excellent health. A+ blood type with borderline high blood pressure. The subject has never given birth, and examinations indicated that she has never been pregnant, making her perfect for the latest drug trial.

"Would you like me to proceed with the injection, doctor?" Helga asked.

"Go ahead," Massengill said, looking at the subject again. She was incredibly beautiful. Even her name was vaguely appealing.

Heather Daniels.

Chapter 27

Bridgett fidgeted, wanting to chew her nails, but she didn't want to mess up her manicure. She forced herself to place her hands behind her back and try to look at ease. Lucas Ross made her nervous in a way that no other man could, and she didn't want him to ever comprehend the depth of that insecurity. Bridgett realized that her efforts at nonchalance were wasted since he was totally engrossed in the draft article she had given him.

"Holy shit," Lucas said, shaking his head and flipping a page.

She wanted to sit, but dared not without his permission, and this was not a time to ask or take liberties. There was danger in the air. *Will he blame me for this?* she wondered.

He threw the report down and pushed it away from him, disgusted. "I thought you had control over him?"

Bridgett swallowed and forced what she hoped was a casual smile. "Allen bought the story I told him about Jack Winters. The only problem was he started digging on his own."

"And dug a little deeper than we wanted," Lucas said, cutting his eyes toward the report. "Hell, he found out things my people haven't yet uncovered."

"He *is* a good journalist," Bridgett said.

Lucas sat back in his chair. "Yes, but how committed is he?"

She shook her head. "I don't understand the question, sir."

He picked up the report again. "This is a hell of a story. He's not only uncovered the disappearance of Jack Winters, but also the disappearances of his former girlfriend and four other college friends. One of whom is actually a soldier who is AWOL. I'm surprised he delayed running the story at all."

"I asked him to let us see it first," she said. "Told him given the governor's connection to Jack Winter's father that we might have a comment."

"And now we have to give a comment," said Lucas with a frown. "Otherwise there will be a sentence at the end saying that the governor refused to comment."

Bridgett looked away towards the door, but then forced herself to relax and meet his gaze. "Sir, it was the only way I could think to get him to delay running the story. As it is, he's looking to send it to his editor soon."

Lucas sighed and rubbed his head. "Can you talk him out of it?" he finally asked, looking her up and down suggestively. "Tell me the truth."

She frowned and ran her hands down her slim waist and full hips before forcing her hands together again behind her back. "Sir, Allen is quite fond of me, but he realizes this is a story that he cannot pass up. At his core, he is a journalist. He loves reporting. There's no way I can convince him to just forget about this."

Staring at her hard for several seconds, he finally picked back up the report. He spun in his chair and began to feed the report page by page into a shredder. When he was finished, he turned back to her and seemed more composed.

"All right then," he finally said. "Tell your young and eager reporter that the governor's office would like to speak to him about this story. Stress that this will be off the record, and if he tells his editor we are speaking with him, it's off. Tell him there are some things about Jackson and Jeremiah Winters that the governor knows but has kept secret. That should whet his journalistic appetite."

"And then what?" she asked.

"I'll call Devin and he'll call you," Lucas said. "I imagine he will give you a location where Allen can meet a representative of the governor's office. Stress to your reporter friend that he can tell no one about this. No one."

Bridgett hesitated, thinking about Allen and his strong hands and alligator smile. "Sir, does it really have to come to that?"

His eyes narrowed at her, and his hands knotted together tightly on his desk in front of him.

Her heart began beating even faster, and she felt the fluttering of death around her like a murder of crows swarming the office. She had stumbled into working for Lucas for the exceptional pay funneled from rich lobbyists, but she sometimes wondered if it wasn't enough considering how it all might end for her. She forced herself to smile as seductively as possible. "It's just that we have worked so hard to cultivate this relationship. He could still be useful to us, granted he is such a silly boy."

Lucas leaned forward in his chair, resting his elbows on his desk. "Bridgett, I chose you to be a part of our team because of your considerable skill and persuasive abilities. You have been a valuable member and helped us to accomplish things that are part of the greater good. I judge you can see the bigger picture and understand that things can get messy at times. Can I still count on you?"

Bridgett felt tension in the air and knew her very life was on the line. She thrust her hip out in his direction and tossed her hair back. "Why, sir, of course. He is only a silly boy, after all. We can't let him interfere in what we are doing."

He stared at her with narrowed eyes for a few more moments before nodding. "All right then. Devin will be in touch. Do what he says."

She nodded and turned to leave.

"One more thing," Lucas said.

Bridgett stopped and turned slowly.

"Make sure there is no connection between you and Allen. You'll need to go through his apartment, car, wallet, everything. Throw away the burner phone you've been using to talk to him. Nothing can tie back to this office. Do you understand?"

"Yes, sir," she answered, feeling faint.

"And you've followed my instructions?" Lucas pressed. "No one has seen you out in public? He's kept the relationship a secret?"

Bridgett nodded. "He still believes I'm married and will leave my husband for him. He knows that no one can know."

"Good," answered Lucas. "I'll get you a new target soon."

She turned slowly and moved out of the office as if in a dream.

Lucas picked up the phone and punched in a number.

"Yes?" answered Devin.

"I've got a job for you," said Lucas, staring thoughtfully out the open door at a retreating Bridgett. "Maybe two jobs. I need you back here tonight."

Chapter 28

Deloy Dequese had asked his daughter to go fishing with him in order to try and cheer her up. After her mother ran off, he and Rena spent nearly every day out on the gulf together. The tranquil waters had soothed their rejected and broken hearts and helped them to draw closer together. In many ways, Deloy would say that he had truly become a father in those difficult days. Now Rena seemed more distant from him than he could remember.

He pulled the boat into the cove where he regularly docked and cut the engine. Rena jumped out of the boat and onto the old weathered surface, tying them off. She then unlocked the thick chain and ran it through a ring on the bow to secure it. Thieves were rare, but it never hurt to be careful. They gathered their gear, which didn't take long. The day had been largely unproductive, both in catching fish and reconnecting with each other.

They walked along the worn trail and the silence between them felt pregnant with deeper meaning. Deloy had never been a talker, but the deadness that existed between them was more than he could bear.

"We had no choice," he said simply.

She grunted and shook her head. "We always have choices. Isn't that what you taught me?"

"You know what I mean," he said. "That man was trouble. All the people who go to the camp are. That's why they take them off the mainland and send them here...to start a better life."

Looking at him angrily, she picked up her pace. "Even you don't really believe that. You know what they do there."

"That man was trouble," Deloy repeated. "What were we supposed to do? Hide him? Sneak him off the island?"

They rounded the curve in the trail and walked into the neat opening that surrounded their cabin. She started up the stairs, but Deloy grabbed her by the arm and pulled her back. He meant it to be gentle, but she resisted and it became rough.

Wrenching away from him, her eyes appeared on fire. "We could have tried. That's what we could have done, instead of letting them take him."

He stepped back from his daughter in surprise. Deloy had seen that look on her face before, but never directed at him.

He frowned. "They would have found out and it would have been bad. I had to protect us, protect you. We owe them."

She nodded, angry tears starting to form in her eyes. "Yeah, we owe them. They saved your life when the doctors said there was no hope and I'm grateful for that, but that doesn't mean we're indebted to them forever and have to do everything they say. Especially when it's wrong. Don't you understand? He trusted us and we betrayed him. Why doesn't that bother you?"

Deloy felt his own heat rising. "We have nothing to be ashamed of. He would have died without our help. You saved his life. No need to feel bad about anything."

"Isn't there?" she asked her hands on her hips. "We saved his life only to give it away to *them*," she said, pointing to the west "What do you think they're going to do to him?"

"It's for the greater good," said Deloy, and he hated how weak his voice now sounded.

She shook her head at him. "That's the first time I've ever known you to lie to me. To use their words. Their slogans. Not even when mother left did you try to shelter me by lying. Why are you doing it now?"

"Why does this bother you so much?" he asked. "We've turned in runaways before. This is just—"

"Because I love him!" she screamed, tears running freely now. "Because I love him. And he might have even loved me."

"Oh darling," said Deloy, reaching out for her. "You only knew each other a few days."

She pulled back away from him. "Don't. It's not something you can fix or explain away." Looking down at the ground, she sought words. Finally, she looked up at him. "It bothers me because I'm ashamed."

Deloy didn't know what to say and only stared at her until she turned and walked away into the woods.

"Rena," he called, but she ignored him and continued. He thought about following. She needed time though, time alone in the forest. She had always found peace there. It would heal her again, he hoped.

Picking up their fishing gear, he climbed the stairs heavily and walked into the cabin. After setting the gear on the floor, he turned to the kitchen to begin cleaning the few fish they had caught for dinner. Something made him freeze and peer into the shadowy corner of the room. There was a presence that didn't belong.

"It's me," said an old but strong voice from the chair in the corner. "I'm sorry to come in uninvited, but I didn't really think you would mind."

"Johnny?" asked Deloy. "What are you doing here? I thought you left the island."

"I did for awhile," the old black man answered, "but this is my home. Even if I have no home anymore. My roots are here and bones belong here. Nowhere else seems right."

Recovering himself, Deloy picked up the fish and walked into the adjacent kitchen. "Well, you're welcome to stay for dinner. Where do you plan to live?"

"I thought I would stay here," said Uncle Johnny with a smile.

Deloy laughed nervously. "You know you're welcome, but do you think that's really best? I mean, what do you believe will happen if they find out you're here?"

"Now why in the world would they find that out?" asked Johnny. "Unless you decided to tell them."

"I would never do that," said Deloy, his jaw tight. "You're a guest under my roof."

"Forgive me," said Johnny, "but I couldn't help overhearing some of the conversation between you and your lovely daughter. If I might say, it appears you have done just that. And recently."

The big man turned away and laid out a medium-sized red snapper on the cutting board while pulling the knife out of his belt. As he began cleaning the fish, he realized how easy it would be to get rid of the meddling old man. He would get them into trouble with the camp. It could be dangerous for Rena.

"Whatever you're thinking of doing," said Johnny, "I won't stop you. You can turn me in or...whatever other solution you may have come up with."

Deloy savagely buried the tip of the knife into the board and spun on the old black man. "I didn't ask for any of this. I'm just trying to protect and raise my daughter. Things get all complicated when strange men like you and...well, like you come around."

"Tell me about the other one," said John. "The man your daughter is in love with."

Turning back around, Deloy worked the knife carefully out of the wood so as not to break the point. "Not much to say, just another mainlander. You know the type."

"Yes," answered John slowly. "Why don't you tell me anyway? Indulge an old man."

Deloy shook his head and remembered something. "He actually said he knew you. Wondered what happened to your old house. I told him you had died."

"How very nice of you," said Johnny.

"What was I supposed to tell him?" said Deloy. "That they burned you out and ran you off, nearly killing you in the process? That they still ask about you and would love to track you down? Honestly, Johnny, why the hell would you come back here after all this time?"

"Like I said," answered Johnny, "this is my home."

"Well, *this* is *my* home," answered Deloy. "And you're putting my daughter and me in danger."

The old man chuckled. "You're already in danger. You just don't have the sense to figure it out."

"What the hell do you mean by that?" asked Deloy.

Johnny stood and moved up close to Deloy. "Do you think that when they are done with what they're doing over there that they will leave any witnesses?"

"We promised them we wouldn't talk," said Deloy more confidently than he felt. "We're loyal to them and they know they can trust us. We've never said anything to anyone."

Johnny stared at the big man and smiled sadly. "Why don't you tell me about this man your daughter loves."

"It doesn't matter. He's gone, and we won't see him again."

"Then why are you so reluctant to talk about him?" asked Johnny.

Deloy stopped cutting the fish and sighed. "Fine. His name was Jack. Actually told Rena he was a lawyer, but I doubt that. Only bums and dregs get sent to Bog Island."

Johnny frowned. "A lawyer named Jack? Did he say anything else?"

"Actually he did," said Deloy, turning to face him. "He said he knew you. That you used to work for his father. Called you Uncle Johnny or some such nonsense."

Johnny Crittenton sat down heavily in the kitchen chair behind him.

Chapter 29

Amanda and Brian were together again playing in the woods as they had when they were children. Both of them were grown now, but the years hadn't come between them as in real life. They held hands and talked and shared. Amanda knew it wasn't real, that her brother was dead, but she didn't want reality. It hurt too much. She dove into the wonderful oblivion of her dream and turned her back on reality.

"You hungry?" he asked her, pointing at the rows of bushes pregnant with ripe blackberries.

She smiled and began popping them into her mouth, as did he. Her stomach rumbled, and it felt like she couldn't get enough of them.

"Easy now," he said, putting his hand on her arm. She looked down and saw a spot of blood on his hand and what looked suspiciously like a piece of brain and bone.

"Wha-wha-wah is that?" she asked and realized she had stuttered. Amanda hadn't stuttered since she was ten and hardly ever around Brian. For some unknown reason, the condition was rare in girls. It had never bothered her brother but made her parents embarrassed and disinterested of her.

Three of the soldiers from the clearing emerged from behind trees, except they were dressed like kids from school. "Aw, look at the little stuttering fr-fr-fr-freak," said Jimmer, now dressed in a high school letter jacket.

Lyles and Brennan, who were dressed to match, laughed as well.

"Leave her alone," said Brian, standing between her and the boys. He had always protected her against the bullies and those that teased her. Her brother had taken some serious beatings over the years on her behalf, but he didn't seem to care.

She tried to pull him back. "Don't, Brian. It's o-k-k-kay."

"K-k-k-" mimicked Jimmer while moving close to Brian. "That's the sound your sister is going to make when we pull down her panties and nail her over and over again until she bleeds."

Her brother flew at Jimmer, who kept smiling evilly at her even as punches landed on his face and body.

"Stop it!" she screamed. "He already killed you!"

Both Brian and Jimmer did stop and turned to look at her. She saw that Jimmer's throat was cut and that a large portion of Brian's head was missing.

Her brother gazed at her with sad eyes. "I'm dead, too, you know."

"No you're not," she cried. "Don't say that!"

"It's true," he insisted. "You can't stay in this place. If you do, you'll die."

"I don't care," she answered covering her face. "You can't be dead." Noticing that she wasn't stuttering anymore, she looked up and saw the three boys were now gone.

Brian was unhurt again, but his eyes were full of sadness. "I know it seems impossible now, but you have to go on. You're strong. You can't just lay down and die."

"I'm not strong," she insisted. "You were the strong one. You're my other half, my twin. Without you, I'm incomplete."

"You think that, but it's not true," he answered. "That's why you hated me going off to the military."

"And leaving me," she said angrily.

"And why you couldn't make things work with Travis," Brian continued.

"That had nothing to do with you," she said.

Brian shook his head. "That was the most meaningful relationship you've ever had and you couldn't find a way to share yourself with anyone but me."

"Because he wasn't the right one," she said, crossing her arms over her chest.

"Because you were scared," he said. "But you have no need to be scared. You're stronger than you think, never forget that."

"Stay with me," she pleaded.

"It's time to go," he said, and she noticed he appeared pale and bloodless. "Wake up, Amanda. Wake up."

"No," she said, struggling deeper into her dream.

"Wake up now," he said more forcefully. "Wake up. Wake up. Wakeupwakeupwakeup..."

Amanda realized someone was shaking her and opened her eyes to find strange men in uniform leaning over her. She was back in the cell. Groaning, Amanda closed her eyes and tried to retreat to her dreams again. A hand slapped her face forcefully, and her eyes flew open.

"How long has she been like this?" asked Urchart.

Lyles shrugged. "I don't know. A few days, a week maybe."

"When is the last time she ate or drank anything?" Urchart asked.

"I couldn't tell you," answered Lyles. "We put in fresh food and water and take out the old. The doc recommended bed rest, so we left her alone."

Brennan stepped close to her and knelt. He put a cool hand to her forehead and then fingers to her neck. Finally, he picked up one of her limp hands and pressed down on the fingernails while watching closely.

He turned to Urchart. "Her capillary refill is almost non-existence. I'd say she is dangerously dehydrated. Has a little fever also, and her pulse seems high."

"Get her over to the clinic," Urchart said. "Tell the doc to get her an IV and make sure nothing bad happens to her."

Amanda started laughing, she couldn't help it. *Make sure nothing bad happens to me*, she thought.

They lifted her up, mattress and all, and carried her out of the cell and across an open area. Then she was inside again and felt herself transported down a dim hallway before the mattress was lowered to a floor. Two men then picked her up and laid her on a hospital bed.

"What do we have here?" asked the doctor in a Haitian accent.

"Dehydration, I believe," answered Brennan. "Possibly a fever. Take care of her." He then motioned for his men to follow him as he left the room.

The thin Haitian leaned over and looked at her carefully. His face showed concern and worry. The dark eyes that peered into hers were kind and sad at the same time.

"Let me get some fluids into you," he said finally and hung a bag of saline on the pole beside her. He had a difficult time finding a vein in her condition, but he finally managed to get the drip started. He put a blood pressure cuff on her other arm and began pumping it up while listening to her pulse on the stethoscope.

"Are you really a doctor?" she managed to ask.

He let the air out of the cuff and pulled it off her arm. "I am," he answered simply.

"How can you do this?" she asked, her eyes cutting towards the barred window to indicate the camp.

"I help people." He slipped a thermometer under her tongue. "Even political prisoners like you need medical help. That is what I do."

She started to speak, but he stopped her with an open palm and pushed the thermometer deeper under her tongue.

"You are severely dehydrated," he said, finally pulling the slender piece of glass from her mouth. "Your blood pressure is dangerously low and your pulse is too high. Are you on any medication?"

"No," she answered. "I've only been kidnapped and seen my twin brother murdered. No medications."

He stared at her suspiciously. "I don't know anything about that, but I need to go get you something to lower that fever. I will be right back."

"I'll be here," she answered, looking towards the closed window.

The doctor hesitated, staring at her uncertain. "I'll be right back," he repeated.

"Can you open the curtains further?" she asked. "I'd like to see the sun and the sky."

"But of course," he answered, walking over and pulling the cloth back. Warm light bathed her, and she could see fluffy white clouds floating above her.

"Thank you," she whispered to him as he walked out of the room.

It reminded her of her dream. She and Brian on a warm, perfect day, just the two of them. She closed her eyes and tried to find her way back to that dream.

You're strong, Brian said in her mind.

Opening her eyes, she noticed the light glint off something on the table beside her. Looking over, she reached out and picked up the thermometer and pulled it close to her eyes to examine.

Who uses these old things anymore? she wondered. *Even when I took that EMT course at LSU, we had the digital forehead thermometers.*

Carefully, she reached out and stuck the end of the thermometer into the small crack in the bedside table's drawer. Amanda then tilted the other end down slowly until she heard the sharp crack. Lifting the jagged remains up, thick silver mercury dripped over her hand and rolled in beads onto the floor. She stared out at the fluffy clouds.

"Oh, Brian," she said crying. "You always thought the best of me and were always so wrong."

She tilted her head back and jabbed the sharp glass into the carotid artery in her neck. Amanda watched the clouds until she slipped away.

Chapter 30

Allen Branch had been a journalist for over a decade and was used to confidential sources acting strangely. They all seemed to believe that if the wrong person saw them talking to a reporter it would ruin their life or at least make things difficult. In Allen's experience, this quest for secrecy was not really necessary and he thought that many of them simply liked the sense of excitement.

Even so, Bridgett had seemed nervous and given him a fiercer than normal hug, as if she were sincerely worried about him.

"Don't worry," he had told her smiling. "I've handled many powerful guard dog types. Devin Alders doesn't scare me."

"He should," she said with a drawn face. "Are you sure you want to do this?"

"Of course," he answered, unable to understand her concern. "This is already a good story. Missing supreme court judge's son and friends, but you add in the governor's connection and that makes it just a little more juicy. Even off the record."

She had smiled, kissed him, and walked away looking like she were going to cry.

What the hell is wrong with her? he wondered. *Must be that time of the month or something.*

Now that he was at the abandoned warehouse on the west side of New Orleans, he felt the slightest sense of unease. As a journalist, you paid attention to the stories you heard. Some of them were worth paying attention to, most of them weren't. Those involving Lucas Ross and his personal assistant Devin Alders were the kind Allen believed were at least grounded in truth. Whispered tales hinted that Devin Alders was the sort of man who made problems disappear quietly, tidily, and permanently.

"Come on, Allen," he said to himself, getting out of his car. "Don't be a scaredy-cat. It's just a story." Nevertheless, the old buildings covered in graffiti and surrounded by trash touched a nerve.

He walked quickly from where he had been instructed to park and around to the side of one particular building. Devin Alders had been very particular on the phone. Exact time. Specific locations. Not telling anyone about the meeting. These ex-military types could be such bores. They still believed they were in the military and treated everyone else around them accordingly. Regardless, it had the makings of an excellent story and that made a little bullshit worth it.

A door opened up as he walked towards it, and an angular face looked at him.

"Name please," the man said.

Allen stopped and frowned. "We just talked on the damn phone. What do you mean, *name please*?"

"Just provide your name, sir," he said calmly.

He sighed. "Allen Branch. I work for the *Louisiana Review*. I'm hoping you are Mr. Devin Alders."

The man opened the door wider. "Please come in. I apologize for any inconvenience."

Allen walked through the door and heard it shut and lock behind him. He looked up into a large open warehouse. The interior was bare but clean. Skylights eliminated most of the shadows. The angular man in jeans and a sport coat smiled at him and indicated for Allen to follow as he walked further into the warehouse.

They proceeded around a corner and entered what must have once been a break room for whoever had worked there before. The small room contained cabinets and a refrigerator. A round table sat in the middle of the linoleum floor with two plastic chairs arranged opposite of each other.

"Want some coffee?" asked Devin, moving over to a full pot and pouring himself a cup.

"No thanks," answered Allen, setting his shoulder bag on the floor and pulling out a digital recorder and a notebook.

Devin pointed at the items. "You won't be needing those."

"I assure you that your confidentiality is safe with me," said Allen. "I simply need to make sure I get the facts straight."

The man stared at him silently for a few moments and then sat down with his coffee. "Fair enough," he finally said. "But we'll need to get a few things straight first. Please sit."

Slowly sliding into the chair, Allen reached out to turn on his digital recorder, but the other man grabbed it and pulled it out of reach.

"Hey, now," said Allen in protest.

"Not yet," said Devin, putting the recorder in his jacket pocket and, with the same hand, pulling a small pistol with a silencer out of a shoulder holster and laid it on the table. Devin kept his hand on the pistol even while it rested on the cheap, round tabletop. The small hole at the end of the silencer pointed at Allen.

It took a minute for Allen to get his voice back. "What the hell is this?"

"This, Mr. Branch, is a conversation," Devin explained. "Maybe the most important conversation you have ever had in your life."

"Okay, but can you put the pistol away?"

"No," Devin answered. "I may need it."

"You don't need it for me."

"That remains to be seen," Devin said. "Look around you. Does this setting strike you as odd?"

Allen nodded. "Yes, but sources are odd ducks, no offense."

Devin tilted his head and smiled. "I am not your source." He rolled his eyes. "Let me paint you a picture. You come to an isolated warehouse in the middle of nowhere to meet a stranger. No one knows you are here. I even have a cell phone jammer in the corner in case you are trying to transmit our meeting. I have a small caliber silenced pistol pointing at you. Small caliber, so as not to make a big mess. You are sitting on a plastic chair that rests on a linoleum floor. Bleach and cleaning supplies are in the corner, and I've got a large canvas bag there filled with plastic sheets and duct tape. It will be short work for me to weight you down and drop your carcass in the nearby harbor. Then I clean up everything and dispose of your car. What do you think is going to happen next?"

Allen's eyes had grown wide as the man talked. "But why? I haven't done anything to you. Why would you want to kill me?"

"I don't want to kill you," Devin answered. "It's just a job. You've stumbled upon something you shouldn't have."

"Jack Winters' disappearance? Why is that such a big deal? I wouldn't even have known about it if my girlfriend hadn't put me onto it."

"Bridgett is not your girlfriend," said Devin.

Allen felt a moment of anger. "*Yes* she *is*. I think I would know. You probably don't even know her."

"That's not even her real name," said Devin with a pitying smile. "Her job was to seduce you and feed you information that Lucas Ross wanted to get into the press."

"I don't believe you."

The man shrugged. "Think about it. All those tidbits and morsels of info? Ever go out with her in public, meet her family, learn her background? Ever date a woman as beautiful and captivating and...uh, more accommodating?"

Allen thought. "Well no, but she loves me."

"Then why does everything have to be secret?" asked Devin.

"If you must know, it's because she's still married," insisted Allen. "She's in the process of getting divorced and then we'll be together. Bridgett just needs to keep our relationship secret for now until it's all over."

Devin chuckled. "You sad boy. That woman is a piranha who has never been married. At least as far as I know. She duped you, but don't be too hard on yourself. She is very good at what she does."

"Why are you telling me this?" Allen asked again.

"Because you need to believe me when I tell you that I don't want to kill you."

"Okay," said Allen. "Then don't. Just let me go, and we'll both forget about all of this."

"That won't be possible," said Devin. "If I don't kill you, someone else will and then come for me. But there might be another way."

"I'm open to alternatives," said Allen nervously.

"Good." Devin smiled. "You will need to disappear. Tonight, in fact. You will never again talk to any friends or family. It will be as if you dropped off the face of the earth."

"I can't do that," said Allen. "My mother is ill."

"Would her illness take a turn for the worse if I shot you the face?" asked Devin, tapping the pistol with his index finger.

Allen sat silently staring hard at the gaunt man.

"Anyway," continued Devin, "I've got a bag for you with money, new identity documents, everything you need to start a new life."

"A new life?" asked Allen. "Doing what?"

"Anything but journalism," answered Devin. "That's a little too close to the truth. The new identification docs are good, but if someone is looking for you, we don't want them looking for a reporter."

"But journalism is my life," protested Allen.

"Is it worth your life?" asked Devin, patting the pistol. "What else do you like to do? Look at this as an opportunity. Stop being such a sorry sack of shit."

Allen thought. "Well, I do like to write. I've been thinking of starting on my novel."

"There you go," said Devin with a smile. "That's the spirit. Just please don't dedicate the book to me."

"No danger of that," said Allen. "And that's it? I just disappear somewhere and forget about all my family and friends? Write books and hide?"

"Not quite," said Devin. "I'm taking a big risk here. I want something in return."

"What?" asked Allen.

Devin pulled out a small scrap of paper. "On here is an email account and password. It doesn't tie to you or me. I want you to check it the first of every month. You'll get an email from someone mentioning lemons."

"An email mentioning lemons?" asked Allen with a confused look on his face.

"Yes," said Devin. "It should come from a different email address each time. You should get it by the first of the month, the third at the latest."

"Who are the emails from?" asked Allen.

"From me, dumbass."

"Why? What am I supposed to do with them?"

"Nothing," answered Devin. "It's what you do if you *don't* get the email."

"I don't understand," said Allen.

The man sat there for a moment looking at the pistol. "I need some insurance. Lucas has begun looking into me. He wouldn't do that unless he's already thinking of me as a loose end. I need some insurance."

"Like kill you?" asked Allen. "The governor's chief-of-staff? That's crazy."

"You don't know him," said Devin. "Not the way I do. He is quite capable of murder and more."

"So go to the police or something," said Allen.

Devin smiled sadly. "He already has the police in his pocket. I need something else."

"I'm figuring that's where I come in," said Allen.

"Yes. If you don't get that email by say...the fifth of any month, you write the story I'm going to give you. I recommend you don't publish it under your own name, but that's up to you at that point. I'll be dead, and if you want to join me, be my guest."

"What story?" asked Allen.

The man looked at him intensely. "The true story of what happened in Oman. I was there. I saw it all. I know what happened."

"Everyone already knows that story," said Allen.

"No, they don't," said Devin. "That is only what they wanted everyone to think. The true story is beyond belief." The man holstered his pistol and reached into his jacket pocket to pull out the digital recorder and handed it back to Allen.

"As a bonus, I'll also tell you quite a fine tale of what the governor and Lucas have been up to and plans for the future, but first Oman."

Allen looked at him with a blank face.

Devin tapped the top of Allen's notebook and recorder. "Now you can use these."

Allen turned on the recorder and began to write as the story unfolded.

Chapter 31

Deborah Mitchell drove slowly through the north section of the French Quarter. She was off duty and terribly tired, but almost without conscious thought found herself on the opposite side of New Orleans from her townhouse apartment.

She pulled into a curbside parking spot and looked across the street. There sat an unassuming concrete building conspicuously free of graffiti or piles of trash. She supposed this is where she had known she was coming since getting off work.

A placard proclaimed, "French Quarter Department of Social Welfare and Services." Below this hung a bright banner that read, "Take Back the Streets One Heart at a Time."

Deborah climbed out of her sedan and walked across the street. Somewhere she could hear blues music playing, but it seemed far away. The fading sun cast long shadows and glinted off hidden bits of broken glass in the thin weeds.

Opening the door, she was met by a thick wall of air conditioning and then a receptionist. The receptionist was the typical government gatekeeper, there not to assist those who entered the building's hallowed halls, but to convince them to go someplace else for help if possible.

"May I help you?" the thin librarian-looking woman asked with a face that made it clear she did not want to help anyone.

She put on an air of authority. "Yes, I am FBI Special Agent Deborah Mitchell. I'm following up on a missing person's case and hoping some of your...residents...might be able to help me."

The receptionist frowned. "I don't see how any of these people could help you. They were all homeless until recently."

"The missing person was also homeless," Deborah replied patiently.

"Oh," the woman answered, the word carrying considerable weight. She looked over her glasses at Deborah. "You know these people often just wander off. I doubt whoever you're looking for is missing."

"Thank you for your expert investigative experience," Deborah answered. "Might I keep your name and number on file in case the FBI needs your assistance with anything? Say, maybe catching a serial killer or possibly defusing a bomb?"

The woman sniffed. "You don't have to snarky."

Deborah sighed. "Look. Let me talk to them, and then I'll be on my way. Shouldn't take more than a few minutes. No one here is suspected of anything and I'm not going to cause trouble. Also, not to put too fine a point on it, but I don't really need your permission. Me explaining my business to you is a courtesy, nothing more."

The receptionist's face scrunched up tight as if she were sucking on a lemon. "I will need to call my director and get her approval." She pointed to a small waiting area. "You may wait over there in one of those chairs."

"Thank you," said Deborah. "Can I use your bathroom?"

She sighed in a long-suffering manner. "If you must. End of the hall to your right."

Deborah made her way down the hall and then began listening for voices. She heard children playing and found a room filled with youngsters. Some were gathered around a television showing a cartoon movie while others played with toys or blocks. A teenager reading a fashion magazine looked up at her.

"Can I help you?"

"No thanks," Deborah answered, closing the door and moving onwards. She opened several other doors until she heard a loud television behind a double-door towards the back of the building.

Entering felt like going into one of many low-end retirement homes she had visited over the years. Elderly men and women sat alone or in groups. Some were gathered around a television game show with the volume so high it made Deborah's eardrums cringe.

Now that she was here, she realized that she had no plan. She looked around the room and spotted an elderly woman sitting beside a dirty window. The woman looked vaguely familiar. Walking over, Deborah pulled out the most recent picture she had of her missing brother.

"Excuse me, ma'am. Have you seen this man?"

The woman jumped and turned to her with startled eyes as if Deborah had snuck up on her. Her frightened and confused eyes met the FBI agent's before clearing slightly and flickering to the picture.

Her voice was surprisingly clear. "Looks like my Tommy."

"Have you seen the person in this picture?"

The woman's eyes were welling up with tears. "He would have been thirty next week. Damn fool stuck too much of that poison in his arm."

Deborah backed away and turned to find a thin elderly man with penetrating eyes gazing at her.

"Can I see that picture please?"

Deborah showed it to him. "Have you seen him?"

He pushed the picture away. "Why are you looking for him? You're police, right?"

"I'm an FBI agent."

"What's Moses done?"

"So you do know him?" she asked eagerly.

"Maybe I do and maybe I don't," the man answered, crossing his arms.

Deborah heard loud voices in the hallway and suspected the receptionist had discovered she wasn't still in the toilet or patiently reading her magazine. "Look, Moses is my little brother. He runs off a lot, but it's been a long time since I saw him last. I just want to make sure he's okay."

"He did mention an older sister," the man answered, "but not that she was a cop. Guess we all got our little secrets we're not proud of."

"When did you last see him?"

The man tilted his head up to the ceiling in thought. "Must have been a couple of months ago. They took us together that same night."

"Took you together?" she asked. "Who?"

"Soldiers," the man answered. "But not really soldiers. I was a soldier myself in Vietnam, and these were a little different. Anyone ever tell you how hot it can get in the Mekong Delta? They say it gets hot and humid here, but they got no idea."

"What about Moses? What happened to him?"

The man shrugged. "They brought some of us here and took the others somewhere else. Not sure."

"What do you do here?"

"Pretty much whatever we want," the man answered. "We can even leave if we choose, but no one wants to stay gone for long."

"Why is that?"

"Because this is where the food and beds and clean clothes are at," the man explained. "Besides, they got cable. You stay gone too long and someone else might get your spot. This is a pretty good deal."

"So they're not giving you classes or making you work or anything?" she asked.

"Hell no," the man laughed. "Most of us would be gone in a minute if that were the—"

"Ma'am," yelled the receptionist from the door. "I thought I asked you to wait in the lobby."

Deborah nodded. "I think you did, too."

"My director says you are not allowed in here to talk to any of the guests without a warrant or a court order."

"A warrant *is* a court order," Deborah explained.

"Be that as it may, I doubt you have either," the woman said with a smile. "My director told me to inform you that if you do not depart the premises immediately I am to call the local police."

"I was just leaving anyway," said Deborah with a smile. "You have been most helpful, and this is quite a tight ship you run around here."

The woman's face clouded in confusion as if not certain whether she was being complimented or insulted.

Before she could speak, Deborah brushed past the small woman and walked down the halls and back outside where it had become dark. She climbed into her vehicle, pulled out a notepad, and began to make notes of what she had seen and learned.

Soldiers, she wrote and then crossed it out. *Not quite soldiers, but almost.*

Rounding up homeless people. Some are brought here, others go elsewhere.

Residents can leave if they want. Are not kept here by force.

Sounds like a free retirement home. How can the government afford that?

She thought for a few moments and wrote two more notes.

Where is the money coming from?

Where is Moses now?

Chapter 32

The unmistakable sound of a vehicle engine made Moses Mitchell freeze in the underbrush. He tilted his head and listened carefully, determining the sound was coming from the west of him. He headed in that direction.

Moses moved quickly but carefully. This was an unfamiliar part of the island and he had been about to end his day's exploration until he heard the sound. He crept through the woods until he came to a dirt road with twin beaten paths leading away to the south. He could hear the sound of the receding engine down the road.

What the hell do you think you're doing? asked Billy in his head.

Dumbass is trying to get himself caught, that's what, answered Nate.

"I am not," whispered Moses as he walked slowly south along the road, listening for any other approaching vehicles.

The lengthening shadows told him that there wasn't much more light left. Moses knew he should probably be headed back to his makeshift camp hidden deep in the forest, but he had to find out about the vehicle.

No you don't, said Delores. *All you need to do is get away from here. Nothing good can come of walking down this road.*

He ignored her and kept going. Soon, he heard men talking, and he crept into the cover of the thick moss-covered trees along the side of the road. Once there, he carefully made his way forward until he could see the vehicle parked in front of an old wooden boat dock. Tied up adjacent to the dock was a flat-bottomed john boat with an outboard motor at the back.

"A boat," whispered Moses in surprise.

"Hurry up," said one of the men to the other. "We're running out of daylight."

Moses looked carefully and saw they were two men from the Evil Dog Camp. Two of the ones who had been mean to him, Lyles and Fred. They were in a jeep without a cover.

"We're *supposed* to be running out of daylight," Fred told Lyles. "This is a job we do when it's dark so the chance of anyone seeing us is less."

"Put a sock in it," Lyles told him, lowering the tailgate. "I don't need you telling me what I already know. Just grab her."

Moses watched them lift a black plastic bag out of the rear. Two handles were on each end, which the men used to lift something that was obviously heavy and awkward.

That's a body bag, said Delores. *You can guess what's in it.*

And what they're doing to the body, said Billy. *Lyles told you himself one night to try and scare you. They take a meat hook and pass it through the Achilles tendons of the bodies after they've stripped it down. They have a chain attached to the hook that is attached to a boat anchor. They take the body out to deep water and drop it. After a week, the fish and crabs will have picked the body clean.*

"No," whispered Moses and shuddered. He'd had nightmares for several nights after Lyles had told him this story. The image of dozens of skeletons floating together at the bottom of the ocean still scared him shitless.

"Hang on a second," said Lyles, setting the bag back down. "This one was a looker, if I remember correctly." He unzipped the bag and a sheaf of blonde hair fell out from a beautiful pale face. The woman was naked inside the bag, and Kenny reached out and squeezed one of the dead woman's breasts.

"Gross!" said Fred. "That's sick, dude."

Lyles smiled. "You should try it. Give you something to think about tonight when you're coaxin the groundhog out of his hole."

"I don't even know what that means," said Fred, zipping the bag back up. "Let's hurry up and get this done so we can get back to camp."

"You're no fun at all," answered Lyles, picking up the other end of the bag. They carefully carried the body and laid it in the bottom of the boat. Then they came back, and Fred grabbed a heavy boat anchor from the rear of the vehicle while Lyles picked up a length of chain and a curved meat hook.

"It's true," whispered Moses.

Of course it's true, answered Nate. *What do you think happened to all the people from the camp who disappeared? They sure didn't release them, and I ain't seen any graveyards around here.*

He wanted to run away, but knelt there frozen and watching as the men unlocked a padlock attached to chain that secured the boat to the dock. Then they started the engine and pulled the boat carefully out into the water.

Now you can get out of here, said Billy.

Moses ignored him. That woman with the blonde hair was someone he had seen before. He thought for a minute and then it came to him. She had been at the pool of water when he'd been running from the camp.

So what? asked Nate. *That dead white girl ain't nothing to you. Besides, she's dead. You couldn't help her even if you weren't an imbecile.*

"Shut up," whispered Moses.

It's time to go, said Delores. *They come back and catch you, it will be bad.*

Moses stood, looked out over the water, and hissed, "Shut up, now."

I don't know what you're thinking, said Nate. *All I know is that it's not good. You need to leave the thinking to us and do what we say. Now get the hell out of here.*

"Leave me alone," Moses said and was surprised that none of them responded. "We have to do something. We have to find a way to stop them."

How? asked Nate. *You can't do anything.*

Not without help, said Delores. *There's no help for you here. Not on this island.*

Moses slipped silently back into the woods and made his way back to his makeshift camp.

Tears of frustration and grief fell unnoticed from his face.

Chapter 33

Dr. Xavier Simone frowned and shook his head at the big man. "You're going to get yourself killed."

"No, I won't," answered Charles, his eyes closed against the alcohol the doctor was rubbing into the gash on his brow.

"If you don't stop, you'll put them in a position where they will kill you."

"I know what I'm doing," answered Charles with a smile. "I've gotten smarter about it."

"Really?" asked Xavier, pulling out a suture kit to bind the gash. "That doesn't look too smart to me."

"But it's just stitches," answered Charles. "I've learned to not mess with the guards when they have anything in their hands like a baton. Fists I can take. The Tasers hurt like a bitch but also do no real lasting damage."

"This gash is pretty nasty. I've seen men maimed for life from just fists. This could have been your eye that's cut open."

Charles nodded in agreement. "I didn't notice one of them had a ring on."

"Stay still," said Xavier, injecting a painkiller into several key locations around the wound. "You would do better to cooperate and do as they say. That way, you can get out of here and go home."

"You still believe that bullshit?" asked Charles. "You see any *indoctrination* classes going on around here?"

Xavier ignored the question and inserted the curved needle under the brow.

"Have you seen Jack?" asked Charles.

The doctor nodded. "Three days ago. I passed on your message, but there's going to be a problem soon. His wounds are healing. Won't have much need to come here regularly. He may also need to get his ass beat regularly, I guess."

"We need a better way to communicate."

"Haven't I been saying that to you?" said Xavier with a heavy sigh.

Charles ignored this. "What about Heather or Amanda?"

The doctor froze in his stitching before resuming. "Haven't seen them."

The big man pushed the doctor's hands away and stared at him. "You're lying."

"No," answered Xavier. "The one girl, Heather…I haven't seen her in a few days. Sometimes they go away for a while before they come back."

"But they don't always come back, do they?"

Xavier didn't answer for several moments. "No, not always."

"Where do they take them?"

The doctor looked away. "I don't know for sure; besides, it is none of my business. I have to look out for my family."

"Do you really think they are going to let you leave this place and go back to your family? After all you've seen?" asked Charles.

"Yes," answered the Xavier fiercely.

"Have you spoken to your family?"

"I write them letters every week that they deliver for me."

Charles smiled sadly at him. "So they say. Have you gotten any letters or calls in return?"

"No, but that is for their safety."

"You're getting played, my little Haitian friend. They aren't delivering your letters, and your family doesn't know what has happened to you."

"That's not true," answered Xavier, trying to begin sewing up the gash again.

Charles pushed him away. "It is true. Use your head. This is a bad place; these are bad people. Tell me, where did they take Heather?"

Xavier didn't answer for several moments. "I don't know for sure, but..."

"But?"

"They say there is a laboratory nearby," Xavier said slowly, as if measuring the reaction of each word. "I've heard men talk, like they are experimenting or testing drugs on people."

Charles stared at Xavier. He wanted to be surprised or angry, but part of his brain had already figured this out. Some of the threatening remarks the guards had directed at him made more sense now: *Don't they need a black aggressive man down there yet?* or *Wait until they strap you down and have their way with you.*

"Sometimes they come back," continued Xavier. "Sometimes they don't. I have no idea what happens to those who don't come back."

"We have to get out of here," said Charles. "You, too. They'll never let you leave this place alive. Help us."

Xavier knew he was in dangerous territory. He didn't want to believe what the big man was telling him, but the logic of it made sense. Xavier pushed Charles back down and started working on the gash again. His face was clouded with indecision and doubt.

Charles let him think and work in silence. When the doctor was done and bandaged the wound, Charles reached out and grabbed his arm. "What about Amanda?"

The doctor's face drooped. "She killed herself two days ago."

Charles' hand tightened on the man's arm. "Killed herself? That can't be right... You sure you know who I'm talking about?"

Xavier nodded sadly, pulled Charles hand away. "She was here. I ran an IV. She was terribly dehydrated and had stopped eating. I just stepped out for a minute and she cut her own throat."

The big man's eyes widened, and he looked around, realizing he was on the bed where she had died. "Here?"

The doctor nodded. "I'm sorry about your friend. The guards said her brother died in an accident earlier. I guess she took it badly."

"His name was Brian and it was no accident," said Charles. "They murdered him. Plain and simple, just like they are going to murder me and then you."

Xavier didn't protest this time, simply cleaned up his instruments. "You should go. The guards outside will start to get suspicious."

"You have to help us."

"I have been helping you," answered Xavier.

"You have to help us to get out of here. All of us."

"How?" asked Xavier.

Charles shook his head. "I don't know yet, but I'll figure something out. The first thing we need to do is find another way to communicate. You're right about that, and I am tired of getting my ass beat."

"What did you have in mind?" asked Xavier.

"We'll get to that in a minute," said Charles. "First things first. Are you with us?"

The Haitian looked at Charles steadily for a long time, his eyes dark and expressionless. He thought of his family back in Haiti, possibly worried. Maybe even believing him dead.

A random memory flashed in his head. He had just started his medical training at Haiti's University Hospital in Port au-Prince. There had been a rare guest lecturer. An elderly man talked about how he had worked at a "re-education center" under President Jean-Claude Duvalier. "Baby Doc," President Duvalier had been called since assuming power from his father Francois "Papa Doc" Duvalier.

The man spoke about being the doctor at such a camp where, supposedly unbeknownst to him, torture and experimentation were going on all around him. Xavier had sat in the audience and thought how ridiculous the man's assertions were; he had to have known. Maybe this was simply a story he told himself at the time to stay alive and now that old man reaffirmed it to stay sane. Xavier had walked out of the lecture with disdain and righteous anger at the cowardly doctor for not doing something.

Xavier stared out the window at the camp. Finally he said simply, "Yes. I am with you."

Charles nodded, and then looked down again at the bed where his friend had died.

Chapter 34

Port Allen Chief of Police Andrew Bolton looked at his sergeant as if he were not sure he understood the words coming out of his mouth. "Say again?"

Sergeant Tooms shrugged. "Avery Island PD said they had been told to stand down on this. It's now state police jurisdiction."

"For a simple missing person case?" said Bolton. "There has to be something else going on."

"Well, either no one knows what it is, or no one is talking."

Bolton rubbed his chin. "Did Avery PD tell you anything helpful before this got taken from them?"

Tooms smiled. "Actually, yes. Remember how Evan Athers' car had been abandoned and then towed from the marina?"

"Yes," answered Bolton. "Told you to check and see if any boats were reported missing."

"And none were," said Tooms with a smile.

Bolton just stared. "And how the hell is that news at all?"

"Oh, but there *was* a boat missing," Tooms said. "I couldn't get a name, but evidently one of the marina fishing boats was rented for the weekend and never returned. When Avery questioned all the boat owners, none of them admitted to missing a boat, but they did tip them off to one guy. Used to have a twenty footer registered in Alabama, but now no longer does."

"What happened to it?" asked Bolton.

"Avery PD questioned him, and he got real squirrely," said Tooms. "Claims to have sold the boat, but couldn't remember the name of the individual or have any records of the sale."

"Good," said Bolton. "That's who the state police should start with. Should be able to follow that lead back to wherever Mr. Athers is. Speaking of which, we need to reach out to them. Regardless of what they tell Avery, we still have our own missing person's case."

"Chief," came Gina's voice from the next room. "Call on line two."

"Take a message," Bolton yelled back.

"I think you're going to want to take this," she said.

Bolton sighed and picked up the phone. "This is Chief Bolton."

"Yes," responded a polished and overly cheerful voice, "Chief of Police Bolton, how very nice to talk to you. My name is Adrian Fisk."

"*The* state attorney general?" asked Bolton, standing up straighter.

"Why, yes," Fisk answered. "So very nice of you to recognize my name. I'm afraid we have never had the pleasure of meeting in person."

"Uh, no, sir," answered Bolton, not sure how else to answer.

"We'll have to remedy that sometime in the future," said Fisk, "but I can tell you that the governor is very pleased with Port Allen's low crime rate and school patrol program you have instituted. Very progressive and in line with his agenda. Loyalty goes a long way with the governor."

"Uh, yes, sir," answered Bolton, feeling like he couldn't get his balance. "Thank you, sir."

"A man like you could go far with the right friends," said Fisk. "Keep up the good work and it will pay off, I can promise you that."

"I appreciate that, sir. What can I do for you?"

"Oh, my," Fisk chuckled. "I almost forgot why I called. Going on and on, thank you for reminding me. I understand you are working a missing person's case?"

"That's true," said Bolton. "A Mr. Evan Athers, CPA here in Port Allen."

"Very good," answered Fisk cheerfully. "I'm going to need you to turn over everything you've got on the case to the state police and cease all investigative activity."

"Sir? I'm not sure I understand."

"Really?" said Fisk with a smile that could be heard through the phone. "I'm declaring state jurisdiction on this case. I appreciate the efforts you and your department have made, and I'll put in a good word for you with the governor, but there's nothing more for you to worry about from this point forward."

"But for a missing person?" repeated Bolton. "Has this turned into a murder case or something?"

Fisk's voice lost its smile. "Now, Chief Bolton, you don't know that, and we don't want anyone to go spreading rumors. As a matter of fact, I'm going to have to insist you don't speak to anyone further on this case except for members of the state police and my office. Especially do not answer any requests from the media."

"What exactly did Mr. Athers get mixed up in?" asked Bolton.

"Again, no need for you to concern yourself. State police now has jurisdiction; they'll be in touch soon. The governor sincerely appreciates your cooperation. Can we count on your support?"

Bolton wasn't sure what to say. He had effectively been given an order and then asked if he would support it. "Certainly, sir," he finally answered.

"Splendid," said Fisk the smile back. "I'll pass that along to the governor's office. Again, keep up the good work. We'll be watching you closely. Don't let us down."

"Uh, we won't, sir."

"Excellent, you have a great day now," Fisk said and hung up the phone.

Bolton pulled the phone from his ear and stared at it for several seconds before placing it slowly in the cradle.

"That was an awful lot of *sirs*," said Tooms.

"Yes," answered Bolton. "We've been ordered to relinquish jurisdiction of the Athers' case to the state police."

"Why?"

"I'm not rightly sure," said Bolton thoughtfully. "But any time you get an order from the state attorney general, you do what you're told."

"That was Adrian Fisk on the line?" asked Tooms, looking impressed.

Bolton nodded.

Tooms whistled appreciatively. "Wow. Well what do we do now?"

The chief thought for a moment and then sighed. "We do what we're told. The state police will be in touch soon. Turn everything over to them and then forget about it."

"Seems odd," said Tooms.

"That it does," admitted Bolton. "First Avery Island PD gets jurisdiction taken and then we do...but that doesn't change anything. Let's turn it over."

Tooms nodded slowly and then walked out of the room.

Something isn't right about this, thought Chief Bolton, flipping through the case file one last time.

"Where did you say that missing boat was registered?" yelled Bolton.

"Alabama," answered Tooms from the adjacent room. "Why?"

"No reason," answered Bolton. "Do me a favor and make me a copy of everything...unofficially."

Tooms paused before answering. "No problem, boss."

Bolton was impressed the man didn't ask any further questions. He was glad. Bolton wasn't sure exactly what he had in mind, only that something wasn't right. He was running on intuition.

Alabama, he thought. *A boat registered in Alabama missing in Louisiana technically makes this a federal issue. A weak one...but still...*

Bolton began to smile.

Chapter 35

Rena fled into the forest wanting to be away from her father, yet also in a way hoping he chased after her. Simultaneously, she craved his love and rejected what he had done...what he had allowed her to do. She slowed to a walk when she realized he wasn't following her. That she was alone.

The forest had always been a refuge to her. Filled with life and beauty, the island was home as surely and true as the tides. She walked slowly and, after a moment, closed her eyes. Rena didn't need her sight to see where she was going; she could sense the trees and plants and animals around her. Moving slowly, she let the tension and heartache flow out of her.

Opening her eyes, she hadn't fully realized she had stopped. The birds sang their evening songs from the trees around her. She knew she should head back home soon. As angry as she was at her father, she didn't want him to worry about her.

Rena closed her eyes once more and tried to soak in as much peace as she could before going back. Very faintly, she heard an odd sound in the distance. Opening her eyes, she looked around, but could not see the source of the noise. Rena forced herself to relax and closed her eyes again. There it was. A very soft high-pitched hitching noise, so like an engine that wasn't running properly. How odd, yet familiar.

Her brain worked to place the sound into context and all manner of potential origins popped into her mind before one dominated the rest. Once it was identified, it was difficult to imagine how she could have failed to identify the source or think it could be something else.

It was crying. Softly. In the distance, but not far.

Intrigued, Rena carefully picked her way through the underbrush towards the sound. On occasion, she had to stop and listen again to make sure she was going in the right direction.

She could now see a faint light in the distance that was certainly a small fire. There was something else as well. A voice.

"We should have done something." A pause. "I don't know, something." Another pause. "Stop calling me that!" The voice sounded near tears again.

Rena moved closer and found a slight trail. She followed the trail in towards the fire and the voice. Carefully and slowly, Rena crept forward.

A small snap at her feet caused her to look down. She saw that she had snagged on taunt fishing line. Something made her look up, and she saw a heavy log attached to a vine swinging down from the tree branches headed her way.

The path was narrow, and the swinging log swung along its axis. The right side was blocked by thick vegetation, but the left was open. Just as the swinging log was almost upon her, Rena threw herself onto the flat ground to her left...and continued to fall.

She dropped about six feet before coming to an abrupt stop on freshly dug earth, knocking the wind out of her. Rena turned on her back and looked upwards out of what appeared to be the bottom of a freshly dug grave.

Might be mine, she thought. *Caught neatly in a tiger pit.*

The silhouette of a dark man appeared in the sky above her. He was naked from the waist up and carried a three-foot branch with a wickedly curved knife attached to one end.

"You," the voice said in a surprised whisper.

Rena struggled to get her breath and bearings. The outline above her seemed vaguely familiar.

The man smiled. "What should I do with her?" He tilted his head to one side before shaking it furiously. "No! That's bad. Moses gets in bad trouble for hurting other people."

"Moses," Rena managed to gasp out. "Let me out of here."

He focused back on her. "You helped the bad men. Moses trusted you, and you gave him over to the bad men."

"I know," said Rena. "That was wrong. I'm sorry."

"They hurt me. Try to kill me. They are very bad. They put the bodies in the water for the crabs to eat on."

Rena wasn't sure what to make of this last statement. "Listen. You need to let me out of here."

He shook his head. "You'll tell the bad men about me. They'll kill me for sure this time. Can't let them catch Moses."

"I won't tell anyone," insisted Rena. "It was a mistake before, and I see that now. I'm very sorry."

Moses seemed uncertain and tilted his head as if listening to other voices.

"You can't keep me down here forever," said Rena.

"Bury her?" asked Moses aghast. "Bury her alive?"

A chill went through her. "Who are you talking to?"

"My friends," Moses answered without looking her way. "We're talking about what we should do. Stop interrupting, it's not polite."

Oh shit, she thought. This was one of the reasons they had turned Moses over to the Chiron folks. He was certainly crazy and needed help, yet she was also convinced that those people had no interest in helping anyone.

"You need to get off the island," she told him. "There are only so many places you can hide. Eventually, they'll find you."

He looked at her and then tilted his head again. "How? They want to know."

"A boat," she answered. "We'll need to find you a boat somewhere. I would give you Poppa's, but he keeps it locked up."

"Same with the bad men at the dock nearby," he answered.

She looked at him quizzically. "What dock?"

"The one close to where they sink the bodies," he explained. "They lock the boat up there."

"Moses, if you take me to this boat, we might be able to get it free and then you can go to the shore. Get off the island."

He thought for a very long time. "You promise not to tell the bad men about me?"

"I promise," she said.

He walked away and didn't return for a very long time. Rena's fear mounted. When he did come back, it was with a long vine. Moses handed it down to her, and when she had a firm grip, he hauled her up with a surprising display of strength.

Rena looked at the lean and wild figure before her. He still held the makeshift spear in his hand and clearly wasn't entirely sane.

"Why don't you get whatever you need together and let's go to the boat?"

He looked around and then started throwing a few things into a green duffle bag. "I'm ready. Follow me."

The last rays of the sun were on the water when they made it to the dock.

"I recognize this place now," said Rena. "I was here years before, but there wasn't a boat then."

"They use it to sink the bodies in the water," he said again, pointing out towards the dark smooth surface.

Rena peered at him closely. "Moses, did you actually see them put dead bodies in the water?"

Moses nodded. "The blonde lady from the stream. She's out there now getting eaten by fish and crabs." He shuddered.

She thought about her life on the island. How they were isolated and protected from the world. Her and her father living a peaceful, happy life. Yet there was something very wrong here, something possibly evil that no one dared talk about. She hesitated only a moment before coming to a decision.

"Moses, once you get to shore, you need to go find the police. Tell them everything you've seen. Everything that's happened."

Moses shook his head. "Police are mean to Moses. Make him move from the good spots."

"This is important," stressed Rena. "The police can help. Not all police are mean."

"Like Deborah?" he asked hopefully.

"Sure," said Rena, not certain who Deborah was. "Find the police and tell them what happened."

Moses looked at her skeptically, and Rena realized it was likely the best she could hope for.

They used an old pipe to pry the chain off the dock. Popping the chain loose from the rotting wood of the dock was much easier than trying to bust the lock off. Rena helped Moses climb into the boat and handed him his gear.

"Do you know where you're going?" she asked.

Moses pointed confidently south out into the open gulf.

"No," she said, shaking her head. "The other way."

He pointed north with less certainty.

"Yes," she nodded.

"Are you sure?" he asked.

"Very certain. Now you want to use the last bits of sunlight. If it gets too dark to see, either head towards the lights of shore or just turn off the engine and drift. You won't go too far before morning and then you can head north again."

"The engine," he said uncertainly, looking at it for the first time.

"You ever driven a boat before?" she asked.

Moses smiled and shook his head.

Rena sighed and climbed down into the boat. She gave him a quick class on how the outboard engine worked along with the yoke and throttle. "The trick is to take everything slow," she said.

"Got it," he answered. "Take everything slow."

Rena climbed back onto the dock and tossed the chain into the boat before pushing it out into the open water. She then had a thought.

"Here," Rena said, pulling a folded piece of paper out of her back pocket. She threw it across the short stretch of water between them and into the boat. "Take this and give it to the police. Tell them this is someone the bad men have."

"I don't like the police," he said, as if Rena had forgotten this all-important fact.

"You can do this," she stressed. "Please, I'm counting on you."

Moses nodded, bent down to pick up the paper, and put it in the front pocket of his pants.

"Go ahead and start the engine. Remember what I taught you."

Moses did it perfectly on the first try and then carefully got the boat headed out into the water. Just as he was nearly out of sight, he lifted a hand in farewell.

Rena waved back as the last rays of the sun fled from the sky.

Chapter 36

Heather woke up slowly as if from a bad hangover. She looked around at the clean and stark white surfaces. A regular beeping sound seemed to coincide with her slow and relaxed heart rate. Heather realized that she felt terrible.

She started to touch her face, but the movement was stopped by a restraint. Opening her eyes fully, she saw she was on a hospital bed with an IV in both arms. Her wrists and ankles were restrained to the metal railing of the bed.

"Hello?" she called out weakly and then with more force. "Is anyone one there?"

There was a slight rustling from an adjacent room before a short, squat, middle-aged woman with silvery hair appeared with a smile.

"There you are, dear," the woman said. "How do you feel?"

"Tired," Heather answered. "Who are you? Where am I?"

"I'm Helga," said the woman. "I've been looking after you. You've been terribly sick, but we think you're all better now."

"Sick? I don't understand."

"Let me take some vitals first," said the nurse. She stopped Heather's questions by putting a thermometer under her tongue and taking her blood pressure and heart rate. After several long moments, she nodded, satisfied, wrote several notes on a clipboard. She started to walk away and then returned to retrieve the thermometer. "Let me go get Dr. Massengill; he wanted to speak with you as soon as you awoke."

"Wait," cried Heather, "why am I in restraints?"

"The doctor will answer all your questions," she said with a reassuring smile and then departed.

Heather looked around her. There were cabinets lining the walls that contained microscopes, centrifuges, and test tube racks. It looked more like a laboratory than a hospital room.

"Ah, good evening, Ms. Daniels," said the tall doctor striding in the room efficiently and briskly. He carried the clipboard Helga had been writing on. "How do you feel?"

"Okay I guess," Heather answered. "Can you tell me what's going on?"

"Certainly," answered Massengill, "but first, we need to get some information from you. You see, you have been terribly sick, but now we think you are much better."

"Sick?"

"Yes. Can you tell me your full name please?"

"Heather Ann Daniels."

"And your age?"

"Thirty-one."

"Very good," said Massengill. "Who is the President of the United States?"

"Janice Wilkens," said Heather. "Unless I've been out longer than I thought."

Massengill smiled, but didn't look at her. "And the Governor of the State of Louisiana?"

"Eric St Keel," answered Heather. "Why am I restrained?"

The doctor turned to Helga. "Is her blood work back?"

"Yes, doctor," she answered, handing him another piece of paper.

Massengill smiled and shook his head. "Remarkable. Simply remarkable."

"The nanos still appear to be doing their work," Helga said. "Even after attacking the cancer cells, they are now patrolling the bloodstream looking for more bad cells."

"Cancer?" said Heather, feeling cold. "I don't have cancer. I was just on a boat trip with my..." Her voice trailed off as she remembered what had happened.

"Unfortunately," said Massengill, "you had a very aggressive form of ovarian cancer. I say *had* because we have managed to eliminate the cancer. You are a very lucky young lady."

"Where are my friends?" Heather asked, pulling on her restraints. She raised her voice. "Why am I restrained?"

"It is for your own good, dear," said Helga soothingly.

Massengill looked down to the floor, thinking. "NCF-102 eliminated the cancer cells, but didn't pass into the kidneys and out the body when done like we thought."

"Some must have," said Helga. "The number of nanos is much lower. Maybe only those that discharged the peptide left the body. The nanos that have not yet encountered a cancer cell are still looking for them."

"It could definitely serve as a preventative medicine," said the doctor with wonder in his voice. "Like a vaccine."

"Let me go," said Heather, straining at the restraints. She could hear the machine that monitored her heart rate beeping faster and faster.

"We'll need to fully test the residual effects," the doctor said.

Helga smiled. "I've already prepared another batch of cancer cells."

"Ovarian?"

The nurse paused. "I thought it wise to maintain the same target until we knew the nanos capabilities."

Massengill nodded approvingly. "Very good, it's like you're reading my mind."

Heather saw the nurse pick up the long needle and turn towards her. "Help!" she screamed and thrashed. "Help me!"

"Better put her out," said the doctor with a tired sigh.

Helga laid the syringe of cancer cells aside and picked up a sedative, which she injected into Heather's IV line.

Heather continued to struggle and fight for several seconds, but soon felt heavy and tired. The room became fuzzy and light.

"Don't worry, dear," she Helga, laying a comforting hand on her forehead. "Everything will be just fine."

"She has no idea how big a role she will play in changing the world," said the doctor.

Heather drifted off into a drugged sleep.

Chapter 37

Justin respected his partner, generally even liked her, but he hated it when she got into one of these moods.

"Just because the boss chewed your butt doesn't mean you have to take it out on me," he said from his cluttered desk.

"Not everything is about you," Deborah responded without looking at him. She had been staring down at a series of notes on her otherwise clear desk without speaking for half an hour.

He shook his head. "You had to know going to that place and asking about your brother was going to get you into trouble."

"Would you please be quiet for just a second?" she asked. "I'm not brooding over the chief and the weak-assed counseling he gave me. I'm actually trying to think."

"If you would just listen to me a little more often," he chided, "you wouldn't be in so much trouble all the time."

"First," she said, finally turning to him, "I'm not *in* trouble all the time. And second"—she picked up a notepad on her desk and showed it to him—"doesn't it seem a little odd to you that only young and healthy men and women are missing?"

"You're not back on that again, are you?"

"Twenty-six reported missing the last three years from New Orleans area," she said, "and since these are homeless people, most of those who are missing likely were never reported. The number could be three or four times higher than that."

"And you think what exactly?"

Deborah dropped the notepad in frustration and turned away. "I don't know. This whole Take Back the Streets thing just seems off to me."

Justin snapped his fingers. "If you're so concerned, take that list of missing persons and check it against the program's participants."

She looked at him as if he were a simpleton. "Already tried that. Good thing I'm the brains behind this outfit."

"Well, what did you find out?"

"Nothing," she answered. "Cited privacy laws, said they couldn't provide that information to me without a warrant."

"And you can't get a warrant because it's not your case," he said. "Hell, it's not even in our jurisdiction since, as far as we know, none of these missing persons has crossed state lines."

"The state police are supposedly looking into it."

"There you go then," her partner answered triumphantly. "They've got it covered and probably don't need your help. Didn't you tell me Moses has done this many times before and always shows back up again?"

"Yes."

He tilted his head at her with a smile. "I'm sure he's fine. Besides, we have our own case load."

"Our cases are cleared," she answered. "Just need to write up and submit all the reports."

"Exactly," he answered. "Maybe you could help with that a little."

She smiled at him. "I haven't heard you strike a single key on your keyboard in over an hour so don't lecture me about report writing."

He turned away. "Just catching up on email. Besides, I got a courtesy copy of an open case from a friend up at the Port Allen PD."

"What type of case?" she asked offhandedly, her mind already on other things.

"A missing person's case, interestingly enough," he answered.

Deborah froze and then stood to walk to and look at her partner's screen.

"Sure," he said, scooting out of the way. "Help yourself. Don't even bother asking."

She read quickly, scrolling through the email and then the attachments.

"State police have it," Justin explained. "Nothing for us on this."

"This is different," she said almost in a whisper. "An accountant. A lawyer. These aren't homeless people."

"Exactly," he said. "No connection to your personal, off-the-reservation, conspiracy theory-fueled obsession."

"So why did your friend send it to you anyway?" she asked.

He scrolled back up to the top of the email and pointed. "The missing boat is registered out of state, so technically they are required to inform us. But that's all it is, a technicality. The state police have it for action."

She was silent as she looked through the documents and one name kept catching in her mind.

"This name seems familiar," she said, pointing.

"Yeah, me too," he answered. "I did a little checking."

"You?" she asked. "Did a little checking? You mean like actual investigative work?"

"Very funny," he answered. "This case is probably going to be big in the news soon. Surprised they haven't picked up on it already."

"Six missing persons do that," she said while reading again.

"Especially if one of the missing is the son of a former Louisiana Supreme Court Justice and personal friend of the governor."

"Who..." she stopped, and things clicked into place. "Winters."

"Bingo." Justin smiled. "Jackson Winters. Only son of Jeremiah Winters. Missing with five of his college friends after heading out to sea on a vacation. Probably all drowned, I'd guess. That missing boat is sitting on the bottom of the ocean if you ask me."

"You're certainly optimistic," she said.

He shrugged. "Just stating the facts. Most missing persons who aren't found within three to five days are never found." His face fell when he realized what he had said. "Of course, that doesn't mean that's the case with Moses."

Deborah ignored her partner and turned back to her notes. She knew he was right and, in that moment, felt like crying.

Instead, she dug in even deeper. What she found frightened her worse than she could have imagined.

Chapter 38

It was dark by the time Rena returned to their small cabin in the woods. The faint glow of an oil lantern burned in the window.

An oasis. Her home. The only one she had ever known.

Have I put all that in jeopardy? she asked herself. *And for what? A fit of conscience? Some strange man who may have already forgotten me?*

That's not why you did it, a voice answered in her head. *You did it because you know what's going on here is wrong. You're either complicit or you try to help.*

"Bullshit," she said to herself. Rena climbed the stairs and paused before opening the door. She heard voices and felt coldness in her stomach.

Do they already know what I've done? Are they here to get Poppa and me?

She listened carefully but couldn't make out the words. Two voices speaking softly, one her father's.

Rena realized there wasn't a vehicle in front of their cabin. The men from the camp always brought the cage truck whenever they took someone away.

Slightly less concerned, she opened the door and walked inside. Her father stopped talking. He rose and walked towards her. A short but powerfully built old black man sat in a chair regarding her calmly. He looked vaguely familiar.

"Where have you been?" Deloy demanded.

"Just walking in the woods," she said.

He grabbed her and gave her a surprisingly fierce hug. "You can't go running off like that. Not now...not the way things are."

She slowly returned the hug, letting her head rest against his giant muscular chest. His scent of salt and earth was soothing. After a moment, the presence of the stranger in the room caused her to feel self-conscious and pull away.

"Who is this?" she asked, tilting her head in the old man's direction.

The old man pushed himself to his feet and walked towards them smiling. "Has it really been that long, Rena? You certainly have blossomed into a beautiful young woman."

"Johnny?" she asked, a smile coming unbidden to her lips. "Is that you?"

"The same." He smiled in return, opening his arms to her.

She rushed into them. "I thought I'd never see you again. When you left, you said you couldn't come back."

"That was true," he answered, "but not entirely accurate. It would have been better for me to say I *shouldn't* come back."

"Because of them," she said. "The men in the camp."

"In a sense," he said. "Let us just say we reached a point where it was impossible for us to peacefully co-exist. I thought it best if I left...on my own terms."

"After they burned your cabin down?" asked Deloy. "You could have been killed if you were in it."

"Who knows? Maybe that was their intention," Johnny answered. "Regardless, the point was made. May have only been a message to keep my nose out of where it wasn't wanted."

"How can they do that?" asked Rena. "You have a right to live here just like we do. Who are these mainlanders to run us off and try to scare us?"

Deloy had been on the verge of defending them, but the term "mainlander" had struck a nerve with him. Their family had lived on this island for over a century and half and relished their independence as much as they distrusted outsiders.

Johnny saw the man struggling internally. "I'm not asking either of you to do anything that could get you into trouble. If you can live in peace with these people, then you should. As for me, there can be no peace. Especially if they might have harmed someone dear to me."

Rena remembered the conversation several days before. "You know Jack. He asked about you. Said you worked for his father."

"I did," answered Johnny. "His father was the best sort of man."

"One who paid regularly?" Deloy asked with a smile.

Johnny kept his eyes on Rena. "A man of quiet dignity. Someone who never spoke without a purpose. A man who treated everyone he came into contact with as if they mattered."

"And Jack Winters was his son?" asked Rena. She found it hurt to say his name.

Johnny nodded. "We all know that unless something is done, he will never leave this island alive."

Rena was quiet for a long time. Finally, she told them about her interaction with Moses. She started out haltingly, looking hesitantly at her father, but gathering strength as she went along. When she was finished, Johnny smiled at her, his face beaming in pride. Her father, on the other hand, had a downcast face and slumped shoulders.

"This could bring trouble to us," Deloy said softly.

"Trouble has already come to us," Rena said more angrily than she intended. "The things they are doing aren't right."

"We don't *know* what they are doing other than healing people. Do we really need to know more than that?" asked Deloy.

"Yes, we do. This is our island, our home," she said. "We sit still and mind our business and keep quiet. Meanwhile these mainlanders are doing horrible things to innocent people. And for what?"

"We don't know any of that," said Deloy.

"We know enough," said Johnny. "We know that it isn't right, otherwise why all the secrecy? Isn't that enough?"

"I thought you weren't asking us to get involved," said Deloy. "Besides, what are we supposed to do? Take on a bunch of armed men? Now that Rena sent Moses to tell the police what's happening, we should stay out of it. Maybe they'll come, and then things will go back to the way they were before."

"Things never go back to the way they were before," answered Johnny.

Rena frowned. "They may not believe him. Moses doesn't seem totally right in the head. He also wasn't real keen on going to the police. Seemed to see them as all bad."

Deloy threw his hands up angrily. "Doesn't matter. This is not our responsibility. We don't need to bring any more trouble to our doors." He turned to Johnny pointing an angry finger at him. "And you don't get to decide to put my family into danger. It's easy for you to talk about charging in, old man. You're only risking your skin. I have far greater responsibilities."

Johnny was quiet, looking from Deloy to Rena. Finally, he nodded. "You're right. I have no business influencing you to do anything that might endanger you. I respect that and appreciate you not throwing me out the door. I've no business involving you in any of this."

"What do you plan to do?" asked Rena.

"Rena," her father said warningly.

She turned to him. "I want to know, and if I can help, I want to. I can't go on any longer pretending we know nothing about what is going on. It's killing me." She grabbed his arm and held on. "What if it were me in there?"

Deloy turned away from his daughter, but she held on tightly, insistently. He finally turned back to meet her gaze. He could still see her as a little girl and remembered her devastated face when he had told Rena her mother wasn't coming back. The years between then and now flashed in his mind. *Has it all come to this?* he wondered with a sinking feeling in his stomach. After a moment, he nodded.

"What do you have in mind?" he asked Johnny.

"I actually have an idea."

"That makes me feel better," said Deloy. "Could you be a little more specific?"

"There's a storm coming," he answered with a smile. "My old bones can feel these things."

"Great," sighed Deloy.

Chapter 39

Helga carried the plastic bag of Heather Daniels' personal belongings to the incinerator. This was one of her more menial tasks. Before the patients were brought in for treatment, they always retrieved their personal belongings from the camp custodian. Sometimes these gave them insight into the health of the patient.

Heather Daniels' personal belongings had given Helga insight, but not into the woman's health.

She was no longer responding to the treatment. Perhaps they had given her too much cancer and it was spreading throughout her body faster than the nanos could track down the offensive cells and eliminate them. Even this setback was not a failure. They needed to know the limits of the miracle drug so that it could be improved. Doctor Massengill had given her another large dosage of the nanos. Time would tell if they worked to kill the cancer.

Pulling open the metal opening that led down a small chute, Helga looked around to make sure no one was watching her. Instead of dropping the bag in, she opened it and took out the nice leather wallet and pulled out the money. Looking around again she pushed the considerable wad of cash into her front pocket. Didn't make sense just to burn up the money. Besides it didn't harm anyone.

Quite a bit more cash than you are used to getting, she thought.

Indeed it was. Most of the derelicts and homeless vagrants they dealt with barely had ten dollars. Helga did this out of an inability to waste anything rather than greed or a need for money. She had been raised during tough times of want and understood the value of things.

This woman isn't a vagrant or homeless, she thought. *This is a nice wallet, same for the purse.*

Helga tried to push the thought aside, but pulled out the woman's driver's license nevertheless. Tossing the plastic identification down the chute, she then pulled out several credit cards and tossed them one by one down into the fire.

You already knew she wasn't like the others. Manicured nails, clean and well-cut hair, even the polite talk. This woman wasn't trash like the semi-human subjects we normally work on.

Helga pulled out the New Orleans Port Authority identification badge and looked at it closely. The woman looking back on the photo was smiling professionally and confidently.

The nurse's hands shook slightly, and she pushed the rest of the items roughly through the chute and slammed the small door roughly. Helga turned away and walked back down the hallway. It was dinnertime.

They told me we would only be working on criminals or homeless people. Those outside of society who contributed nothing. Testing the revolutionary treatment on them gave the losers an opportunity to serve a purpose. It was really the best thing for them. The only possible meaning their life could ever serve. But this woman was different, and Helga couldn't get the beautiful face out of her head.

She had tested the drug on dozens of patients, many of whom did not survive. None of them had given her the slightest pause...until now.

This isn't right. You shouldn't use respectable and upstanding citizens as guinea pigs. All of that was fine for the trash. They were just barely above animals, after all. But not people like Heather Daniels.

What should I do?

"Nothing," Helga said out loud, startling herself slightly. *Keep your mouth shut and do your job. If they can make someone like this woman disappear, then they can make an old hag like you disappear.*

Helga walked into the small cafeteria filled with lab techs and researchers and looked at today's special. It was salmon, normally one of her favorites, but she turned away.

She no longer felt hungry.

Chapter 40

Moses did just as the dark-haired girl had told him. He headed north towards the lights on the distant shore.

Don't know why you trust her, said Nate in his head. *She did turn you over to the bad men.*

But she also helped you get away this time, said Delores.

That remains to be seen, said Nate smugly. *We're not safe yet.*

The conversation went on, but Moses pushed the details to the rear of his mind until it was simply background noise. He didn't need to hear every word to know what was being said. It was enough that they were with him and he wasn't alone. Being alone was the worst thing in the world.

It was spooky out on the open water at night. The only sounds were the small drone of the motor and the lapping of the waves against the boat's edge. Moses kept remembering a movie that had scared him as a child. He couldn't remember the name, but there had been a giant shark that came out of the ocean and destroyed the boat that the three men were on. It was named *Crunch* or *Teeth* or *Chomp* maybe. That boat had been much bigger than the one Moses was on.

He again tried to twist the throttle further, but the little engine was already maxed out.

Moses calmed himself by looking at the clear sky above him as he had on countless nights before. This was one reason he could never stand to live indoors. How could you see the beautiful sky and stars if you were inside?

There were few lights on the shore, but Moses picked out the closest and aimed for it. He was ready to get off the boat and away from the schools of giant sharks he could almost feel circling underneath him.

Jaws, he thought and shivered, *that was the name of the movie.*

After nearly a half hour, Moses could make out a small dock jutting out into a small inlet. A light from a pole at the end of the dock had been his guiding beacon. More light from a tiny home on a nearby hill cast menacing shadows on the water. Several times Moses could have sworn that cresting waves were the images of shark fins.

He pulled the boat up to the dock and tossed the chain onto the wooden surface in an attempt to hold him in place. It made a loud thump. Moses grabbed his meager belongings and carefully climbed from the boat to the deck. He stood and looked around, trying to figure out what to do next.

A door slammed at the tiny house. "Hey, who's out there?" a voice cried.

Moses froze, but then realized he was under a bright light. He grabbed his belongings and sprinted down the dock towards the land and darkness.

"Stop right there!" yelled the voice. "I got a gun and, by God, I'll use it."

This declaration only made Moses run faster. This was not the first time someone had threatened to shoot him and the threats were often carried out.

He caught sight of a small elderly man holding a shotgun. Moses ran past him and they made eye contact, the shotgun barrel following him accurately, but no blast came. Moses ran up the home's driveway and out onto a dark road.

Stopping to catch his breath and get his bearings, Moses peered right and left. There was no sign of anyone else, but it was a remote country road. Fortunately, the night was clear and moonlight filtered down to illuminate the dark paved path through the towering Cyprus trees on either side.

"Which way?" he said out loud.

Right, answered Delores.

Moses turned right and began walking. After an hour, the small road intersected a slightly larger road labeled by the number eighty-three in a white circle. Delores again told him to go right and he did.

Several pickup trucks drove past him on the dark road. Moses fought the urge to jump into the nearby ditch, afraid that the bad men from the camp had come looking for him, but none of the vehicles slowed. After another couple of hours, he saw a sign that said, "Baldwin - 6."

Moses had never heard of a town called Baldwin, but something about the sign made him realize where he was going. New Orleans. Home. He had hitchhiked before and could do it again.

Have to be careful, said Billy. *Some people aren't nice.*

And watch out for the police, said Nate. *They'll hurt you if they can. Might even turn you over to the bad camp men.*

Moses didn't always like Nate, but admitted he was often right. He should definitely avoid the police.

Chapter 41

Lucas Ross walked into the governor's office and closed the door. His friend was on the phone thanking a contributor for a recent donation. St Keel made eye contact with Lucas and used his hand to mime someone talking and talking. He motioned for Lucas to go ahead and sit.

"You bet, James," the governor said, "you and Eva both. Great to talk to you." He prepared to hang up the phone but then listened again, his head dropping in exasperation.

"Indeed, you're right," St Keel said. "I'm just as concerned, and let's talk about it more sometime over whiskey and cigars." He shrugged at his chief-of-staff apologetically.

Lucas didn't mind waiting. It gave him more time to think through the unsavory task he needed to perform. He tuned out the governor's conversation.

The governor finally hung up the phone. "Good Lord that man can talk. You would think someone who was running one of the largest oil businesses in the western hemisphere would have work to do, but evidently not."

"I need to tell you something," said Lucas. "Want to make sure you're not blindsided should someone ask you about it."

The governor froze. "Uh-oh. That doesn't sound good."

Lucas sighed. "We found out about a developing situation. Four men and two women rented a boat down on the gulf and, after six days, haven't returned."

"Have we informed the coast guard?" asked St Keel. "Probably capsized or had engine trouble."

"They know and have been searching, but nothing yet."

St Keel thought for a moment and then nodded. "Okay, seems pretty straight forward. Appreciate the heads up."

"That's not all of it," continued Lucas. "One of the men was Jackson Winters."

The governor stared at him intently for several long seconds. "I'm presuming you are telling me this because it is the same Jackson Winters who is the son of Jeremiah."

"The same," said Lucas. "We're doing all we can to try to locate them, but after six days...who knows."

"I want him found," said St Keel in a commanding voice. "Do whatever it takes. He could be in serious trouble. We have got to find him!"

"You need to prepare for the worst," said Lucas. "I know he was your friend's son, but the reality is grim."

"I know that, but even the worst case...I want him found. He deserves to rest beside his father and mother."

"Yes, sir," answered his chief-of-staff. "We will, but we need to work on a media response."

"Have they picked up on it yet?"

Lucas shook his head. "But it's only a matter of time. There's already missing persons' reports on several of the group. I've taken the liberty of assigning the case to the state police."

"Good." St Keel nodded. "Keep me informed. I want to know of any developments immediately."

There was a knock of the door, and the governor's secretary stuck her head into the room. "I'm sorry to interrupt, but there is an incoming call from Senator Clemens."

"Oh, yes," said St Keel, reaching for the phone on his desk. "Have to take this, Lucas. Remember, do whatever it takes. I want that boy found."

Lucas nodded and stood as his boss picked up the phone and donned a smile and overly friendly manner. He walked out of the governor's offices and down the hallway.

Devin was waiting for him.

"Did you take care of that thing?" Lucas asked.

Devin nodded. "Even with that reporter gone, we won't be able to keep a lid on this for long."

"I know," answered Lucas. "We'll just have to make sure it spins our way."

"Like Oman?"

Lucas gave the man a look filled with warning. "This is a very critical time for the governor. He is on the cusp of a presidential run. Do I need to tell you what that could mean for all of us?"

"I understand," said Devin after a pause.

Staring at his old deputy for a moment, Lucas felt a note of unease. "That's good. Have you checked into the situation at Site Iaso?"

Devin nodded slowly. "Something's off down there, but I'm not sure if Urchart has lost control or not. If I had to guess, I would say not."

"Doesn't mean he doesn't need a talking to," answered Lucas. "Maybe you need to go down there and make sure things are under control."

"Whatever you think best."

"Good, it's settled then."

Devin shifted. "What if Jackson Winters and his friends are there? What if they've fallen into our net?"

Lucas didn't answer for a long time. "Crazy homeless bums are one thing. No one would believe them even if they did escape. This is something else. Someone might believe a lawyer, especially one who is the son of a Supreme Court Justice."

"I understand," answered Devin.

"Are you sure?" asked Lucas.

Devin nodded. "If they are there, none of them can ever leave that island."

Lucas smiled and nodded.

It was such a relief not to have to explain everything.

Chapter 42

"You sure about this?" asked Deloy, leading a bound Johnny through the woods towards the prison camp.

"Nope," answered Johnny, "but we don't have any better ideas. Besides this will prove your loyalty to them and take away any suspicion they might have."

"Someone could go for help," said Rena from behind Johnny. "Or we could wait for Moses to tell the police."

Johnny laughed. "Ain't no policeman going to believe a crazy story like that. Especially not from a loony black homeless man. They wouldn't believe it from us. Even if they did, they would only call the park service, who happen to be the evil thugs we're trying to outsmart."

"Is that what we're trying to do here?" asked Deloy. "I thought this was about saving your friend's son."

"Same thing," answered Johnny.

They walked slowly down a forest path still wet from the night's dew. Rays of sun knifed through the dense foliage to highlight clouds of mist rising into the air.

"I thought you said there was a storm coming," said Rena, shielding her eyes from the sun.

Johnny nodded. "It's coming, never fear, and it's going to be a whopper."

By the time they approached the front gate of the camp, it was nearly noon and they were all soaked with sweat.

"Hold right there," said a commanding voice from the guard shack. "This is a federal facility and you are trespassing."

Deloy held up the rope in his hand that was attached to Johnny's bound wrists. "Tell Mr. Urchart that Deloy Dequese is here with someone I think he would be interested in seeing."

The guard hesitated for a moment before speaking indistinctly into a radio and then listening carefully. He then stepped out of the shack, his hand on the pistol at his belt. He peered at the trio carefully. "He'll be out in a minute. What exactly do we have here?"

"Kidnapping, torture, experimentation, cover-up, conspiracy," said Johnny. "You know, the typical secret government facility bullshit."

"You got a big mouth," the guard told Johnny. "Especially for a tied-up old man out here in the middle of nowhere."

Johnny smiled. "You have no idea, son."

The guard took a step forward, but Urchart arrived. He glared at Johnny as he walked up to Deloy.

"Where did you find him?" he asked.

"We didn't," answered Deloy. "He came to our house last night asking for a place to stay. Said he came back to the island yesterday."

Urchart shook his head at Johnny. "Dumb idea, my friend. You were home free; we weren't even looking for you anymore. Everyone just assumed you'd died somewhere along the way."

"One of many bad assumptions I would say," answered Johnny, looking at the camp perimeter behind them.

"We don't want any trouble," Deloy told Urchart. "You folks have been decent to my family and everything's been good on the island between us. I'd like to keep it that way."

Urchart nodded and stuck his hand out to Deloy who shook it. "Thank you very much. Some people just don't understand the importance of what we're doing here."

"What will happen to him?" asked Rena.

Her father gave her a warning look, but Urchart only shrugged. "We'll give him a place where he can rest and stay out of trouble. Get the doctor to check him out, bet he's off his meds. He'll get good meals and probably a better night's rest than he's had in months."

"Exactly why I'm here," said Johnny with a smile.

Urchart waved the guard forward. "Take him in to Kevin, who will process him. I'll keep an eye on the gate until you get back."

The guard walked forward and took the lead rope, jerking Johnny roughly forward. He pulled him through the metal gate before closing and locking the gate.

There had maybe been only five seconds to peer into the camp, but Rena discovered she was holding her breath. She made herself let it out. Urchart looked at her curiously.

Her father put his arm on her back and steered her away from the camp and back towards their home.

"Thanks again," Urchart called after them.

Deloy raised his hand in response but picked up his step.

"Did you see him?" she asked almost in a whisper.

"Just keep walking," her father said.

The glimpse had been brief and from a distance. Much of the view had been blocked by Johnny and the guard. The man she had seen in the orange jumpsuit could have been anyone.

But she knew it was Jack.

Her soul ached.

As she marched through the woods towards her home that pain was slowly replaced by something else. Something she welcomed.

Fury.

Chapter 43

Cliff had been true to his word. The Kingston Shelter Director had called Deborah at work the day before. Her heart had been racing as she drove in a frantic and absent-minded trail of angry car horns across town. The whole way she kept telling herself it wasn't him. It wasn't her brother. She couldn't bear the heartbreak and disappointment. Deborah had even begun to have nightmares of being called to the city morgue to identify Moses.

But she had been wrong.

She looked over at him sleeping fitfully on her couch. At times he would moan and mumble in his sleep, but his body was clearly exhausted and his slumber was deep if not peaceful.

As always, he had greeted her as if they had seen each other that morning. Her barely contained emotions obviously confused him, so she did her best to keep it under control. Once back home, she had allowed herself to go into the bathroom and cry quietly for ten minutes. Then she had gotten it all together.

After feeding and cleaning her brother, she had given him clean clothes...his clean clothes. She always kept them around her apartment for Moses' sudden resurfaces.

He frequently was not in the best state of health after one of his vanishing acts, but she was shocked by how skeletal he appeared. Always thin and wiry, bones protruded from every angle of his protesting skin covered with countless sores and old insect bites. When she brushed his think tangle of matted hair it came out in clumps. Not only that, but there were several scars that she had never seen before. Ugly jagged lines or thick puckered keloids punctuated his shattered body like road signs in a forgotten desert.

Her brother was in bad shape.

Deborah had wanted to take him to the hospital, but this caused her brother to launch into hysterics. Fortunately, she knew enough about physical trauma and first aid to convince herself that he didn't suffer from anything life-threatening. She would try to get him to a doctor once he recovered...or at least after he and had gained some weight and a sense of security.

"Where have you been?" Deborah whispered towards him.

He mumbled and then slowly opened his eyes to gaze at her expressionlessly.

She walked over and put her hand on his head. Deborah took it as a good sign he didn't try to draw away. "How are you feeling? You need anything?"

"Rena," he said softly.

"I'm sorry, what?"

He cleared his throat and sat up on an elbow. Taking a drink of water from the glass on the table beside him, his thin hand trembled.

"Moses," she said, taking his other hand in hers, "where have you been?"

His eyes looked away and glazed. "The dog camp, but not for dogs. We lived in the kennels."

"Dogs?" she wondered if some sick freak hadn't captured and mistreated her brother. She kept the anger out of her face with difficulty.

"Rena helped me escape. Nate told me to kill her, but I didn't."

Deborah knew Nate and hated him. She knew it was ridiculous to hate an imaginary voice, but she did nevertheless. Inwardly, she groaned, worried that the voices in his tortured mind were increasing. Now evidently there was a new voice, Rena. These voices were carving out pieces of his personality and smothering the brother she loved.

"Did bad people hurt you?"

He looked at her now and nodded. "Others, too. I ran. Fast. Hid in the trees." He smiled, but then it slowly melted away. "Couldn't help them. Wanted to."

Deborah's voice had taken on a steely tone. "Tell me where you were?"

"The island. Bad place. Lots of angry voices."

She sighed to calm her frustration. Getting information from her brother had grown increasingly difficult over the years. She had learned to use her honed investigative skills. It was the only way to learn what had happened to him.

An island, she thought. *There is no way Moses could get to an island on his own with no money. Of course it might not be an actual island, but just a name or an invention of those damn voices in his head.*

"Did you go on a boat?" she asked regardless.

He smiled. "Never driven a boat before."

"Did you steal someone's boat?" she asked.

Moses dropped his eyes. "Rena told me to do it."

That new damn voice, Deborah thought. *Encouraging my brother to a life of crime. Great.* She paused and thought back to something he said earlier.

"Moses, you said that you ran and you hid. Were people chasing you? Did they try to hurt you?"

He looked away again and pulled his arms in close and his knees to his chest. Closing his eyes, he said, "Tired...so tired." He turned away from her, pulling the blanket over his head. There he lay not moving.

Deborah fought the urge to pull the blanket down, to force him to talk to her. It would be no use, she had tried before, but the need to know what had happened to him was nearly unbearable. Instead, she reached out a gentle hand and patted his shoulder.

Walking back into the kitchen she saw the pile of Moses' dirty and smelly clothes. That reminded her of the drive home and that she would have to get the inside of her now filthy car detailed.

Her first instinct was to throw the clothes away, but her brother could be nearly autistic at times with his attachment to routine and comfortable things.

After putting detergent into the small washer, she picked up the pieces of stiff and dirty clothing with the very tips of two fingers, using her other hand to cover her nose.

She froze as she looked at the clothing more closely. It was one piece and so covered in mud and filth that at first it had been impossible to see that the color was bright orange.

A prison jumpsuit? she realized. *What the hell?*

Turning the smelly cloth blob around to the back, she used the kitchen cleaning brush to scrub off an area where a label of some sort normally went. A warning to peaceful citizens should they spot dangerous escaped inmates in their midst. Something like Louisiana State Correctional Facility. She scrubbed other spots, but discovered nothing more than bright orange nylon in sharp contrast to the dark black and brown of the remainder of the garment.

She felt something out of place towards the waist, the entire garment was stiff with petrified sweat, oil, and dirt, but this was different. Fishing into a pocket with a tight face, her fingers found a small piece of wet paper and pulled it out.

After a few seconds, she dropped the kitchen brush and re-read the note. Her head turned in slow motion towards the slumbering form of Moses on the couch.

Who is Rena?

Her brother moaned in his sleep.

Chapter 44

Johnny and Jack had seen each other the day before. The guards were complacent and the end of Jack's one hour of freedom in his little dog run had coincided with Johnny's beginning time. They were at least three empty dog runs between them, but there had been no mistake.

Jack's eyes had widened and his mouth had begun to open.

The old man shook his head ever so slightly, and Jack looked away.

Fortunately, the relaxed guards hadn't caught the moment.

Now Johnny sat in his cell thinking about his dead friend's son. It had been almost a decade since he had laid eyes upon him, but there was no mistaking his identity. He was a spitting image for his father forty years before.

The first step was over. Johnny had confirmed that Jack was in the camp and still alive. Jack now knew that Johnny was also inside. They needed to find a way to communicate and fast. They didn't have much time before the storm arrived.

Actual escape was also an unknown. Johnny had lied to Deloy and Rena about that. He had told them he had someone on the inside who would help him escape, but that was untrue. He knew if he had told them the truth, that his plan was to get inside and then count on figuring a way out, they wouldn't have agreed to help him.

They would have considered it suicide, he thought. *And for good reason.*

One thing at a time. How to talk to Jack?

There was a scraping at the door, and the small metal panel pulled back. A pair of narrow eyes looked in at him, staring critically.

Johnny laid on his bunk, his hands behind his head, and stared back.

The face vanished as the panel was slid back closed. A few seconds later, a key turned in the door, and it opened with a thin squeal of metal.

The guard turned to a thin black man beside him.

"This is one of the new ones; want me to come in with you?"

"It is okay," the man said with a Haitian accent. "I will be fine."

The guard nodded. "Okay, you know the drill. Pound on the door when you are done."

The Haitian nodded and stepped inside, carrying a small medical bag. The door closed and locked behind him.

"My name is Dr. Xavier Simone," the man said. "I am here to check your health."

Johnny didn't move.

The doctor looked around nervously. "Might you introduce yourself since I have kindly done so?"

"You already know my name and why I am here," Johnny said.

Xavier nodded. "Nevertheless, it is courtesy to introduce oneself."

Swinging his feet to the floor, Johnny sat up on his thin bunk. "Why are you really here?"

Xavier shrugged. "It is just as I said. The camp commander has agreed to allow me to come check on all the...uh, guests in their...uh, quarters. Sickness has been going around, and I thought it best to keep a close eye on everyone."

"Is that so?"

The Haitian took this as agreement and moved forward to sit beside Johnny. He pulled out a number of instruments, including a thermometer, stethoscope, and blood pressure cuff along with a notebook.

Johnny shook his head. "Keep your hands to yourself."

Xavier put on the stethoscope. "Please indulge me." His eyes dropped to the notepad on the bunk beside them.

The first words caught his attention: *Uncle Johnny.*

Placing the stethoscope on Johnny's chest, Simone leaned in close. "They may be watching, play along."

Johnny did and looked down at the notepad. He slowly read the entire message.

Uncle Johnny,

What are you doing here? We were captured nearly a week ago. My friends Brian, Amanda, and Evan are dead. I've seen Charles, but not sure where Heather is or even if she is still alive.

Dr. Simone is a friend and can be trusted. We're trying to come up with a plan to escape or at least get a message outside for help. So far we have come up with nothing.

I'm sorry if we somehow dragged you into this. Sorry about a lot of things.

Write back through Simone. Don't trust anyone else. This is a terrible place. For God's sake, please be careful.

J.W.

Simone had moved on to taking his blood pressure by the time he had finished reading the note several times.

He leaned over near the doctor's ear. "How do I even know if this is real? It could be his handwriting, but maybe not. I was their handyman, not his school teacher. You might just be trying to set us both up."

"He thought you might feel that way," said Xavier as he slid a small smooth object into Johnny's hand.

The old man looked down at the ivory-handled knife. The one he had lost many years before.

"I doubt anyone at this camp would give that to you under any circumstances," whispered Xavier.

Johnny stared at the knife and had to admit the man was right. Even if they were trying to gain his trust enough to unintentionally betray Jack, they would not give him a knife. Not in this place.

"Perhaps you can help me take notes," the Haitian said in a conversational tone. "I tell you the vitals and you write them down for me. This will go much quicker that way."

Johnny nodded and picked up the notepad. He tuned the doctor out while he wrote his dead friend's son a message.

Chapter 45

Devin Alders stepped off the small boat onto Bog Island. Urchart walked forward along the dock to meet him.

"Great to see you, Brent," said Devin, shaking the man's hand warmly.

"Been a little while," answered Urchart, smiling himself. "How is it working with the governor and the general?"

"A nest of snakes," answered Devin, "but it's a job and it pays well."

"Well, you've got me beat there."

Devin held his arms out to encompass the island around them. "Yeah, but it's all about the benefits."

Urchart chuckled and clapped Devin on the back. "Come on, let me show you the operation."

They drove through the swampy island forest making small talk and catching up from their time in high school together. Neither had kept up with much of anyone but still knew stories and pieces of information that the other had not, and the time passed quickly and comfortably.

After going through the camp's security, they made their way to Urchart's office.

"I'll give you the grand tour in a bit, but perhaps we should go to my office to talk about everything first."

Devin nodded and followed the man into a small building. They walked down a small hallway to a large office in the back with an almost pleasant view of the forest.

"Want a drink?" Urchart asked, holding a bottle of Woodford's Reserve over a couple of glasses.

"Hell, yes," answered Devin. It was early in the day, but who gave a shit?

Urchart poured the glasses, set one in front of Devin. Both sat, clinked their drinks together, and sipped.

"So I understand this isn't a social call," said Urchart. "It's also not 'just procedure' or 'a normal visit' before you say it. No one, especially not from the governor's officer, ever comes out here. That's the whole point of a covert operating location."

Devin rolled the liquid on his tongue. Urchart might be isolated, but he evidently didn't skimp on his bourbon. "Why don't you start with the recent prisoners you acquired?"

"How did you know about..." Urchart stopped and shook his head. "Never mind. A group of six civilians. We ran across them while chas-...well, while on patrol. It wasn't a big deal, we sometimes get visitors, but one of the new hires went all over the top and ended up shooting and killing one of them."

"Shooting him? For what?"

"Making a satellite phone call," said Urchart. "911. Luckily the call was ended before he said much of anything, but you can understand why the idiot freaked out. Not excusing his actions, you see."

Devin nodded, several pieces of the puzzle starting to fall into place.

"Anyway, he got what was coming to him in the end."

"Don't we all?"

"Yes." Urchart smiled. "Anyway, one of these six visitors evidently had some training. Probably military. Before anyone knew anything, he rushed my guys with a knife. Killed Jimmer, who was the guy that started this whole mess, and then three more before we put him down."

"I see."

"We took the other three prisoners and brought them back to the camp."

"I thought you said there were six of them," said Devin. "Two died on site, that leaves four. Forgive me if I'm wrong, as you well know I am a product of the Mississippi public school system."

Urchart looked away and took a sip of his drink. "A mild complication that resolved itself. We now have the remaining four here...well, sort of. One of the four had an unfortunate accident and is no longer with us."

"This just keeps getting better and better," said Devin, putting his drink down and leaning forward. "You had six civilians potentially compromise our operation here. We have protocols for this sort of thing. Stay in role, play your part, and send them on their way. Now we have three dead civilians and four dead guards. How could this happen?"

Urchart frowned. "I don't get the best material to work with, you know that. Jimmer was a meat whistle, who I wouldn't have trusted to watch my dog for the weekend, but we work with what we have. Am I right?"

Devin sighed. "So, who are these six?"

Urchart turned away and shuffled papers on his desk. He finally isolated one and pulled it out.

Taking the piece of paper, Devin watched Urchart kill the rest of his drink and get up to refill it.

"Want another?" he asked Devin.

Shaking his head, Devin looked down at the piece of paper that had six names, dates of birth, and residences. He presumed they had gathered the information from identification documents, but understood it could have come through torture as well.

His eyes locked onto one name at the bottom and feigned surprise.

"Jackson Winters?"

"So?" Urchart shrugged, sitting back down and taking a large drink.

"Only son of former Supreme Court Judge Jeremiah Winters? Friend of our governor?"

"Oh shit," said Urchart, setting his drink down and rubbing his hand over his head.

"Oh shit is right. You do know the police have a BOLO out for him and all of his friends. The media hasn't put all the pieces together, but they will soon."

"I didn't know," said Urchart, a little pale. "We get all sorts here. I thought we could contain it ourselves."

"You don't get all sorts here," said Devin darkly. "You get one sort. The castoffs. The forgotten ones. Poor souls no one will miss or even believe if their story somehow gets out." He lifted up the piece of paper. "These are not that sort."

"What was I supposed to do?"

"You should have let me know," said Devin, pulling the compact pistol from the small of his back and sitting it on the table beside his drink. "You knew that; don't act like you didn't."

Urchart nodded slowly. "Yeah, I knew, but we also know what kind of man Lucas Ross is." His eyes went to the gun. "We both knew how this was going to end one way or the other."

"I said you should have let *me* know," answered Devin.

"No offense, buddy, but we all know you're Ross's pit bull."

"That doesn't mean I'm his loyal dog. It's a job, and I can make up my own mind."

Hope had begun to appear in Urchart's eyes, which kept cutting back to the gun. "So how does this go down?"

"That depends on if you let me help you. I'd like to do that, but you have to do exactly what I say from here on out. I can be your fecal matter umbrella, but only if you tell me everything and do as I say. Have you told me everything?"

Urchart's face pinched up in pain. "There is one more little thing."

"Isn't there always. Tell me."

"When we ran into the six civilians, we were chasing an escaped subject. Man named Moses Mitchell, a real mental case. A nobody like the rest of them we bring here. Unfortunately, we haven't yet found him."

"He's *still* missing?"

Urchart shrugged. "The guy's probably gator turds by now."

"Or he could be off the island talking to the police."

"Even if by some miracle he did get to the mainland, no one would believe this guy. He's more screwed up than most. Voices in the head and other crazy shit. Trust me, you don't have to worry about that little loose end."

Devin gave him a warning look. "I'll be the judge of what to worry about and what not to worry about. I'll need you to give me everything you have on Mister Mitchell."

"Of course," answered Urchart, looking pointedly at the pistol. "What now?"

Devin put the pistol back into the small of his back and finished his drink. "I need to borrow your phone."

Urchart turned the phone on his desk around and pushed it in Devin's direction.

Devin called a fictitious cut-out number that was registered to a muffler supply company that had been belly up for half a year. He got a message about how Jimmy's Mufflers had closed and hoped to blah blah blah.

He punched in a twelve-digit code. Afterwards, there was a brief pause and then an answering machine beep. He punched in a four-digit code and then there were a series of beeps. Once the beeps stopped, he said, "They're not here. Everything is under control, no need to be concerned."

He then hung up the phone and looked at Urchart.

"Thank you," the man answered, relief on his face.

"Don't thank me yet," Devin answered. "We're all living on borrowed time; it's an occupational hazard."

"I know, but thanks all the same."

"You're welcome. Now why don't you give me that grand tour?"

The two stood and walked outside into the sweltering heat and humidity. There were dark clouds growing in the distance from some tropical storm, but the sun still beat down on them mercilessly.

Urchart showed him the storage areas and the entrance to the testing facilities saying they would save that area for last. He then led him to the dog kennels where the subjects were kept. Two thin men sat in the outside shade of the fenced-in dog runs.

Devin eyes were drawn to a guard who was escorting a black man from one kennel entrance to another. He saw the man slide something white from his palm into a front pocket.

"Who is that?" Devin asked, nodding in the man's direction.

"Dr. Xavier Simone," Urchart answered. "Haitian doctor here as part of the relocation program. Fell off a boat on the way over here. Another one nobody is going to miss."

"I'd like to talk to him...quietly."

"Now?" Urchart asked.

"Yes."

Urchart yelled at the guard escorting the doctor. "Hey, Brennan. Grab the doc and have him follow us."

The Haitian's eyes looked up in alarm and met Devin's. There was surprise and then instant comprehension. The man pulled the note from his pocket and put it in his mouth.

"Hey! Stop him!" yelled Urchart.

Brennen forced the man to the ground, but the Haitian kept chewing, and when Urchart forced open his mouth, it was empty.

"Take him to the questioning room," Urchart ordered him.

Devin shook his head. "When I said *quietly*, I didn't mean he and I were going to have a quiet conversation. I meant, take him quietly so that we didn't alarm him."

"Oh, I see," said Urchart. "Sorry."

"It is both a comfort and a concern to know that you are the most competent person here," said Devin, following after the Haitian.

Chapter 46

There was a light knock on Deborah's apartment door. She looked worriedly at Moses, but he was still fast asleep on her couch.

Walking over, she looked through the peephole and then opened the door to see Justin, her partner, standing there.

"Did you bring it?" she asked him.

"Good to see you, too," he said. "How about a 'thanks for coming through for me'? Maybe a 'I'm sorry about asking you to stick your neck out for me'?"

"Yeah, all that and more," she said hurriedly. "Did you bring it?"

"Yes, I brought it." He indicated a shoulder bag and then brushed past her inside. "And, oh yes, I will come inside. So nice of you to ask."

"Aren't you touchy today?" she said, closing and locking the door.

Justin froze in the living room, staring at the sleeping form on the couch. "Is that who I think it is?"

"It is," Deborah said. "Meet my brother, Moses."

Justin turned to her and smiled. "You found him."

"Actually, it was a combination of luck and us finding each other, I think."

Her partner turned back to him. "He doesn't look too bad...physically, I know he's got…you know...issues in the head and stuff."

"You're one to talk."

"Still, the streets can be tough, I know."

Deborah didn't speak for a few seconds. "I don't think he was on the streets."

"What do you mean?"

"Let's move into the kitchen," she said. "He's dead asleep and needs his rest. Don't want to wake him."

Deborah led them into the next room and quietly closed the adjoining sliding doors. She then sat across from Justin at the table. "Can I see it?"

He shook his head and sighed before pulling out a thin binder and laying it on the table. "You know how much trouble I could get into for taking this out of the office?"

"Of course I do," she answered. "Done it myself several times."

"Yes, but the difference is this is you getting me in trouble."

She was flipping through the folder. "You worry too much."

"Are you at least going to tell me what this is about? Maybe start with how your missing brother is back."

Deborah pulled out a report and showed it her partner. "Would you believe the two are connected?"

Justin took the report that had combined six missing person's cases. Once they had uncovered that the six knew each other and were on a trip together when they disappeared, this had only made sense.

"Your brother kidnapped these people?"

Deborah looked at her partner and shook her head. "How in the hell did you ever make it this far?"

"Good looks, I guess."

"No, he didn't kidnap them," she said patently, "but he might be a clue to where they are."

"What has he said?"

"Not much really," she answered. "That's not the real clue, though. Wait here a second."

She departed into an adjacent room before returning with a small piece of stained paper. She slid it across the table to her partner.

Justin picked it up curiously and read out loud. "My name is Rena, and I live on Bog Island with my father. There are people on this island running a prison camp, and I'm pretty sure they are killing people. They took my friend Jack Winters after shooting him. Moses Mitchell escaped from their camp, and the story he tells is true. Please send help. Rena."

He turned from the note to the report and back again.

"Jack Winters? What is going on here?"

Deborah shook her head. "I don't know yet, but I will. Some very sick assholes had my brother, and I think those same freaks have our missing persons."

"Maybe he made the note up."

"No," answered Deborah, "it's not his handwriting, and how would he even know about Jack Winters?"

"Why all the cloak and dagger routine? We should take this to the chief."

"So he can turn it over to the state police? So they can take my brother and mentally tear his head off to get at the information inside? I won't let them do that to him." Her eyes started to tear up. "I can't."

"Why don't you start by telling me everything," Justin said.

"Can I trust you not to go to the chief?"

"It's a little late for that question," said her partner. "If you didn't trust me, you shouldn't have asked me to bring the case file. You *have* to trust me."

"Good point," she said and reached across the table to take his hand. "And I do trust you. You're my partner."

"Thanks for that."

"Now," she said, pulling away. "I'll break it down for you so you can understand. If I talk too fast or use big words you don't understand, stop me and I'll draw pictures."

Over the next hour, she told him everything about Moses' return and what she had uncovered in examining his clothing. She also talked about the bizarre conversation she had with Moses.

"So what do you think is going on?" Justin asked her after she had finished.

"I don't know exactly, but I think it's something big. I also think nothing goes on this big and gets covered up without the government being involved."

"Here we go again," said Justin with a roll of his eyes. "You believe everything is a vast government conspiracy, right?"

"No, but some things are, and this one involves my brother." She tapped on the note from Rena. "It also involves six missing persons...at least in some manner."

"So you're just going to go off the reservation on this one?"

Deborah shook her head. "We just had cultural sensitivity training last week. You can't say stuff like that anymore."

"Stuff like what?" he asked. "Off the reservation? How is that offensive?"

"Native Americans? Being confined to reservations?"

"That phrase has nothing to do with Indians; it's about getting your name taken off a reservation at a restaurant or something."

Deborah closed her eyes and took several deep breaths. "Anyway, I'm going to look into this and see what I can find out."

"You do realize you'll—correction, *we'll*—be withholding evidence in a missing persons' case? That's a felony offense for a civilian. As federal agents, we'll be cooked if this goes badly."

"Like you said, Moses could have made up that note himself. We don't know anything yet and therefore don't have any evidence to withhold."

"That's good," said Justin. "Keep rehearsing stuff like that for your union rep when we're hung up by the internal affairs folks at Justice."

"It'll be fine," said Deborah with a smile. "Play it cool. We're doing the right thing here. Besides, it's my brother we're talking about."

Justin looked towards the closed doors that separated them from Moses. "Okay," he finally said. "Under two conditions."

"Shoot," she said.

"First, you bring me in on everything. No more holding stuff back from me."

"I'd figure you'd want some deniability if things go south."

"Like I said earlier, it's too late for that. If I'm going to be in on the plane crash I might as well be in on the plane takeoff. This will also allow me to moderate your craziness."

"Fine," she said. "And I'll overlook that craziness comment. My brother does have a mental issue, you know."

"And second, we go to the chief the very second we get anything credible regarding the location of those missing persons or evidence of criminal activity."

"Sure. Anything else?"

"As a matter of fact, yes."

"Oh God, what?"

"Repeat after me."

"What?" she asked.

"Just do it. Repeat after me."

"Fine," she said, rolling her eyes and crossing her arms.

"Justin..."

"What?"

"Just say it, Justin..."

"Justin," she said with exaggerated slowness.

"You're the smartest, cutest, best FBI agent in this galaxy, and I'm humbled to be in your presence each and every moment of my miserable life."

"Go to hell."

Justin smiled. "Close enough."

Chapter 47

Damn that little Haitian straight to hell, Helga thought not for the first time that day.

The adjustment for Helga hadn't been easy. The nurse was much more suited to dealing with subjects than actual patients who had needs and wants and voiced their opinions. One of the reasons she had gotten into research in the first place.

It did help that the subjects she dealt with at least knew their place. Most were too frightened to speak to her without permission and compliant. That big black man frightened her, but fortunately, she hadn't had to deal with him yet.

This is supposed to be Xavier Simone's job, she thought, giving a waif of a woman an antibiotic to fight an infection. *I didn't sign on for this.*

Dr. Massengill hadn't been happy either, but recognized that if the subjects didn't come to him relatively healthy and free from outside influences, it could skew the test results. Besides, a new doctor should hopefully be on the way soon.

Speaking of which, what happened to Dr. Simone? she wondered. One day he was here, and the next he had decided to go back home to Haiti? No one decided to go back home to Haiti. Helga suspected Dr. Simone had never left the island, and would never go anywhere else again, but knew enough to keep her thoughts to herself.

There were likely rumors of course, but if you were smart, you didn't spread them at Site Iaso. There was just no way of telling if someone could be trusted or not.

"We got one more for you, Doc," said a guard. They kept calling her doctor no matter how many times she told them she was a nurse.

"Did you search him?" she asked. Urchart and the strange visitor had given instructions that each of the subjects was to be physically searched more often. When Helga had asked one of the guards what they were looking for, he answered "messages" and shrugged.

Messages? Messages from where and for whom? So much around this place doesn't make sense.

Remember the work, she told herself. *Remember why we are here. There is no finer mission or more important goal.*

Helga realized the guard was still looking at her expectantly. "Yes, show them in."

A not unattractive man with the hollow eyes and the thin skin of someone recently sick entered and sat without permission. His hands and feet were shackled.

"You can wait outside," she told the guard, who nodded and took up a post outside the door.

"Who are you and where is Dr. Simone?" the man asked.

"Don't speak to me unless I ask you a question," Helga told him. "I will be taking care of you now. What seems to be the problem?"

The man didn't say anything for a few seconds, but finally pointed with shackled hands across his chest to his opposite shoulder. "My wound is festering again."

"Well, let's have a look," said Helga, standing up. "Put your arms above your head and lay on your stomach."

The man complied, and Helga pulled down the edge of the man's jumpsuit. She was surprised at what she saw. "This looks like a gunshot wound. A fairly recent one."

"You're telling me."

"How did you get shot?" she asked, poking tenderly at the edges of redness around the wound.

"It happened when I was captured on the other end of the island," the man said. "I guess I should count myself lucky. Two of my friends were killed instantly by those sadistic thugs out there."

On the island? she thought. *That seems unlikely. The subjects are brought from the mainland. Bums and dregs. The lowest of the low.*

The man hissed as she began to excise the wound and apply a new bandage. How did you get here, Mister...?"

"Winters. Jack Winters," the man answered. "My friends and I were here on a fishing trip."

My friends and I, she thought. *Most of the uneducated masses would have said, 'me and my friends' or 'my friends and me' or 'us bros.'*

"What did you do for a living?" she asked with outward casualness. "Did you have a job before you came here?"

"I was...am...a lawyer," the man answered. "Specialize in trial defense like my father."

He's lying, she thought, but another part of her wasn't convinced.

"What happened to your friends that came with you?" she asked.

265

"Three of them are still here...at least I think they are. The other three are dead."

"Oh, my," said Helga with sympathy she didn't really feel. Years of habit died hard. She applied a topical cream to the wound and reset the bandage.

Jack looked at her hopefully. "Have you seen either of them? A big black man and a redheaded woman?"

Helga paused at the mention of the redhead before pushing the thought aside.

"Go ahead and sit up," she told him and then went over to the medicine cabinet and came back with a small pill and a cup of water. "Take this."

"What is it?" he asked.

"It's what I'm telling you to take."

When the man just stared at her, she finally huffed in exasperation. "It's an antibiotic. For your shoulder. Good grief, if I wanted to hurt you, this wouldn't be the way to do it."

"I know that's true," Jackson answered and took the medicine.

Helga opened the door and looked at the guard outside. "We're done here. I'll need to see him each day to complete the round of antibiotics."

"See you soon," said Jack, smiling at her. "And no offense, but you're no Dr. Simone."

The man left, and her thoughts were drawn to the small box of the woman's stuff she had taken. Heather Daniels was her name. She had worked at the New Orleans Port Authority.

Not a bum or a castoff. A person of substance...like Mr. Winters.

Someone that would be missed. Someone that they might all go to prison for if anything ever got out.

Helga felt a tightness in her chest as she locked up the medical office for the evening.

Chapter 48

Candice Stapleton felt like she was on the crest of a rising wave. One she hoped to ride all the way to the beautiful shores of fame, stardom, and wealth.

She admitted to herself that much of this success was not due to any particular abilities she had, although these were not insignificant. Rather it was due to the man sitting across from her, Governor Eric St Keel. The man who had chosen her show *Our Nation* as his primary outlet to speak to growing throngs of loyal supporters.

She had even been able to finally convince him and his chief-of-staff to do a live broadcast. Granted, she had agreed to provide her questions ahead of time and promised not to deviate, but it was still a major journalistic coup.

St Keel was on the way up, anyone could see it, especially after tonight's show.

"Your Take Back the Streets Program continues to be a big success," Candice said. "Crime and unemployment are down while tourism and voter confidence is up. Any encores?"

St Keel smiled at the compliment. "Thank you, Candice. We have been pleased with the progress we've made so far, but still have lots of work to do."

"Some have lauded your work in the medical field. Specifically your efforts in working with various pharmaceutical companies to produce low-cost effective medications and your support of the quest to find cures to major diseases, specifically cancer. Will this area be where you turn your efforts next?"

"I don't believe as the governor I have the luxury of really focusing my efforts on any one thing. This job requires extreme multitasking. With that said, you are correct about my passions. Our citizens deserve affordable medications, and we as a people need to finally get serious about curing cancer."

"How do we do that?" Candice asked, leaning forward.

"By investing our very best efforts, our very best minds, and our very best resources into this fight. I don't think it's unreasonable to look at something similar to the Manhattan Project. If we can produce a nuclear weapon in a few years, what could we do if a similar level of dedication was placed on curing cancer?"

Candice nodded. "Some have criticized your close connections to big pharmaceutical companies. Concerns have been expressed regarding campaign donations and big business involvement in your administration. How do you address these concerns?"

St Keel cut his eyes briefly to Lucas. He hadn't wanted this question, but Lucas said it was important to address the issue head on before anyone thought to use it to attack him.

The governor nodded. "I too share the voters concerns about the influence of big business and lobbyists. As you recall, it was one of my major platforms when I ran for governor. I can assure you I am not in anyone's pocket. I am committed to serving each and every citizen of this great state with integrity and honor. Regarding these pharmaceutical companies, we have to recognize that at the end of the day they will be producing any cancer cure we find. They will be integral to that discovery as well. Given my commitment to finding that cure, I will not turn away any potential ally in that worthy cause."

"Well said," answered Candice. "I'd like to shift gears for a second. How do you respond to the report this morning of the disappearance of Jackson Winters, attorney from Lafayette? Mr. Winters is, of course, the son of former Supreme Court Justice and personal friend of yours, the late Jeremiah Winters."

St Keel looked at Lucas again, this time with slight annoyance. Lucas had assured him everything possible was being done to find the young man, but there was still no news.

"I read it with extreme concern and alarm. The state has mobilized every possible resource to find him."

"There are also reports that he may have been with several friends of his, some of which may be missing as well."

St Keel nodded seriously. "The state police have been able to determine that Jack and a group of friends rented a fishing boat for the day last week, yet never returned." The governor looked away for a second as if trying to control his emotions before looking back. "To date, no wreckage has been found, and after more than a week, our worst fears may become reality."

"Let us hope Mr. Winters and his friends are somewhere safe and are found soon."

"Yes, indeed," answered St Keel.

"Let's shift back to the upcoming presidential election." Candice displayed a coy smile and leaned toward her guest "What are your overall thoughts on how this campaign season will shake out?"

St Keel looked pained. "Well, as you know, I believe President Wilkens has done many fine things, but hasn't responded as well as she could on a number of issues."

"Such as the scandal surrounding Vice President Tipton?"

"That is one example, but there are a multitude of others. I am loyal to my president as a fellow party member, but as a voter and citizen, I am concerned."

"How do you respond to her criticisms of you? Specifically that you are planning to try and steal your party's nomination from her in the upcoming primaries."

The governor laughed. "I don't think it's possible to steal a presidential nomination. Her statement either implies that she does not understand the process or is resorting to baseless accusations. Sadly, such irresponsible and irrational behavior has become only too common during her administration.

"I also believe the people of this great country deserve choices. Just because someone has held an office for the previous four years doesn't mean they are a shoe-in to be nominated the next time. Our country deserves better and our voters certainly deserve better."

"Are you saying you might run for president next year?"

St Keel smiled wryly, as if in surrender. "I have been approached too many times by too many concerned citizens to ignore the calls any longer. As you know, I have resisted such calls, as my responsibilities lie in other areas, but it seems new and greater duties may be thrust on me yet. I was raised never to shirk my responsibilities, and I don't plan on starting now."

Candice looked startled by the revelation, although she had known it was coming for several days. "Are you saying you plan on running for your party's nomination for president?"

St Keel nodded. "It is with humility and pride that I have agreed to run for president next year."

"You heard it here first, folks," Candice said, turning to the camera. "Governor St Keel has announced for the first time that he will be running for President of the United States in the next election."

She turned back to her guest "Thank you so very much for your time, Governor. Good luck, and I hope to have you back on our show soon."

"You can count on it," said St Keel as the camera moved away to transition to a commercial break.

"We're clear," yelled a stage engineer. "Clock is running. We're back on in three minutes forty-six seconds."

St Keel sat still as a technician took off his attached microphone. He said his farewell again to Candice, who was consulting notes for her next guest, a disheveled-looking man on the edge of the stage, there to talk about rising sea levels.

An intern led him back into the makeup room where he sat in the same chair he had occupied an hour earlier, only this time the makeup lady was cleaning his face off rather than applying cosmetics.

He saw Lucas appear behind them both in the mirror in front of him. "What did you think?"

Lucas smiled. "Couldn't have gone better. It all starts here tonight."

"Anything on Jack Winters?"

"Nothing," Lucas answered, "but we're still looking."

"Leave no stone unturned," ordered St Keel. "I'm serious. That young man is the only son of the closest thing to a father I ever had."

"I understand," answered Lucas, and moved away and out of the mirror.

St Keel wanted to believe his friend and chief-of-staff, but a suspicion was starting to grow in the back of his mind.

After all, when was the last time Lucas Ross had been unable to accomplish something he set his mind to?

Chapter 49

Dark clouds filled with menacing flashes of light, and hidden power had been building out in the Gulf of Mexico for days. Those clouds had absorbed moisture and rising heat. The swirling motion and energy that had begun off the coast of Africa months before had reached a crescendo of howling winds and fury.

New Orleans breathed a sigh of relief when Hurricane Humphrey veered to the southwest away from the city still reeling from several destructive hurricanes. Yet, Louisiana was not expected to be completely missed, and the right edge of the storm would hit the western half of the state hard.

Including Bog Island.

Most other islands and coastal areas were encouraged to evacuate, but the people there were a hardy and resilient lot. Most decided to remain. Those on Bog Island never gave it a thought. They either had important work to do and leaving was not an option. Residents wouldn't dream of leaving their land...or they were prisoners locked in makeshift cells and unable to leave.

Johnny lifted his head and smiled at the howling wind. *This is what I have been waiting for.* This is what his arthritis had told him was coming for over a week and Deloy, with his decades of experience on the ocean, had confirmed. A hurricane was approaching, and it had finally arrived.

It was the signal for them to finally escape.

Johnny didn't have the whole plan worked out when he had surrendered himself, only a part. He had been a handyman most of his life and was confident in his ability to fix things or figure them out. He had known this time would likely be no different.

Still, he had gone through the routines for several days. He watched and listened and learned what he could, but his swirling nebulous plan didn't obtain any solidity.

Until Dr. Xavier Simone had passed him the note...and his knife. It had been the tool he was missing and the plan obtained solid form almost immediately.

Johnny reached under his mattress and pulled out the knife and a small piece of curiously carved hardwood. He had been able to hide the piece of wood down one pants' leg during a day of labor outside the wire. One of the benefits of being an old man, he had discovered, was that people rarely thought him a threat or worthy of close scrutiny.

He looked hard at the piece of wood. Johnny had acquired skills through the years the way some people obtained business cards. As a handyman he had become a competent mechanic, electrician, plumber, carpenter, builder, mason, and even...a locksmith.

The mail order course had come after watching a man take twenty minutes to open Mr. Winters 'car with the keys locked inside and then charging fifty dollars. Mr. Winters hadn't minded paying the bill, but Johnny had been appalled and decided he wouldn't put his boss in that position again.

The course showed him what he should have realized was self-evident. It was still all gears and mechanics. Tumblers and pins. He had obtained his license and locksmith tools and, except for three or four occasions afterwards, never used the skills again.

But he had not forgotten. Johnny had studied the keys the guards used to open their kennels. All the kennels used one common key and that key was a simple mortise type.

Which looked much in shape like the piece of wood he held in his hands.

He already knew it would work. For nights, he had carefully filed and carved on the wood with his old pocketknife. Occasionally, he would try the wood in the lock and encounter resistance and pull the wood out. He would study the indentations in the wood and work on those spots until one night the key had activated the pins and tumblers ever so slightly.

Johnny knew he could have used the key then to escape, but forcing the wood might break it, and he needed it to work more than once. The action must be smooth so as to not strain the wooden key. So, he filed and carved until it turned the lock's mechanism as smoothly as butter.

Now the time had come.

He suspected the camp was on lockdown. All the guards were buttoned up inside their barracks to get away from the torrential rain and dangerous winds. The security lights were dimmed by the swaying trees and swaths of water that passed in front of the lights.

Johnny said a quick prayer and then walked slowly to the door. He slid the key in and turned carefully, feeling the lock's mechanism engage and then flip over. Pulling the key out, he eased the door open to peek outside.

The door was nearly wrenched from his hand by the wind where it would have banged loudly against the opposite wall. Of course, in this noise, no one was likely to notice, but best not to take chances.

Johnny fought against the wind and pushed the door back shut until it latched. For good measure, he went ahead and locked it back in case any of the guards checked during the night.

He made his way three kennel doors down to the right. By the time he slid the wooden key into the lock, he was completely drenched and cold water ran in rivets off his head and down into his orange jumpsuit.

As he pulled the door open slowly, a mountain of a man materialized out of the shadows.

"I was beginning to wonder if I'd gotten the wrong signal," Charles said. "Maybe you meant we escape during the *second* hurricane or maybe during the next lunar eclipse."

"You're welcome, young man," said Johnny over the howl of the wind. "Come on."

They made their way down two more doors and unlocked it to find Jackson sitting in his cell.

"Should we come back later?" Charles asked him.

"We still don't know where Heather is."

"She's not in any of these kennels," said Charles.

"We leave without her," said Johnny.

"The hell we do," growled Charles.

Johnny stepped into Jackson's cell motioning Charles in after him. He then closed the door, and the drop in noise level was almost startling.

"When was the last time either of you saw her?" asked Johnny.

Charles looked at Jackson with uncertainly. "Maybe a week ago. She was pulled out of her cell and hasn't come back."

"She's not dead," said Jack. "Don't even go there."

"I wasn't implying she was dead," Johnny answered. "Only that she is somewhere else that we can't get to her. At least not now. The best thing we can do for her is get out of here and go get help."

"We could look through some of the nearby buildings," offered Charles.

Johnny shook his head. "We have a narrow window of opportunity here. Every minute that we waste, the chances of us getting caught increase. We need to get out of here now."

Jack looked up and met Charles's eyes for a second and then nodded.

Johnny turned to Charles. "You lead the way. This is your part of the show."

Jack followed his friend out into the storm while Johnny locked the cell behind them. All crept around the kennels using them to screen their movements from anyone in the guard shacks or larger buildings. They were forced to sprint across fifty yards of open ground before they made it to the edge of the fence-line. Jackson kept waiting to hear sirens or gunshots or alarms, but all they heard was the howling of the wind.

Charles walked along the edge of the fence and pointed at an area where water was pouring down the nearby hill and under the fence. The runoff had already taken a considerable amount of soil and rocks leaving a gap a foot high under the fence.

"Stupid shits never fixed the fence," said Charles.

"Good luck for us," answered Johnny, turning to Jackson. "You first."

Jack hesitated and then thrust himself into the rush of water, shimmying his way under the chain-link barrier as cold water flood into his face and down into his clothing. He had a mental image of himself as a salmon fighting upstream and had to suppress the urge to laugh.

Finally, he was on the other side and pulled up the fence a little higher for Johnny who came after him. Just as Johnny's legs cleared the edge, a spotlight from one of the guard shacks turned on with an audible pop and swiveled in their direction.

"Go!" said Charles. "I'll distract them."

"No you won't," yelled Jack. "Get under the fence."

"We won't make it very far if they're right on our heels," said Charles. "Go on and go. Get help, and come back for Heather and me."

"He's right," hissed Johnny. "Let's go."

Charles didn't wait for an answer. As the light swung in his direction, he took off running across the yard, and the light struggled to stay on him. A moment later, the alarms Jackson had been anticipating blared weakly in the mighty wind.

Johnny dragged him away from the fence and into the dark forest. After a few feet, Jack stopped fighting and followed the old man. The darkness was oppressive, and Jack was not sure how the old man found his way at all. Vines and branches constantly seemed to reach out for his feet, and Jack fell half a dozen times it seemed between each bright lightning flash.

Then they were out of the woods and on a trail.

"Where are we going?" asked Jack.

"This way," said Johnny. "Hurry now." He prayed Deloy and his daughter had remembered the part about meeting him during the night ahead of the hurricane landing...and that they hadn't changed their minds.

Jack followed him down the gently sloping trail and soon could make out the ocean by the flashes of lightning. A dock with a boat rocking mightily on the waves awaited them.

Two figures huddled in the bottom of the boat filled with bundles. A large man and smaller woman.

"You!" yelled Jack, recognizing Deloy and Rena. He turned to Johnny. "This is how we're escaping? You do know they are the ones who turned me in, don't you?"

"Yes," answered Johnny, "and they now regret that decision."

"Jack, please," said Rena.

"We're just supposed to trust them?" Jack asked the old man. "After everything that has happened?"

Johnny sighed. "We need off this island. What would you recommend?"

"In that little thing?" Jack pointed at the small boat. "It's suicide to go out in that during a hurricane."

"A fact we are hoping the guards recognize as well," said Deloy. "Rest assured, I can get us to the mainland. I would not risk my daughter's life if I did not believe this."

"What's all that?" Jack asked, pointing to the bundles along the bottom of the boat."

"Ballast," said Deloy. "We'll need it in seas like this."

"And our belongings," said Rena, looking sadly into Jack's eyes. "We're not planning on coming back. We're leaving our home."

"You need to make up your mind, son," said Johnny. "Whatever you do, do it quickly."

"Fine," growled Jack as he climbed down into the boat and sat next to Rena with Johnny following. Deloy untied the boat and pushed away from the dock. He then cranked an engine and steered them away from the shore while consulting a luminous compass. Winds and high waves threatened to throw them back up onto the shore.

"Jack?" said Rena.

"Let's save our breath. There's a good chance we won't make it despite your father's assurances."

"True enough," she said. "That's why I want you to know that I'm sorry. For what has happened to you. For what has happened to your friends. Most of all, for what I did."

Jack turned towards her with anger in his mouth, but a flash of lightning showed him the tears and anguish on her face, and his fury subsided.

He turned back away from her. "I'm sorry, too."

The dark night swallowed the small boat and tossed it upon the turbulent seas.

Chapter 50

Lucas Ross sat at his desk heavily. It had been an extremely busy week, but things seemed to be under control. The worst of the hurricane was evidently past, but winds still howled outside, and parts of the state had experienced severe flooding and would have power outages for days to come.

He saw one of the lights blinking on his secure phone. Ross picked up the receiver and pushed the indicated button. A computer-generated voice said, "Four. Two. Six."

Lucas ended the call and almost didn't check the message that had been left. Dr. Edward Massengill was a good source of information on what was going on down at Site Iaso, but the man complained about everything. It was almost not worth having him as an inside man.

Finally, overcoming his hesitancy, Lucas called another number and entered the six-digit code to unlock the message. He listened.

The man's elitist and unconscious condescending voice came on almost immediately. "I can't understand why I'm not able to simply call and talk to you. This is ridiculous and a waste of my time. Anyway, I thought you should know that things down here seem to be chaotic, to put it mildly. Several guards have died as well as some valuable subjects. You should also know that I saw the news. That Jackson Winters fellow everyone was looking for...he was here. Until he escaped. Have a nice day, and please make sure my payment gets where it belongs on time. It has been late the last two months."

The call then ended with a click.

Lucas listened to the full message two more times before putting the receiver down and thinking for nearly a quarter of an hour.

Jackson Winters *was* on the island.

Urchart has been lying to me, he thought. *None of this has been in his reports. Massengill is a blowhard, but doesn't lie. That bastard Urchart has been lying to me.*

And not just Urchart, he thought.

Lucas called two men from the governor's security detail into his office. They were old soldiers of his. Loyal, obedient, discrete, and capable. He briefed them on the situation, and then asked his secretary to find Devin and tell him to come to his office.

Within a half hour, the man walked into his boss's office without knocking, but froze as he saw the two security personnel.

"Close the door," said Lucas.

Devin slowly shut the door, but stood with his back to the wall with the two other men flanking him.

"Do you have any weapons on you?" Lucas asked.

"You know damned well I do."

Lucas indicated the table off to his right. "Place them there for now."

"Why?" the man asked, his whole body tense.

"Because I want to have a tough conversation with you. We both know you can sometimes leap to violent conclusions, and I need us all to remain calm so we can get to the bottom of this and move forward."

Devin didn't move for several long seconds. "Fine," he finally said and strode over to the table. While being closely watched by the security detail, he pulled a compact automatic pistol from a holster in the small of his back and a snub-nosed revolver from an ankle holster. He then added a few extra magazines and a speed loader for the revolver."

"Happy?" Devin asked.

"As I recall, you always carry a knife," said Lucas. "That, too."

A vein had started to throb in Devin's forehead.

He's angry, thought Lucas. *That's the right response if he isn't guilty. Is it possible he was also fooled by Urchart? That he went down there and didn't realize what was happening?*

Doesn't matter, Lucas realized. *To be that incompetent is a worse sin than betrayal.*

Devin laid a spring knife on the table.

"Now sit," said Lucas, pointing at the chair in front of him well away from Devin's weapons.

The man obeyed while cutting his eyes to the two guards standing behind him.

"You recently visited Bog Island and reported that Site Iaso was running without complications. Nothing to be concerned about is what I believe you said."

"Did I?" asked Devin.

"We both know that isn't correct."

"Nothing runs completely smooth in covert ops. We both know that."

Lucas leaned forward. "Don't play games with me. This is not about your impression being different from mine. This is about you intentionally deceiving me."

"Now why would I do that?"

"I'm not exactly sure, and I don't care," said Lucas. "Also, that's not a denial. You're trying to divert. That's a guilty response."

"I can't deny something when I don't know what you're talking about."

Lucas had planned to go through the whole elaborate interrogation-questioning sequence. To string it out until Devin was forced to admit what he had done. To realize his goose was cooked. Lucas had wanted to see that realization on the man's face.

Now, he realized he was tired. Bone tired.

"Devin, you know how this works. You kept critical information from me about what was going on down at Bog Island. You also intentionally didn't tell me about Jackson Winters and his friends. If I can't trust you, I don't need you."

Lucas looked up at the two men along the walls and nodded to them before looking back at Devin. "Your services are no longer required."

"Wait a minute!" said Devin, starting to rise. "If you do anything to me, then—"

His voice was cut off as one of the security detail sent fifty thousand volts of electricity through his body from a Taser. Devin fell to the floor and convulsed and flopped. After ten full seconds, the man stopped the electricity flow, and Devin lay still on the ground.

"Get him out of here," Lucas told them. "Remember what I told you about disposing of him. Screw it up and you'll get a lesson on how it's done correctly...firsthand."

"We understand, Mr. Ross," said one as they lifted Devin to his feet and used flex cuffs to secure his hands behind his back. They then marched Devin out the door.

"Close the door!" Lucas yelled, but the men were already gone.

His secretary stuck her head in the door with a worried expression. She looked back and forth between the two security men dragging Devin away and Lucas. "Is there anything I can do, sir?"

"Yes, close the door and leave me alone."

She jerked her head back and pulled the door shut behind her.

Lucas walked over to the wall and opened his safe. He then deposited Devin's weapons from the side table inside and relocked the safe before sitting back in his chair.

Depression descended upon him. He and Devin had been comrades-in-arms. Been through the fire together. How could he do such a thing?

"Focus on the now," he told himself.

First thing was to find Jackson Winters before he could talk to someone. They also needed to discredit him in case they were unsuccessful.

A flicker of an idea came to mind. Perhaps they could kill two birds with one stone. Let the police do their job for them and at the same time make them unwilling to listen to any crazy story.

They would also have to shut down Site Iaso. Feds would be crawling all over the area soon enough.

Lucas began to make notes and plans, but his mind was drawn back to the confrontation with Devin.

What had the man been about to say before the guard tazed him? If anything happens to me, then I'll...

Then what?

Lucas shook his head. What could a man possibly do when he was six feet under?

Chapter 51

Deloy had kept his word and gotten them to shore alive...but not by much. His boat was nearly swamped by the time he pulled it into a small cove. They had all been exhausted and sick from hours of bailing cold water on the sea that felt at times like a trampoline.

They rode the next day out deep in the interior of one of the many swampy glades. Deloy had managed to remove the engine and wrap it in plastic and then turn the boat upside down. For the next twenty-four hours they had used sheets of plastic along the sides and then tried to shelter themselves inside from the wind and rain.

By the next morning, the worst of the hurricane seemed to have passed. Exhausted, they climbed out from under the boat and spent the morning trying to dry their wet clothes and get warm around a fire.

The sound of an approaching motorboat caused them all to stop and listen.

"We should hide," said Deloy.

"Hang on," said Jack. "Let's see what we got. Besides, we can't hide the boat that quickly. Someone will know we're here."

Within minutes, a fifteen-foot boat filled with soldiers in camouflaged uniforms and orange life vests pulled into view. A few dazed civilians in blankets sat in the middle of the boat. The side of their watercraft had Louisiana National Guard stenciled on the side.

"Hey, you folks okay?" called out a soldier from the front.

"Better now that the wind and rain stopped," answered Johnny.

"Ain't that the truth," the soldier replied. "I'm guessing you tried to move inland using that boat and got caught up in the surge."

"It's almost like you were there," said Johnny.

"You need anything?"

"Some food and water would be nice," Johnny answered.

The soldier pointed ahead of them. "There's an aid camp a mile ahead of us our battalion set up this morning. They've got food, water, and shelter there. We'd offer you a lift, but we're already full."

"Our boat's still good," Deloy said. "We can make our way there."

"Want us to wait on you?" asked the soldier.

"Don't bother," said Johnny. "We'll be along shortly. Thanks for the info."

The soldier gave them a parting wave and moved on down the river.

"Think it's safe to go there?" asked Rena. "They might be looking for us."

"It should be okay as long as we don't use our true names," Johnny said. "If this aid camp is like any of the others I've seen after a hurricane, we should be able to blend into the crowd. Get shelter and food, and unless we ask for something, most people will ignore us."

"Besides, we don't have much choice," said Jack. "We won't last another night out here. We'll either get hypothermia or dehydrated."

They packed their meager belongings, righted the boat, and headed in the direction of the camp. After a half hour, they could hear the sounds of generators and see thin ribbons of exhaust in the sky. Soon, the large camp came into view.

It sat back from the water in an open field. Dozens of large green army tents were arranged in neat rows. Civilians mingled about with each other as a few soldiers watched listlessly. A group of children chased each other around the perimeter of the camp.

"Looks like the right place," said Johnny.

They unloaded their boat, and Deloy chained it to a tree with a padlock.

"You really think someone's going to steal it?" asked Jack.

"Best not to leave the temptation out there," said Deloy. "I know mainlanders aren't as trustworthy."

Jack decided to let the comment go, as he was the only "mainlander" among them.

The four moved slowly up into the camp, and soldiers directed them to a nearby tent. He stated they could pick out a cot, drop their belongings, and then go register at the administration tent. After that, they could get food and maybe a shower.

"Registration doesn't sound good," said Deloy from a cot near the edge of a large tent.

"Why not?" asked Jack. "We can finally talk to the police and tell them what has happened. These army folks might be able to help as well."

"I'm not so sure," said Johnny. "We don't yet know what we're dealing with. Don't forget that what happened at Bog Island *was* the government. Don't stick your head out there yet until we know what's flying around above us."

"Fine," said Jack, "for now. But they're going to want to have a name for their registration. Maybe even want to see identification."

"Make up names," said Rena. "Say all our identification was lost. Daddy, Johnny, and I are all family that fled the storm, and we picked you up along the way."

"Because I'm white?" asked Jackson.

"No," answered Deloy, "because you *aren't* part of the family."

"Yes," said Rena. "One of these things is not like the others," she sang.

"Whatever," said Jack. "Let's go get this over with so we can get something to eat. I'm starving."

A half hour later, they were sitting at a long table in a food tent. The registration had been surprisingly perfunctory. They had added their names and addresses to a list and been given a blanket, pillow, and meal card.

"Damn, beef stew never tasted so good," mumbled Jack.

Other groups of disheveled refugees moved around them, but everyone mostly kept to themselves. Many had the dazed look of someone who believes they have lost everything.

Johnny who had eaten and departed to get information returned and sat beside them. "Found a soldier who had a newspaper he let me borrow. It's from yesterday. *New Orleans Tribune*."

"What's it say? Hurricane coming?" asked Deloy.

"No," said Johnny. He opened the newspaper to the inside page and then turned it so Jack could see.

Jack's spoon froze halfway to his mouth. He was looking at a picture of himself in a suit smiling. The title read, "Police on Lookout for Missing Attorney, Suspect in Multiple Disappearances."

He took the paper and began to read.

Jackson Winters, an attorney at Riley and Associate Law Firm in Lafayette, LA, has been missing since Thursday the 28th of May. Jackson is the son of former Supreme Court Justice the Honorable Jeremiah Winters. Authorities state that he and five friends went on a fishing trip and never returned. At first, it was believed that they might have been the victims of an accident, but recent evidence has surfaced that Mr. Winters has psychological issues and may have been responsible for the deaths of his friends on Bog Island. Authorities are currently investigating, but if anyone has information about the whereabouts of Jackson Winters, telephone the state police immediately. Under no circumstances should anyone attempt to approach the suspect, as he is considered extremely dangerous.

The suspect, thought Jack. *That's me. Killed my friends?*

"Good thing we didn't use our real names," said Rena.

Jack looked at his picture and then around the tent self-consciously.

"Don't worry," said Johnny. "No one's going to recognize you. Not with that beard and scraggly hair. You've also lost at least fifteen pounds."

Jack turned back to the paper and read the story again. "Those bastards," he finally said.

"What now?" asked Deloy. "We obviously can't go to the police."

Jack thought for several long moments. "Do we have any money?"

"Some," answered Deloy. "We brought all we had...but it's not a lot."

"I don't need a lot," Jack answered. "And don't worry, I'll pay you back."

"That's not what I'm worried about," answered Deloy.

"What are you thinking?" asked Rena.

Jack smiled. "What my father would have done."

"And what's that?" asked Rena.

"Come at them sideways," Jack answered.

Johnny smiled.

Chapter 52

St Keel was on the phone when Lucas entered the office. The governor kept talking and motioned for Lucas to come on in and take a seat.

Lucas sat and gazed around the office. It was filled with mementoes and pictures. There was a rather large photograph of the governor in black robes the day he had graduated from Tulane. A dignified middle-aged gentleman stood beside him. Jeremiah Winters had his arm around the governor's shoulders, and his face beamed with pride.

This is going to be hard, Lucas thought.

St Keel hung up the phone and shook his head. "There are many things about this job that I love, but catering to donors who might give me ten dollars and a friendly nod is not one of them."

"I'm afraid I have some bad news," Lucas said. "I've been digging into the media stories about Jackson Winters."

The governor was already shaking his head, sensing what his chief-of-staff was going to tell him. "I don't believe it."

"I'm afraid it's true. There are witnesses who will testify that Jackson Winters took his friends to Bog Island. He then sunk the boat out in the ocean and systematically hunted and killed his five friends. It is also likely that he killed four personnel at our...special site there."

"He's a lawyer for God's sake! I know this kid. He's no killer."

"Believe me," said Lucas. "You never really know who is a killer and who isn't. There are some indications that he was suffering from psychological issues. In that case, I guess it could be argued that's he's not entirely responsible for his actions."

St Keel ran his hands through his hair and looked over at the picture Lucas had noticed earlier. "Any idea where he's at?"

"Not yet, but all the authorities have a picture and description. He can't stay hidden forever."

"Maybe he's still on the island."

"We know that he left during the recent hurricane. Our guards there confirmed as much."

"Guards?" said the governor. "I thought we have a research laboratory there. Why are there guards?"

"They're doing high-level sensitive research," Lucas explained. "Corporate espionage is a serious concern, and when it comes to stakes, a cure for cancer is as big as they get."

St Keel thought for a moment. "Perhaps it's time I go see this operation."

"That's not a good idea. This is not a sanctioned operation. Keeping it hidden comes with a cost. One that our friends at the big pharmas are willing to pay, but in order to protect you, there needs to be some distance."

"But if we're not doing anything wrong, why do we need to go through all of this?"

"Trust me," said Lucas. "This is for the best. Perception is sometimes worse than doing wrong."

What are you not telling me? St Keel wondered. *What are you trying to protect and what's in it for you, my friend?*

"It's going to get out now anyway," said the governor. "The media is going to know that Bog Island is the...scene of these horrific acts. They're going to descend on the park soon."

"By then, everything will be shut down and moved elsewhere," Lucas said. "The hurricane has helped in that regard because it has delayed getting people out there. By the time the blood-suckers descend, our operation will be gone, and the park service will have cleaned everything else up."

"Moved elsewhere? Where exactly?"

"Sir, it really is best you don't know."

St Keel let the silence hang in the air for a few seconds. "You do know that if you are telling me everything and it turns out anything criminal or immoral has been going on...it's all going to stop with you."

"That's exactly how it is supposed to be," answered Lucas. "My job is to protect you, and that's what I'm doing now."

St Keel sighed. "I guess you're right. I've trusted you this long and have no reason to stop now."

"Thank you, sir."

"Just make sure we find Jack Winters. I don't want anything bad to happen to him. Make sure everyone knows he might be mentally incapacitated. I don't want some Barney Fife to go in all blasting the first time they see him."

"Understood," said Lucas.

"I still can't believe it," said St Keel. "I'm glad his father didn't live to see this day. It would have crushed a very fine man."

"Will that be all? I've got some things I need to wrap up."

"Yes," said the governor, waving in his direction but looking away outside. "I think I'd like to be alone for a while anyway."

Lucas left the office. He now knew that whatever happened, Jackson Winters could not be taken alive. If anyone else talked to him, they wouldn't believe his story and would chalk it up to the fabricated psyche reports his people had planted.

But not Eric St Keel. He felt his owed the boy's father. He would listen and just might believe.

Jackson Winters most definitely had to die.

Chapter 53

Jack sat at the small hotel room desk and tried to compose his thoughts. They had checked into the small third-rate establishment the night before using some of Deloy's money. Jack had spent most of the time trying to organize his thoughts around how to legally get out of the net they had constructed for him.

"Why don't you take a break?" asked Johnny, his roommate. Deloy and Rena were in the room next door.

Jack looked up at Johnny lying on the bed watching the news. "Wouldn't do any good. This is all I can think about."

"You're just like your father," said Johnny, shaking his head.

"What do you mean?" asked Jack, but was interrupted by a knock on the door.

Johnny answered it to reveal Rena. She was in a sweatshirt and must have just taken a shower.

"Would you mind letting me come in and talk to Jack alone?" she asked.

"Not at all, honey," said Johnny, stepping outside. "He needs a little break time right now for sure."

Jack sighed heavily as she closed the door. He knew what this would be about. "Look, you don't have to apologize anymore. What's done is done."

"I'm not going to apologize. I've already done that."

"Well, good...I guess."

She sat on the bed across from him. "You do realize that my father and I have lost our home. We're fugitives from the law. We're funding everything you do right now."

"I guess you could say it's the least you could do."

"After what we did... Isn't that how you want to finish the sentence?"

Jack grunted. "You said it, I didn't."

"My father and I were put into a very difficult position. We made the wrong decision, but then risked everything to make it right the only way we could. Just a little bit of acknowledgement of that fact would go a long way."

Jack glared at her. "Acknowledgement? I'm still working on acknowledgement that all my friends are dead or locked up in some sadistic experimentation camp. That's taking me some time to deal with, so forgive me if I don't fully *recognize* your generosity and sacrifice."

"We helped you."

"And then betrayed me."

"I saved your life," she said.

"To give it away to people who tortured me."

"I loved you."

Jack's angry retort froze in his throat. He really looked at Rena for the first time and saw she was crying.

He shook his head. "How? We knew each other for like five minutes. How could you possibly love me?"

Rena wiped her eyes and nodded. "You're probably right. What would I know? Silly little island girl who falls in love for the first time. Tell me you don't feel anything for me and I'll leave you alone. Better yet, tell me that and my father and I will go. Maybe we can still salvage something from our old life."

Jack felt like he couldn't get his breath. "I...just...it's, you know...how—"

"Oh, never mind." She stood up and stormed towards the door, throwing it open. "Let me know when you make up your mind, you self-absorbed jerk."

She disappeared before Jack could say anything.

Johnny stepped back inside and closed the door. "Good visit?"

"Don't even talk to me about it."

"Would never dream of it," said Johnny. "Only to say she's a hell of a girl who cares about you and those don't come along very often."

"Said I didn't want to talk about it."

"And I respect your wishes, son." Johnny was silent for a few seconds. "I'll just say your father would have liked her."

Jack looked up to yell at Johnny, but his eyes locked onto the television screen. He pointed. "Turn it up. Turn it up."

Johnny picked up the remote and raised the volume. A reporter was talking about Governor St Keel's presidential run and an address he would be making the following night in Baton Rouge.

"I think I see a way out of this," said Jack. "He was my father's friend."

"Doesn't mean he's *your* friend," replied Johnny. "There's nothing slipperier than a mud eel except a politician running for office."

"My father trusted him," Jack shot back at him.

"So what are you planning on doing?" asked Johnny. "You get within a mile of him and the police will snag you."

"I'll wear a disguise."

"And then what? Jerk it off when you shake the governor's hand? That's likely to get you shot, even if they don't recognize him."

Jack growled in frustration. "There has to be a way to get his attention and pass a message along without everyone knowing. I think if I could get ten minutes alone with him, I could make him believe me."

"Maybe there's a way after all," said Johnny thoughtfully.

"How?"

Johnny smiled. "You're not the only one from the old days the governor remembers. Just leave it to me."

Jack shook his head. "I don't want you doing anything dangerous on my behalf."

"It *way* too late for that, son," said Johnny, pointing his thumb towards the closed door. "*All* of us are doubled-down on you whether you like it or not."

Chapter 54

St Keel could feel the buzz in the air. It reminded him of the time as a young boy he had been caught outside in a lightning storm. He had felt a similar charge, an energy that had made his hair stand on end, right before a bolt of lightning had struck a tree not twenty yards away from him with a thunderous clap that had thrown him to the ground, dazed.

He had given hundreds, maybe thousands of speeches at rallies and fundraisers such as this, but it felt different.

Eric St Keel was running for President of the United States. And people were excited about it. They were rooting for him. He was leading in early polls. All from a poor boy who no one likely would have believed could even get into college.

It was all coming together, just as Lucas said it would.

The big donors were pouring in even more money, especially the pharmas. He was the darling of radio and television talk shows. Even the Republican Party leadership was starting to abandon President Wilkens and get on his bandwagon.

Still, something didn't seem right. There was something off.

St Keel knew it at least partially had to do with what was going on down at Bog Island. He understood Lucas' logic of not telling him everything for his own protection, but he had a nagging feeling as if he were being used, or worse, played for a fool.

And really, how much could you trust a man like Lucas Ross? He was a childhood friend, but he had always been someone who lived on the ragged edge of morality and usually seemed to find a way to get what he wanted.

And this business with Jack Winters. A mass murderer? St Keel still didn't buy it. He had known the boy well. Sure, he had likely been devastated first by the loss of his mother and then his father, but he was stable. His father's son.

His thoughts were interrupted as an aide approached him and gave him a warning. He turned his attention back to the overly long introductory speech as he heard, "It gives me great honor and pleasure to introduce to you my friend and your governor, the next President of the United States, Eric St Keel!"

He walked from backstage and into the noise and light. Shaking hands with the chairman of the Louisiana Republican Committee, he turned and faced the crowd with the man and waved for the cameras.

The chairman then turned back to him and smiled. "This is it, Eric. Give 'em a show." He then walked off stage.

If anything, the applause got louder, and he lifted his hands to thank everyone. His speech was in a binder before him, and he spotted the sticky note Lucas has put on top.

Don't stop the applause; just smile and wave and look at the crowd. Make as much eye contact as you can. They'll remember it. Each person will think you are looking directly at them.

St Keel did just that. He smiled and waved at all the blue signs reading "St Keel for President" that were bouncing up and down in the crowd.

He waved to the elderly woman in the front who was wearing pink tennis shoes.

Smiled at the huge biker with tattoos and cut-off sleeves. Blew a kiss to his wife, Brenda on the front row. Placed his hand over his heart at the little girl's homemade poster in his honor. Pointed at the elderly black man near the right front now who stood there glaring at him. Waved to the boy in a wheelchair down front.

Wait. Back to the old black man. Did he know him?

St Keel continued to smile and wave, but he was looking at the man who was staring at him so intently.

Was that Jeremiah's handyman?

As if man could read his thoughts, he nodded and slowly turned his "St Keel for President" sign around to the back side. It was blank, but he pulled down a taped-up flap. There was neat magic marker writing.

Jack is innocent. 5 PM tomorrow. The Refuge. He trusts you. Come alone.

St Keel looked away and smiled and waved. His heart thundered in his chest, and he realized he was sweating. Looking back towards Johnny, he saw that the man and his sign were nowhere to be seen.

He nodded and smiled and played the part. The presidential candidate gave an inspiring and moving speech about hope and service and taking care of people. Many were genuinely moved and more inspired. The Baton Rouge News would say the next day that it was one of the best campaign speeches since William Jennings Bryant.

Yet St Keel missed most of the moment. He was there, but his mind was somewhere else.

Thinking of Jack Winters to be exact.

***

"Who is that?" Lucas Ross pointed into the crowd. He had just seen how the governor had reacted strangely to something. No one else would likely notice, but Lucas knew the man better than he knew himself.

"Who?" asked a member of the security detail.

"There," said Lucas. "The old black man. He's leaving now. Get him, I'd like to talk to that man."

The security detail spoke into a walkie-talkie and then departed.

All they were able to recover was a campaign sign with duct tape on the back as if something had been stuck on the reverse side.

Lucas would have to find a way to ask St Keel about it.

Secrets are definitely not good in a relationship, he thought. *At least not secrets from me.*

Chapter 55

Deborah walked into the FBI office and slumped down into her cubicle beside her partner.

"Staying out all night partying again, I see," said Justin.

"It's Moses," she said. "He sleeps all day while I'm at work and then stays up most of the night wandering around and talking to himself."

"You leave him at your apartment by himself?"

"Of course not," said Deborah. "I've hired a nurse to look after him."

"And she can't keep him awake while you're at work?"

"Probably," she admitted, "but he seems to be getting better. I don't want to mess with anything if his mind is trying to heal itself."

"I guess, you know that they have actual hospitals for this sort of thing."

"No," said Deborah, a little more forcefully that she intended. "No. Those places aren't for my brother. They're not interested in helping him, only in keeping him from hurting himself or someone else. My brother isn't suicidal or homicidal, so paying tons to put him there makes no sense."

"Well, he's your brother."

Yes he is, thought Deborah fiercely.

"Hey, did you see this?" asked Justin, pointing at the television and turning up the volume a few notches.

"Yeah," she answered. "Can you imagine a guy from Louisiana as President of the United States?"

"Well, it's been done before."

"Actually, no it hasn't."

"Yes, it has," said Justin slowly.

"Name one."

"How about Jimmy Carter for starters."

Deborah sighed. "He's from Georgia, dumbass."

"No, he wasn't. And what about Truman?"

"I'm pretty sure he was from Missouri."

"Zachary Taylor," said a passing colleague. "He was from Louisiana."

Justin turned to her in triumph. "See, there you go."

She had begun to turn away when her eyes locked onto the television. "Hey, turn that up," she said.

There was a picture of Jackson Winters in a suit. He was smiling and looked like the world was at his feet. The reporter was stating that the manhunt was still on for the suspected mass murderer and that any information should be relayed immediately to the police.

She shook her head. "This is getting out of control."

"What do you mean?"

Deborah ignored him and pulled out the missing person's case file that was sent to them 'by mistake' because the missing boat had crossed state lines.

Someone had wanted them to know about this. She looked through the file until she found a name.

"Come on," she told her partner. "Let's go for a little ride."

***

Port Allen Chief of Police Andrew Bolton had finally managed to sit down at his desk to enjoy his now cold cup of coffee. It had been a bear of a morning with a three-car pileup out on the highway. Luckily, no one had been killed, but two were in the hospital.

Gina, his secretary, stuck her head in the office. "Chief, you got visitors."

"Tell 'em to come back later, or you take care of them."

Gina looked out the door and then back into his office. She had a serious glint in her eyes. "I think you better talk to them. They're two feds."

Good grief, thought Bolton. *That's all I need.* "Probably here to coordinate for that counter-terrorism exercise next month. Go ahead and show them in."

A tall, serious, athletically built black woman walked in, followed by a more relaxed white man. Both wore business suits that were specifically cut to conceal the pistols holstered at their sides.

Andrew rose to greet them, shook their hands, and introduced himself.

"I'm Special Agent Deborah Mitchell, and this is my partner Justin Blake."

"Have a seat." Bolton pointed at the chairs in front of his desk. "Did Gina offer you any coffee? Realize if she didn't, it likely wasn't discourtesy but mercy."

"We're fine," replied Deborah. "Thank you. We'd like to talk to you about the missing person's case? The one involving Evan Athers?"

Bolton took a few seconds to think, but Deborah could tell it was for show; he knew the name right away.

The chief rubbed his chin and looked towards the ceiling. "Yeah, I remember that one. We got a message about a 911 call from his satellite phone. When that was combined with a missing person's report, we thought it sounded like something nefarious might have happened."

"Your report that you sent to the FBI office—"

"Because of the boat," Bolton put in. "I'm required to do that because the missing boat came from across state lines, making it technically a federal matter."

"And we appreciate that," said Justin. "We passed that right over to our Missing Fishing Boat Task Force."

"Why didn't you investigate it?" Deborah asked.

"We did...for a while."

"What happened?" asked Deborah, leaning forward.

Bolton sat back heavily in his chair and sighed. "Look, I don't want to get into any trouble and bring any heat down on me from way up high. I was told in no uncertain terms not to discuss this with anyone."

"Told by who?" asked Justin.

Bolton looked back and forth at them with uncertainty. He finally appeared to make up his mind.

"I may regret this, but what the hell," the chief said and actually smiled. "The damn state attorney general himself called me. Told me to cease and dissent all investigative activity and turn it over to the state police."

"Why would they do that?" asked Deborah. "Is that normal for something like this?"

"Not at all," answered Bolton. "Something didn't seem right about it. Still doesn't, and that's the main reason I sent the file to you guys."

"Not to mobilize the Missing Fishing Boat Task Force?" asked Justin.

Deborah gave her partner a warning look before looking back at the chief. "What do you think is going on here?"

Bolton shook his head. "Oh, I don't want to speculate. I have no idea what is going on...but the news has been all over that lawyer Jackson Winters and the five friends he supposedly killed. The news isn't saying, but we know Evan Athers was one of those friends."

"So?" asked Justin.

"So...it's not a secret that Jackson Winters is the only son of the governor's close friend who just happened to be a Louisiana Supreme Court Justice," said Bolton. "Maybe they didn't want this news out before he could prepare his presidential campaign announcement. Maybe they wanted time to dig in on their own. The bottom line is they have known a lot more that they are letting on to for a lot longer than people think."

"Has anyone from the state police contacted you further about this case?" asked Deborah.

"Not at all," answered Bolton, "which is also a little odd."

"Why?" asked Justin.

"Because they didn't want to talk to any of my people. Sure, we handed them the case file, but you know as well as I do that not everything goes on paper. Typically, a detective wants to talk to everyone to make sure they have all the info."

"And no one from the state police has talked to your guys?" asked Deborah.

"Not one," said Bolton. "I don't know what is going on, but something seems out of place here."

You got that right, thought Deborah.

"And what about *habeus corpus*?" Bolton asked.

"What about it?" asked Justin.

Bolton threw his hands up in the air. "I mean, why has it gone from a missing persons' case to a homicide? As far as I know, no bodies have been recovered. Evan Athers' body certainly hasn't been, as far as we know. And what was the motive? What was the murder weapon? And where is the murder weapon itself?"

"Does seem like a lot of unknowns," Justin said.

Bolton leaned forward. "What I mean is that the state sat on this for almost two weeks and then it's all out in news? This wasn't a leak;

312

it was officially released. Yet we all know no judge would issue a warrant for an arrest on such poor evidence."

"Maybe they just want Mr. Winters for questioning," said Justin.

"But they're painting him in the media as a mass murderer," said Bolton, "and the police are doing nothing to refute that impression. Not a good idea unless you want to have to pay out on a massive lawsuit. Especially when you're slandering and defaming a very respected lawyer."

"Well, at least he'll get his payday at the end," said Justin, "presuming, of course, he didn't do it."

"Oh, I don't think he's ever going to get his payday," said Bolton with a smile. "As a matter of fact, if I hadn't given up gambling years ago, I would lay a grand on them not finding Mr. Winters or any of his lost friends...ever."

"I admit the staties are a little slow when it comes to police work," said Justin, "but that's a bit of a stretch."

"They don't want them to be found," said Deborah suddenly.

"Exactly," smiled Bolton. "Now the million-dollar question is why?"

***

The car was silent as they drove away from the police station.

"You don't believe all of that, do you?" Justin finally asked.

"I'm not sure what to believe," Deborah answered.

"Certainly not the sort of thing we want to get involved in."

"Something very bad is going on here, and it somehow involved my brother."

Her partner looked at her hesitantly. "I know you don't want to hear this...but maybe it's time we handed this all over to the chief."

"Okay."

"I mean, he can put resources against this and contact the guys at Justice, and...wait...did you just agree to turn this over to the chief?"

"I said okay, didn't I?"

Justice sat back in his seat and smiled. "We're coming back on the reservation."

"I told you not to say things like that."

Her partner was thinking. "Maybe when we tell the chief, you should let me do all the talking. I'm not sure he likes you very much."

"Good idea," Deborah answered. "You take the lead on this from here on. Don't screw it up."

"Not a chance." Justin smiled.

Chapter 56

The Winters Estate had been passed down through the family since it was bought in the late 1830s from an upstart merchant named Edgar Luroue. Much of the land had been lost and sold off during the years, but the old homestead and central house still remained as well as a little more than twenty acres.

Jack had rented the place out to a nice family after his father died. He had just started work at his practice in Lafayette, which was too far to drive from Baton Rouge each day.

There was one area of the estate that, by agreement, the rental family steered clear of. Jeremiah Winters had built a small office cabin on the top of a hill along the edge of the property. It overlooked a small stream and was isolated from much of the world.

Jack's father had often gone there to work. Many Supreme Court decisions had been crafted and solidified in that small cabin. Jeremiah called the small cabin "The Refuge" and even had a modest wood-burned placard made to hang over the door.

Eric St Keel made his way through the woods in a tracksuit. He had been able to leave his security detail behind by telling them he was going for a run through the woods in the nearby state park. If he wasn't back in an hour, they would call him and shortly after come looking for him.

The clock was ticking.

Part of him wondered what he was doing out here. He had, of course, been to The Refuge numerous times, but it had been many years. The man Jeremiah had called Johnny might just be crazy or looking to rob him.

Still, the message had intrigued him. *Jack is innocent.* He wanted that so badly to be true.

He stopped walking and looked around. It had seemed so clear at first, but now nothing looked familiar. Where was the hill? What about the stream?

"Over here, Governor," said a deep voice.

St Keel turned to see Johnny standing next to a tree nearby.

"I hope I'm not making a mistake," he told the old man.

Johnny shrugged. "Not for me to say. Follow me though if you want to find out." Without waiting for a response, the man turned and began walking up the nearby hill.

St Keel hesitated for a moment and then followed after him. He led him up and over the hill and found the small cabin not more than a hundred yards from where he had encountered Johnny.

The old man opened the front door and motioned for the governor to enter.

Staring at Johnny for a long moment, St Keel walked into the cabin.

His first thought was confusion. There was an enormous black man standing in front of him flanked by a beautiful girl with raven hair right behind him.

"You came," said a voice to St Keel's left.

He turned to see Jack Winters smiling at him with emotion in his eyes.

"Didn't see how I had much choice," St Keel said. "I owe your father a great deal."

"You could have turned us in; most would have."

"Maybe," the governor shrugged. "Maybe not. Perhaps you should start by telling me what is going on."

They all sat and told their story. St Keel didn't interrupt or show surprise. His face was a mask of calm.

"Is that everything?" he finally asked when Jack was done with his story.

"Isn't that enough?" asked Deloy.

The governor looked around at each of them. "Don't misunderstand me. It's quite a tale."

"You don't believe us?" asked Rena, her color rising.

Johnny held up his hand to calm her. "Oh, he believes us. In fact, he's not even surprised."

"Is that true?" asked Jack.

St Keel stood and moved to look out the window. "I didn't know about any of this, but I knew something was going on at that island. Something that was being kept from me. Many things make more sense now than they did before."

"So what happens now?" asked Rena.

"We blow the top off everything," said Jack. "I go and tell everything. The governor will ensure I get that chance."

St Keel turned from the window and looked at Jack with sad eyes. "It's too late for that."

"What do you mean?" asked Deloy.

"Everything that would corroborate your story is either gone, destroyed, or hidden. You speaking out would get you nothing but arrested at best."

"At least it might save my friends."

"Maybe, but likely not," said St Keel. "Besides, you'll be in prison. These sorts of people could make you disappear inside of a day in prison."

Johnny looked at him sternly. "These are some friends you have, Governor. Mr. Jeremiah might not understand."

"It is what it is," said St Keel hotly, the comment hitting its mark. "What I'm telling is you can't try and fight this, not head-on."

"What do you recommend?" asked Rena.

"You hide or lay low," said St Keel. "I can try and help you."

"Hide?" asked Jack. "Are you serious?"

"Hey!" yelled the governor. "I came here, didn't I? You know the risk I'm taking by even being here? For not turning you in? I'm on your side and I'm telling you the facts of life, son. If you want to stay alive, you have to do as I say."

"There has to be another way," said Rena.

St Keel's phone rang, startling everyone in the room.

He looked down at the phone. "I have to go."

"Yes, you do," said Jack.

St Keel sighed. "Son, keep your head down. Bide your time." Without waiting for an answer, he walked out the door.

Everyone turned to look at Jack.

"What are you going to do?" asked Rena.

Jack's lips tightened. "They murdered my friends. They kidnapped and tortured my friends and me. I'm not laying low. I'm going to make them bleed."

"Well, all right then," said Johnny. "I guess we need another plan."

"Can we trust him not to give us away?" asked Deloy.

"We're going to have to," said Johnny. "We got no place else to go."

Chapter 57

There was a knock on St Keel's door. He looked up to see his pretty secretary.

"Governor, there is an FBI Special Agent-in-Charge Fred Maclan on line one for you. Says it's important."

"Thanks. Fred and I know each other." He picked up the phone. "Fred, how's it going? Still trying to pretend you know how to play golf?"

"I'm afraid I had to give that up, Governor. Just not enough time in the day."

"You're telling me. What can I do for you?"

Maclan hesitated for a few seconds. "We should go have lunch together today and catch up."

"Fred, as much as I would like to, I'm swamped right now with the campaign and everything. I can put you in touch with my secretary and we can schedule something."

"It really needs to be today," Maclan answered. "We have lots of catching up to do. No need to go through anyone, best if it's just the two of us."

St Keel sat up a little straighter in his chair. He looked at his watch. "O...kay. It's a quarter after eleven now. How about we meet at noon?"

"Good. Let's go to Donovan's on Fifth. Both of us should be able to walk there."

"Fred," asked St Keel slowly, "this *is* strictly a social call right? Do I need to bring any of my people along?"

"Definitely not," answered Maclan. "Come alone. See you soon." Maclan then hung up.

St Keel looked at the phone. *Definitely not.* To which question had that been the answer?

He responded to a few more emails, but found himself frequently checking his wall clock. His mind was preoccupied with what Maclan could want. The man was a bore, but he had given him some advance warning on things before. Maclan was old school and believed that no one in power should ever be completely surprised.

Rising, St Keel grabbed his jacket. It was a little early, but he could walk slowly and think. As he strode out of the office, he passed his secretary. "I'm going to grab a bite to eat. Be back in an hour or so."

His secretary looked confused. "Do you want me to have them bring the car around?"

"No, I'll walk. It's a nice day."

"Do you know where you're going? Mr. Ross always likes to know."

"Back soon." St Keel waved as he moved quickly towards the elevators.

Twenty minutes later, he was sitting at a small table in the back of the best Italian restaurant in Baton Rouge. A glass of water and a cup of coffee sat in front of him. He let his mind drift and watched people walk by outside on the sidewalk through the nearby window.

They bustled or strolled or stood and talked. Quite a few were on their smart phones. Most appeared relaxed. Oblivious to the things going on around them. St Keel realized he was a little envious of them.

"Governor?" said a voice nearby.

St Keel looked up to see the tall aristocratic form of Fred Maclan in an impeccable suit. Rumor was that he came from Massachusetts and that Maclan and his family were worth a fortune. Must have broken his father's heart when he went into the FBI rather than the banking industry.

"Fred," said St Keel with a smile. He rose and shook the man's hand and offered the seat opposite him. They both sat and a waitress took Maclan's drink order.

"What are you thinking about for lunch?" St Keel asked. "The chick parm is fantastic."

"Nothing for me, I'm sorry," said Fred. "Actually, I need to get back to New Orleans pretty quick. Things are crazy there right now."

"You sure? My treat."

"No, thank you. Please go ahead and order yourself."

St Keel did. The chicken parmesan.

"So what's going on?"

Maclan looked around slowly to make sure no one was listening. "Sir, I just wanted to give you a head's up on something. I hope it goes without saying that we never had this conversation?"

"Of course."

Sighing, Maclan looked down at his hands. "The Justice Department is going to open a major investigation into the Jackson Winters' case and the missing persons involved."

"Justice Department?" asked St Keel. "I thought that was a state case."

Maclan nodded. "It was, but there are indications of something more going on. Corruption, obstruction of justice, false official statements, you name it."

"How does this tie into Jackson?"

"A couple of my agents"—he paused and his jaw tightened—"*stumbled* upon some information. They presented it to me. At first I wanted to squash it, but the amount of evidence was a little too much to overlook."

"I'm afraid I don't understand."

Maclan leaned forward. "There is something strange going on down at Bog Island, and it appears to involve state and maybe federal persons. There is evidence of a cover-up and possibly foul play."

"So Jackson isn't a mass murderer?"

Maclan shrugged. "We don't know yet. Frankly, that's one of the odd things about this case. No serious investigator should have yet made that leap. There are no bodies, there is no murder weapon, there is no motive, and the primary suspect is on the loose. Who's to say this isn't still a missing persons' case?"

"And you're telling me this because you know of my ties to Jackson's father," said the governor. "I appreciate that, Fred."

"And...because it also appears to involve your chief-of-staff."

"Lucas?" said St Keel. He realized he wasn't surprised.

"We have nothing concrete yet, but every string we pull seems to somehow tie back to him. FBI agents are on their way to Bog Island now. A lot will depend on what they find there and what the people they interview say, but all indications are that something wrong has been going on."

St Keel sat up straight. "Will I be implicated in this?"

"Not as long as you knew nothing about it," said Maclan, letting the question hang in the air, "but you certainly will not come off unscathed in the public eye. Everyone knows that you and Lucas Ross are friends and he's more than just your chief-of-staff."

"I didn't know about whatever it is you are talking about, but...I probably should tell you something."

Maclan leaned forward.

"I saw Jackson Winters yesterday. I spoke with him."

The FBI agent's face relaxed in surprise. "Spoke to him? And you didn't call the police?"

"No," said St Keel. "And while we're in the circle of discretion here, I trust this conversation didn't take place."

Maclan sighed and leaned back in his chair. "What did he say?"

"Surprisingly, many of the same things you are saying. He is adamant that he is innocent. That there is some sort of experimentation lab going on down there on the island. That they captured and tortured and murdered some of his friends while two others are still there being held captive."

"Sounds like quite a tall tale. Do you believe him?"

St Keel shrugged. "I believe he's innocent. As far as the other stuff, who knows?"

Maclan pulled out a business card and slid it across the table to the governor.

"I've got your number, Fred."

"It's for Jackson. We can protect him. I understand why he's laying low, but we need to talk to him to figure out what is going on."

St Keel took the card and put in his pocket. "I'm not sure I'll see him again."

"Well, if you do, please encourage him to call me. It's only a matter of time before someone sees him. The police may not be as understanding as we are, and you know how accidents can happen."

The governor nodded.

Maclan looked at his watch. "I'm sorry, sir, but I have to go. My team should be at Bog Island any minute now."

The FBI agent stood and paused before turning away. "Governor, can I give you a word of advice?"

"Go ahead."

"Get rid of Lucas Ross. The sooner the better. I'm not sure what they'll find down on that island, but he's connected to lots of bad things...not just this issue. Sooner or later, folks like that always go down. Make sure you don't go down with him."

Maclan turned away and walked out of the restaurant.

The waitress returned and set a savory smelling chicken parmesan in front of the governor. It was actually his favorite.

He found he was no longer hungry.

Chapter 58

The last few days had been a torturing hell for Lucas Ross. He felt like he had been juggling flaming chainsaws with the Bog Island cleanup, media misinformation, calming the pharmas down, and greasing palms in the state police and Justice Department.

At last it seemed like everything was under control. No one was going to find anything down at Bog Island except a guide dog training center and a well-run state wildlife preserve, albeit ravaged by the recent hurricane.

"Sir," said Bridgett on his intercom phone. "The governor would like to see you in his office. He says it's urgent."

Lucas sighed. Dealing with that man was so much like dealing with a spoiled toddler. Granted, a very powerful and influential toddler. He imagined this was what tutors or governesses of young princes had felt like in centuries past.

"Tell him I'm on my way."

The General walked from his office down the wide hallways to the governor's office. He passed through open cubicle areas and neat break rooms. Everywhere he went, casual conversations ceased and work productivity increased exponentially. Few met his gaze.

Lucas knocked perfunctorily on the frame of the governor's open door and walked in.

"Please close the door," St Keel told him.

His chief-of-staff eased the door shut and sat in the oversized chair across from his friend.

St Keel stared at him. His hands fidgeted in front of him.

"Whatever it is, just say it," said Lucas. "We'll figure it out together."

"I've gotten word that there is a Justice Department investigation into the Jackson Winters' case. They are also going to be looking into whatever is going on down at Bog Island."

"Gotten word from whom?"

The governor waved his hand. "It doesn't matter. The point is that everything is going to come to a head soon. I'm afraid whatever it is you have been doing is going to blow up and it will splash all over me."

"There's no need for you to worry. I've got folks in the Justice Department that can squash this. Right now everything ties back to Jackson Winters. He's the real criminal here; everything else is just a distraction. Bog Island is a red herring as far as we're concerned."

St Keel didn't speak for a long time. "I don't think Jackson Winters is guilty at all."

Lucas leaned forward and smiled. "You actually spoke to him, didn't you?"

"Maybe. The point is he's being framed."

"No, the point is you met privately with a wanted fugitive and didn't report it to the authorities. Tell me where he is, and I can make this all go away."

"But he's not guilty."

Lucas clapped his open hand on the governor's desk loudly. "It doesn't matter. Don't you understand? This is about controlling the situation. Let the police and the legal process sort out guilt and innocence. Jackson is a lawyer, after all, and should appreciate that."

"He thinks he might disappear somewhere along the line if he were arrested."

Lucas shook his head. "That just goes to show you how mentally unstable he really is. I know you have a soft spot for the man because of his father, but you have to face facts. Jackson Winters is a mass murderer. You shouldn't have gone to see him."

"I had to."

"Let me handle this," Lucas said. "It's why you have me. Tell me where he is, and I can make all of this go away."

"I'm not so sure I want this all to go away."

"What do you mean?"

The governor clinched his fists together in front of him. "I'm sick of this game where things are going on behind my back. I'm sick of dancing to others' strings and not even knowing the song. This isn't why I entered politics. It isn't me at all."

Lucas leaned forward. "Hey, buddy, take a breath here. This is all part of the game, you know that. You have to earn the right to do some good. Part of that is paying for things along the way. Doing favors. Playing the long game. We're in a perfect position, just don't lose sight of the ball."

"That's quite a bewildering series of analogies."

"I judge you get where I'm going though, right?"

"Oh, I get it all right." St Keel reached over and pushed a button on his intercom. "Please go ahead and send them in."

"What are you doing?" asked Lucas, standing.

Within a few seconds, two large state police officers in uniforms entered and stood behind Lucas.

"Gentleman, please take this man into custody. Your commander will provide you with all the details on charges and the like."

"You don't want to do this," said Lucas as the officers pulled his hands behind his back to cuff him.

"You're right about that, old friend, but I have no choice. This is your doing not mine."

Lucas' face was red, and he glared at the governor. "You do realize you're committing career suicide. Everything we've worked for all these years flushed down the toilet. And for what? Some boy you hardly even know?"

"Take him away," said St Keel.

The chief-of-staff smiled evilly. "I'll tell them everything. I know a lot of secrets, Eric. I'll tell them everything."

St Keel looked back at him sadly. "I sincerely doubt that."

The door closed as Lucas Ross was led away.

Chapter 59

This is a mistake, Deborah told herself for the perhaps the tenth time.

"Come on," said a smiling Moses, waving her on after him.

She trudged through the woods. He might be skinny and malnourished, but his energy level was amazing.

"Are you sure we're going the right way?" Deborah asked her brother.

He looked confused. "Is there a right way?"

"Touché," she answered. They were looking for something. One way was as good as another. As long as they didn't get lost.

"Which way is the car?" she asked. The sun was starting to go down, and she definitely didn't want to be out in these woods at night.

"That way." He pointed off behind him without hesitation.

What am I doing? she wondered. She had wanted to leave Moses behind, but the nurse had been sick. Besides, her cover story for getting off work was to check out a hospital for her brother, so bringing him along seemed right.

"Is that it?" he asked, pointing through the deepening shadows of the woods.

"Is what it?"

"No she's not!" Moses said.

"What?"

"Nothing. Nate just said something mean about you."

"Well, you tell Nate if he's says anything else, I'm going to slap the bitch out of him."

Moses froze, sniffing the air. "Food cooking. Smells good."

Deborah looked around. "We're in the middle of nowhere, Moses. Are you sure?"

"This way," he said, taking off, not waiting to see if she followed.

He raced through the trees and she struggled to keep up.

"Moses, slow down! Wait up!"

Finally, he stopped mid-stride, and she stumbled up next to him panting, her hands on her knees.

"Don't...run...off..." she managed to gasp.

"There it is." He pointed at a small cabin on the edge of a hill near a stream. Smoke was coming from a small chimney and lights shone forth into the approaching night.

Now that she was here, she wasn't exactly sure what to do. Her hand rested on the butt of the pistol at her belt.

"Voices from inside," Moses said. "Someone's in there."

"Oh hell," Deborah finally hissed and walked forward to the door and knocked. The voices inside immediately died out.

She knocked again. "I know you're in there. I heard voices, and there's lights on inside."

"Go away," said someone from inside. "This is private property and you're trespassing."

"In that case you should call the police," Deborah shot back.

"What do you want?" asked another voice.

"Hey, it's Rena," said Moses from her left. She looked over to see her brother with his hands around his face peering in the window.

"Oh my God," came a faint female voice.

"I see you know my brother," said Deborah. "Why don't you open the door and let's discuss what we need to discuss. We're not going away, and if we were here to take you away, don't you think this would be going a different way?"

The door creaked open an inch. Out peered a large black man. His eyes cut down to her pistol and the badge at her belt. "You a cop?"

"I'm an FBI agent," she answered. "I'm just looking for a few answers."

The man looked back inside towards someone else.

"Oh, go ahead and let them in," another voice said. "The game is either up or it's not at this point."

The door slowly opened to reveal four figures. The large black man, an old black man, a small dark-haired woman, and a man who, despite his scraggly beard and long hair, appeared to be Jackson Winters.

She stepped into the cabin followed by her brother. "My name is Deborah Mitchell, and this is my brother Moses, who I believe some of you already have met."

"I'm Deloy," said the large man and pointed towards the woman. "That is my daughter Rena."

Deborah turned to Moses. "Is she *that* Rena?"

Moses nodded.

Deborah walked over close to the small woman. "So, you're the person responsible for my brother being kidnapped by a bunch of sadistic thugs and being abused? Do I have that right?"

Rena paled slightly, but didn't step away from the larger woman. "I'm also the one responsible for saving his life and getting him off the island, so I'm guessing those even out."

"Jury's still out on that one," said Deborah, turning away from her. "We'll see how things go from here before jumping to any conclusions like that."

"How did you find us?" asked Jackson.

"I'm very good at finding things out," said Deborah. She nodded towards Moses. "I'm also very practiced at finding people who want to disappear."

"Who else knows?" asked the old man.

"And you are?"

"Johnny. Do we need to run?"

Deborah shrugged. "No one else knows as far as I know. I had to dig a little bit to find that this land was still owned by Mister Winters there. Since you're off the grid, I figured you must have some place to hold up at. Most people go to a familiar spot, and this seemed logical."

"Well hell," said Johnny.

"Why are you here?" asked Jack.

Deborah's fierce eyes softened. "To find out what happened to my brother. I'm getting bits and pieces from him but not the whole picture."

"What are you cooking?" asked Moses, sniffing around the stove.

They all sat around the table and ate a stew that Deloy had prepared while each told their stories and what they knew.

"So the murder charges have been dropped on me?" asked Jack in surprise. "How did that happen?"

"Best I can tell the governor pulled some strings. He probably had the state prosecutor looking into things and realized there wasn't much to go on."

"Why would he do that?" asked Rena. "When he was here, he didn't seem inclined to help."

"He was here?" asked Deborah in surprise.

"He was," said Johnny. "We set it up so he could come talk to Jack, but again, why would he help?"

"Either he did it because he is doing you a solid to protect you, or he really does believe the charges are bogus," said Deborah.

"At least now that they are looking into Bog Island everything will come out," said Rena.

Deborah shook her head. "I was down there. Part of the team. A few off things but nothing that corroborates your story. All new people, everything cleaned up. It's obvious someone has gone to a lot of trouble but no idea who."

"No sign of my friends?" asked Jack with a pained face.

"Sorry, no."

There was a long silence at the table.

"So what now?" asked Johnny.

"That depends," Deborah answered. "What do you all want to do?"

"I want to find my friends and make those responsible pay," said Jack. "I said it before and I meant it. I want to blow the whole lid off this thing."

"That could be dangerous, lots of money and big players," Deborah answered.

"I don't care about that," answered Jack.

"What about them?" Deborah asked. "It's not just your life you're dealing with here. Lots of people can get hurt, you know."

"Don't worry about us," said Rena.

All looked around the table at each other.

"Okay then," said Deborah. "You folks come with me. Time to get moving."

Chapter 60

St Keel hated using the private jet almost as much as he hated going to Washington, D.C., but it was necessary.

The men and women who had put him in power, and could make him president, had summoned him. It was not a summons that could be ignored. Besides, St Keel wanted some answers.

They landed at Reagan International Airport and were met by a limousine and driver. He took his carry-on bag and loaded it in the back. This trip was a turn and burn with no staff and little luggage. It was in a sense freeing not to have to run everything through Lucas.

The limo driver took him to the Ritz Carlton. "Sir, I've been asked to inform you that dinner will be a private affair in the Jefferson Room this evening."

St Keel didn't have to ask who dinner would be with. The leaders of the major pharmaceutical companies or their reps wanted to speak with him. Evidently, Lucas had been their boy and getting rid of him had caused some waves.

Well, to hell with them, thought the governor. *I can have whoever I want working for me.*

He took a quick shower, changed clothes, and went down to the bar for a quick drink. While there he caught the news about Jackson Winters no longer being a suspect, only a potential witness. There were already talking heads discussing how confused the police appeared to be in this case.

"You don't know the half of it," said St Keel.

After finishing his drink, he walked upstairs to the private Jefferson Dining Room. About a dozen men and women milled about the anti-room drinking champagne. He took a glass and joined them.

At first, he had been tense and expecting the worst, but should have known better. These folks came from *society*; they knew better than to ruin a good meal with unsavory talk.

He joked and laughed and talked about the upcoming election. There was no mention of events in Louisiana. When dinner was served they all took their seats and enjoyed a delicious pumpkin soup followed by lamb chops. An apple crumble with cream on top followed for dessert. Wine flowed liberally throughout the meal. Talk and laughter were loud.

They all then retired to an adjacent smoking room. St Keel selected a very expensive cigar and an even more expensive glass of scotch. His cigar lit, he sank down into a plush leather chair.

He noticed that everyone else in the room was sitting around in a circle facing him. Two men and one woman sat closest. Everyone had cigars and scotch, but the jovial atmosphere had vanished.

"We're concerned about what has happened recently down in Louisiana," said Tony Clarion, head of Clarion Drug Company.

"Yes," added Grace Tippleton. Grace was the CEO of Bashier Pharmaceuticals. "We've heard some unfortunate rumors that Lucas Ross has been removed as your chief-of-staff. It's crazy how these stories can be exaggerated. We even heard he had been arrested," Grace laughed. "Surely, that can't be true."

St Keel looked around the room meaningfully.

"The room is clean," said Tony. "We had it swept and everyone in here can be trusted. What about Lucas? Is it true you had him arrested?"

"Oh, but it is true," said St Keel. "The man, I'm sorry to say, was a crook and involved in criminal activity. I decided it was best to get rid of him sooner rather than later."

"I see," puffed Dale Zilbo, founder of Zilbo Medical Research. "Perhaps it would have been wiser to consult with us prior to such a drastic course of action. It will cost us significantly in money and time to right the ship on this one."

"He lied to me," said St Keel.

"So what? They're only holding him on charges of corruption anyway. How long do you think that will stick?" asked Grace.

"What's really going on at Bog Island?" asked St Keel.

"Nothing that you need to worry about," answered Dale. "It's for your protection that you know as little as possible."

St Keel sighed and took a sip of his drink. "I'm sick to death of hearing that line. Besides, it's out of my hands now anyway. The Justice Department and the FBI are involved. I can't cover all of this up."

"We can," said Tony. "We have."

"What do you mean by that?" asked the governor.

"It's simple," answered Grace. "The Justice Department has already decided to stand down and turn the case back over to the state police."

"But what about Bog Island?"

"What about it?" asked Dale. "The feds found nothing there."

"You need to trust us and do what we tell you," said Grace, blowing smoke in his direction. "We can only protect you as long as you are worth protecting."

"I want out of whatever it is you're doing," said St Keel.

"You're in way too deep to get out, Governor," said Dale. "If we go down, you'll be the first to feel the bite."

St Keel's hand tightened on his glass.

Grace reached out and put a calming hand on his knee. "We're all friends here. We're all on the same side. No need to get upset. Play your part and everyone is a winner. No one gets hurt."

"You mean no one *else* gets hurt," said St Keel.

"It's a difficult world we live in," said Tony. "We're talking about curing cancer here. You have to look at the greater good. And not to put too fine a point on it, but without us watching your back and covering for you at D.C., all sorts of unsavory things can happen."

"That's the second time you've threatened me in the last few minutes," growled St Keel.

"Don't look at it as threats," said Grace. "We are simply giving you the courtesy of speaking plainly with you. Whether you like it or not, we are in the same boat here...for better or worse."

"And what is it exactly that you want me to do?" asked St Keel.

Dale smiled. "Simply sit back on this. We'll handle everything else."

"What do I tell the FBI if they question me?"

"They shouldn't," said Tony, "but if they do, you tell them nothing. If you've already told them something, say you were mistaken."

St Keel sat back and sucked on the cigar thinking.

"It's time to decide, Governor," said Grace. "Do you want to be one of those idealists who burns the world down around them on principle and gains nothing...or do you want to be the President of the United States?"

Eric St Keel sipped his drink and made his decision.

Chapter 61

Deborah felt nervous as she made her way through the plain nondescript lobby. It had been many years since she had been to the Justice Department building. The vast hall was open and filled with young professionals moving with purpose.

The six of them had driven in a large passenger van through the night from Louisiana to Washington, D.C. Everyone had been nervous about being spotted. Everyone except Moses who was oblivious to their plight and seemed to enjoy the sights out the window.

They were all exhausted as they entered the building. Deborah pointed to a set of chairs near a window. "Have a seat here. I'll be right back."

"Are you serious?" asked Rena, tilting her head towards Jack. "We're sitting in the Justice Department with one of the FBI's most wanted."

"He's not on that list, and he's only wanted for questioning," said Deborah. "Just be cool, and I'll be back in a minute."

"Why can't we just come with you?" asked Deloy.

Deborah looked meaningfully at the security turnstiles. "My badge will get me in, but you all would have to be checked-in. I'd like to keep you all on the down-low until I'm sure we've got top cover from someone."

"How likely is that?" asked Johnny.

"We'll see," said Deborah. "I used to work for him."

"Is that a good or bad thing?" asked Deloy.

Deborah smiled. "You might have noticed not everyone gets me."

"Oh hell," said Deloy. "Perhaps we should go back on the run now."

"Just be cool," said Deborah, walking towards the turnstiles. She made her way through and took the elevator to the fifth floor. On the way there, she saw several folks that she had known before. Some nodded at her, but most avoided eye contact. She knew she had never been popular with her co-workers.

She paused and took a deep breath before she pushed through the dark oak door at the end of a long hall. The small sign by the door read "Internal Affairs Division."

Walking through the door as if she belonged there, Deborah made her way towards the back where Special Agent-in-Charge Norman Kendricks sat. He had been a mentor to her for many years, and it had broken both their hearts when he had been forced to re-assign her several years before. Deborah's intensity and unwillingness to always follow orders had inevitably gotten her in trouble.

"Deborah?" asked Kendricks' secretary in surprise. "What are you doing here?"

She smiled at the older lady who she had always liked. "Hi, Fay. Good to see you. Is the boss available?"

Fay's smiled slipped a little. "Does he know you're coming?"

Deborah looked at the closed office door and then back at Fay. "No, but it's important."

"You know he went out on a limb for you last time, don't you?"

"I do and I haven't let him down," answered Deborah, fighting down her defensiveness. She knew this little lady was the gatekeeper if she wanted to see the head of the Justice Department's Internal Affairs Division. "I'm not here to have him get me out of trouble or ask for a favor. This is official business that falls squarely in his lane."

Fay stared at her hard for a few seconds. Finally, she sighed and started punching on her computer keyboard. "I can get you in there for five minutes as soon as the door opens."

"Thank you," said Deborah and sat in a chair against the wall.

As the minutes ticked away, her nervousness slowly grew. She had mostly been working on instinct. The magnitude of what she was about to do started to sink in. Agents around the office gave her furtive glances, as if they were already shunning her.

When the door opened, she shot to her feet. Three agents with notebooks emerged smiling and laughing and walked away.

That used to be me, she thought. After a few seconds, she realized the open door beckoned. She turned to find a squat overweight man in a bowtie staring at her from an enormous desk.

"Well, you might as well come on in, I guess," Kendricks said.

Deborah walked into the office and closed the door behind her. "I'm sorry to drop in like this, sir."

"Go ahead and have a seat since you're here."

She sat and found it difficult to start. There was so much history and emotion and disappointment between them. This man had been fair to her. A good boss and mentor.

"Just start at the beginning," said Kendricks. "In my experience, that's always the best place to start."

Deborah felt immense gratitude, and the tension flowed out of her. She told him everything. Showed him the case file from the shoulder bag she carried. She told him about the group of five in the lobby.

Kendricks stood up and opened the door. "Fay, clear my afternoon. We're going to be busy." He then turned back to Deborah. "I'd like to meet these fugitives you've brought here."

***

Kendricks met Jackson, Johnny, Deloy, Moses, and Rena in the lobby.

"This is some situation we seem to find ourselves in," Kendricks said.

"Do you think you can help us?" asked Jack.

Kendricks looked at them each slowly in turn. "I presume all of you are prepared to testify under oath to the things Deborah here has told me?"

"We will," said Johnny.

Kendricks turned to Deborah. "You do know this will probably be the end of your career in the FBI. No one will want you. No one will recommend you for promotion. No partner will want to work with you. Are you ready for that? You sure you want to go forward?"

Deborah smiled. "Let's face it, we both know I never really fit in anyway."

"Okay then," Kendricks said. "Let's go talk to the boss."

"Who's that?" asked Rena.

"The Attorney General," answered Deborah.

Chapter 62

St Keel finally had a day off. He and Brenda planned to spend the day working in their overgrown garden together and maybe go out to eat later. It was a beautiful autumn day. The weather had been perfect after the hurricane had rolled through the gulf.

"Eric," called Brenda from downstairs. "There are some people here to see you."

St Keel could tell from the tone of her voice that something wasn't right. The security detail would have turned away any troublemakers or reporters, so it was likely someone from the office. Brenda was looking forward to their day alone and probably thought whoever it was would get him back into the office.

Not today, he told himself. *Nothing was going to ruin this day.*

He made his way down the ornate spiral staircase to the entryway. "Whatever it is, it can wait until tomorrow," he said loudly.

"I'm afraid not," answered a man in a suit and sunglasses at the front door. Another man stood beside him.

"What is this about?" St Keel asked.

The first man pulled out a badge. "I am Deputy U.S. Marshal Gimbals, and this is Deputy U.S. Marshall Ashley."

"U.S. Marshalls?" said St Keel. "I presume this is about Jackson Winters. I've already told the state police everything I know."

"I'm afraid that is not why we're here," said Gimbals, pulling out a piece of paper. "We're here to execute an arrest warrant on behalf of the U.S. Attorney General."

"Arrest warrant?" St Keel took the paper. "For who?'

"For you, sir," said Ashley.

St Keel looked up from the paper at him in shock. "What in the world is this about?"

"That will all be explained, I presume, at the Baton Rouge Police Station," said Ashley.

St Keel turned to Brenda. "Call the office and tell them to get a lawyer down there. Hell, tell them to get all the lawyers down there. We're going to sue the shit out of everyone involved in this."

"Not really our concern," said Gimbals. "Can we trust you to come along cooperatively, sir? I'd rather not use the cuffs if we don't have to."

"Definitely not," answered St Keel. He turned to Brenda and gave her a kiss. "Don't worry, I'll be home for lunch."

St Keel walked between the two marshals and got in the back of the typical government sedan.

It killed him to see his wife's worried face staring out at them as they drove away.

***

St Keel seethed as he was fingerprinted, booked, and photographed. He vowed to make everyone involved pay.

He sat at a table in a plain gray interrogation room. St Keel was prepared to tell whoever came to talk to him and read him his rights to go to hell, but strangely, they let him be.

After an exceptionally long time, a short man with spectacles and a briefcase was let in the room by a police officer, who closed the door behind them.

"Who are you?" asked St Keel.

"My name is Lucius McCraven," the man said. "I'm your attorney."

"No, you're not. I know all the attorneys at the office and I've never seen you before."

"I'm afraid those are attorneys for the state," McCraven said. "Their job is to represent and defend Louisiana. I'm here to represent *you*."

St Keel shook his head. "I don't understand what is going on."

McCraven pulled off his glasses and polished them. "You have been indicted on obstruction of justice and conspiracy by the Justice Department. Your warrant was executed as part of a series of indictments. I'm still getting read up on the case, so I'll know more soon enough."

"When can I get out of here?"

McCraven frowned. "I'm afraid that's not going to happen. In fact, they only allowed me to talk to you as a courtesy. In a few minutes, they will come and take you to a cell."

"A cell? This can't be happening. What evidence do they have? I haven't done anything wrong."

"I don't know yet, but they've let me know that the FBI has an inside source. This source said you had a meeting with several leaders of pharmaceutical companies and agreed to use your position to inappropriately benefit them. Seems like this source was actually in the room."

St Keel closed his eyes going through the meeting in D.C. in his mind.

"There is also someone on your staff who has implicated you in corruption."

"Who?" asked St Keel.

"Your former chief-of-staff."

"What did he say?" asked St Keel.

McCraven shook his head. "Again, I'll know more tomorrow morning when I come back."

"Tomorrow morning? You mean I have to spend the night here?"

McCraven looked at him sadly. "Sir, I'm afraid you're likely to be here for several days until the arraignment. I'll argue then to get you released on bail and I think any judge would agree."

St Keel's head was spinning. The implications of what was happening were starting to flash before his eyes.

"Does the media know yet?"

McCraven looked uncomfortable. "You know it's almost impossible to keep things like this secret."

A policeman opened the door. He looked apologetically at St Keel. "I'm sorry, sir. Time to go."

McCraven stood. "I'll be back in the morning. I trust it goes without saying that you know not to talk to anyone without me being there."

"It does. You know I was an attorney myself."

"That doesn't always help people," McCraven said. "Lawyers tend to think they're the smartest people on the planet when it comes to the law. Just hang in there and don't talk. We'll have you out in a few days." He then turned and walked out the door without looking back.

The policeman at the door indicated St Keel should exit the room and led him through a series of security doors and down several halls. Soon they were walking on gray concrete floors with cells on each side crammed with inmates. He felt a hint of fear.

"Don't worry, sir," said the policeman, as if reading his mind. "We'll put you in your own cell at the end. No one will mess with you."

"Thank you," said St Keel, hating the sound of abject gratitude in his voice.

"Hello, Eric," said a voice to his right.

St Keel turned to see a smiling Lucas Ross.

"I told you you'd regret this," the man said.

Chapter 63

"Is that it?" asked Jack, throwing the newspaper down in disgust.

"I'm afraid it's as good as it's going to get," answered Deborah. "It's my unfortunate experience that people in power rarely get what they deserve."

"The governor is only facing charges of obstruction of justice," Jackson said. "And he's not even the big fish here."

Deborah signed heavily. "They weren't able to find any evidence of what happened at Bog Island. Everything had been cleaned up. The case might even be dropped for lack of evidence."

"But we gave sworn statements," said Rena. "We told everything. And what about that nurse from down there who agreed to cooperate?"

"They're discrediting her," answered Deborah. "Say she has no real proof of anything. Even the belongings of your friend might have been stolen. If we had any concrete evidence, all your testimony would be the nail in the coffin, but without it..."

"And there's a whole lot of pharma money flowing around," said Johnny.

"That, too," said Deborah. "Just know that whatever else happens, you at least caused it to all be shut down."

"And the governor is certainly done, no matter how this turns out," said Deloy. "Same for that Lucas Ross fellow they say cut a deal with the feds to testify."

"It's not enough," said Jackson. "Charles and Heather are still out there somewhere."

"You've done your best. What else can you do?" asked Rena.

"Use the law, like my father taught me," Jack answered. "I'll chase them with civil cases until I get them. My friends deserve better."

"Your firm going along with that?" asked Johnny.

"No, which is why I'm starting my own firm," said Johnny. "I've got some decent initial investment, but I need some good folks to help me. You all in?"

They all looked at each other in surprise.

"All of us?" asked Rena, staring at Jack with meaning.

"Yes," he said, walking over and taking her hand.

"Well, I'm actually between jobs," said Deborah. "I always wondered what it would be like to be a private eye. Every good attorney needs a private eye on the payroll."

"What about the rest of us?" asked Deloy.

Jack smiled. "Oh, I'm sure we'll find something for you to do."

Epilogue

Captain Ernest Quincy sat in a lawn chair reading a paper. His already deeply tanned skin soaked in the southern Arizona sun. If he had looked up from his paper, Quincy could have seen where the Mexico border was located across about six miles of high desert.

He shook his head in disgust at the headline. It was amazing the level of corruption in the world today. What was everything coming to?

The newspapers came in with their supplies and mail once a week via special cleared courier. Quincy didn't miss the outside world, but he liked to read about what was happening. Most of the time it reaffirmed his current career choice.

There was a man-sized shadow suddenly over him.

"You're blocking my sun," said Quincy. "Makes it hard to read."

"We got a message in on the secure comm system," Conrad, his operations officer, said.

"Can you believe this shit?" asked Quincy, shaking the paper at Conrad.

The big man leaned over and looked at the article.

Murder, Torture, and Corruption in Oman
Louisiana Governor Eric St Keel's already embattled
administration suffered even more scandal yesterday when damning

evidence emerged that his chief-of-staff, former Colonel Lucas Ross, was responsible for the torture and deaths of civilians and enemy combatants while in command of Task Force Shark in Oman several years ago. There are also indications that the Department of Defense covered up these incidents and allowed Ross to retire without further discipline. By some estimates, over one hundred civilians were held prisoner without legal authorization in Task Force Shark's Detention Center. Reports indicate that even by the authorized legal authority of "enhanced interrogation techniques" Ross's unit went far beyond what the U.S. Government authorizes.

The Justice Department has opened an investigation into Task Force Shark and into allegations that the Department of Defense failed to disclose criminal conduct by its senior military commander in embattled Oman. The Oman government is also demanding an explanation, and protests there have continued for the past three days.

President Wilkens pledged to get to the bottom of this incident along with numerous allegations against presidential candidate Eric St Keel.

- Story continued on page 6 -

"Looks like someone stepped in it this time," said Conrad.

Quincy shook his head. "That's putting it mildly."

Conrad held out a piece of paper. "The message. It's marked 'immediate.'"

355

Taking the message, Quincy leaned forward and dropped the paper.

To: Site Eir
From: Headquarters
Subject: Bronze Protocol Alert Notice

Recent compromise of Site Iaso has necessitated initiation of Bronze Protocol through all Project Chiron Sites. Bronze Protocol will continue for thirty days from receipt of this message unless suspended by official headquarters secure message.

All site commanders will acknowledge by authenticated secure message.

"What the hell is Bronze Protocol?" asked Conrad.

"It means we're locked down. All experiments and research are on hold," answered Quincy. "It means those assholes at Site Iaso shit the bed and we have to sleep in it."

"What the hell is Iaso?"

"Who knows?" said Quincy. "Probably some damn mythological figure. Just like Eir is supposed to be the Norse god of healing."

Conrad grunted. "Why couldn't they have just named the sites after football teams or beers or something non-geek like?"

"Because, just like in this job, geeks rule the world. That's why we beat the shit out of them in high school, because deep down we know it will be our last chance."

Quincy looked back at the camp behind him. There were a dozen long square buildings surrounding a central fenced-in courtyard. Around the yard were a number of concrete-lined holes in the ground with metal covers where the test subjects were housed.

There were several subjects taking their hour in the sun. A massive mountain of a black man stared at them with murder in his eyes.

"I don't like that one," said Conrad. "I don't understand why we had to take on the Iaso riffraff anyway. The little Haitian's no trouble, and the woman's a hottie, but that guy's nothing but a problem."

"It's not like they could let them go," said Quincy. "Besides it was worth it to get that guy. And I never believed in Karma."

"What do you mean?"

Quincy pointed at the big black man. "Back eleven years ago, I lost ten grand when LSU beat Texas in the Cotton Bowl. The Longhorns would have won if not for a crazy beast of a defensive end who had three sacks, eight tackles, and an interception. If not for that asshole, Texas would have won."

"Karma? I didn't see it," said Conrad.

"I was actually there, and I promised that if I ever got my hands on that guy, I would take ten grand out of his ass."

Conrad shook his head. "I still don't get it."

Quincy smiled and pointed at the large man staring at them from behind the fence. "That guy right there is the LSU player who lost me my college money. That's Charles Haywood himself."

"Wow," said Conrad. "What are the odds?"

"A million to one. Nothing short of a damn miracle."

Charles Haywood stared back at the men, hoping he got a chance to make them pay and knowing somewhere out there Jackson would be looking for them.

A stiff wind wiped into Site Eir and tore the newspaper out of Quincy's hands. The paper blew up into the air and away.

Authors' Notes and Acknowledgements

Dennis and I thank you for reading *Project Chiron* and hope you enjoyed the story. Please take time to leave a review of the book as it will let other readers know if they will like the book or not.

This book has been a collaboration between the two of us that began several years ago. Dennis had a story idea and asked me to join him in putting that idea into the format you now hold in your hands. It has truly been an adventure.

No author completes a book in a vacuum and it is frequently a team effort. That is certainly the case here and many have actively supported us in this endeavor. I would like to especially thank my wife and fellow author, Kristin King, who reviewed numerous versions of this book and made relevant and insightful recommendations. I also want to thank Sherman Chaudoin for reading the rough draft and helping make it better.

If you enjoyed this book, and I sincerely hope that you did, please consider signing up for my reader's newsletter at Ryan King Newsletter, you can unsubscribe at any time. For signing up you will immediately receive a free book in addition to the latest information on new releases and free giveaways.

Thanks again,

Ryan King

www.ingramcontent.com/pod-product-compliance
Lightning Source LLC
Chambersburg PA
CBHW021527250626
47154CB00006BA/2005